SEASON
OF THE
SWORDS

BOOK ONE

THE SWORDS OF VALOR

DOMENIC MELILLO

Phase Publishing, LLC
Seattle, WA

Phase Publishing, LLC first paperback edition
October 2018

ISBN 978-1-943048-66-3
Library of Congress Control Number 2018957933
Cataloging-in-Publication Data on file.

DEDICATION

This book is dedicated to Joseph A. Melillo,
Mr. Better-than-Good.

My father, my mentor, my hero.

A true example of virtue and valor.
A true giant.

OUR SWORDS SHALL SING

Our swords have sat there silent
Rusting on the wall,
While we have rusted also,
Ears deaf unto their call.

We have ignored for far too long
The call to take up arms,
To fight the scourge of hatred
That threatens all that's calm.

The clarion call is far too strong
For us to still ignore,
Beckoning to our hearts and minds
To fight a virtuous war.

The Swords of Terror have been loosed.
Their fear and horror swell.
Their songs of taunting and of wrath
We must attempt to quell.

The Swords of Valor must now rise
To answer and to save
The last remaining vestiges
Of the bold and brave.

Rise, oh Swords of Valor!
Rise, and sing your songs!
Fill our hearts with words of love
And make our meek hearts strong.

Sing to us a virtuous song.
Sing it loud and clear.
Sing it out across the land,
So humble men can hear.

Today we must take up the cause.
No longer shall we tremble.
Heroes now with swords in hand
And promises to remember.

INTRODUCTION

I will tell you the story of a family. My family.

I, Domenic, am but a minor player. I was born to tell this story, and it was born for me to tell. I have a brother, a fellow prophet. He is the Prophet of Action, with the power of inspiration. I am the Speaker. My power lies in storytelling and remembering.

All stories are first born of action; then they are reborn as tales. They don't exist without both parts. I'm here to ensure that my family's most important stories are told and remembered.

Stories also need heroes. Sometimes they are born, and sometimes they are built. I will tell you how the heroes of this story were both born and built. Heroes need guidance and direction. They need focus and a purpose. Most of all, they need valor and virtue.

How they obtain these qualities is often painful. It is always a process. But in the end, without virtue and valor, they will fail. Yes, it is possible for heroes to fail. Failure has nothing to do with valor and even less to do with virtue. Sometimes, heroes face loss, but they are never defeated. Death may challenge them, yet they live on. It is never about an individual battle. Outcomes are not as important as conduct and character. Heroes' experiences are less about legends and more about legacy.

There is a bit of hero in each of us, and as with all

heroes, the greatest truth of life is what we leave behind for others to find; what path we leave for them to follow; what light we may bequeath to help them find their way when the night falls and their hope is dying.

May this story be a lamp unto your feet, a beacon in the night, hope when you face despair, and a reminder, most of all a reminder, that it is never too late. It is never too late to find virtue, never too late to find valor, never too late to find the hero within.

Remember, it takes but a day. Anything can happen in a day. Anything.

PROLOGUE

As Rob sat before the roaring fire in the great room of his family's upstate New York vacation home, he felt what he could only describe as satisfaction. After ten long years of college and schooling in Functional Neurology, he had his PhD and was now looking forward to implementing all that he had learned. His doctoral dissertation had been well received by most of the dissertation committee, but not all.

Frankly, he had expected more pushback since his theories on the cause and treatment of autism were so cutting-edge and outside the currently accepted theories. The support he received was encouraging.

Now, here he was, meeting with his father, getting ready to outline a plan for putting his theories into practice. They were going to spend some time together planning out the next steps for what Rob believed would be a lifelong career helping families deal with the struggles and challenges of autism.

It had become such a scourge over the past decade, and Rob was convinced he had the understanding to make a significant difference. That was his passion, all he ever really wanted to do; help children and families overcome their struggles.

"Rob, are you up for a little more wine?" his father

asked as he grabbed a couple of glasses from the dinner table and a bottle of Chianti.

"Sure dad, absolutely," replied Rob.

His father poured the wine and handed him his glass. As he took his seat across from Rob in front of the crackling fire, they toasted to his success and accomplishments.

"Rob, you know that I am immensely proud of you." His father smiled. "I want you to be able to fulfill all that you have planned for yourself, but there are a few things you need to know before you begin. You need to have all the facts, so you can make a fully-informed decision."

A muffled explosion made the wine in Rob's glass vibrate and quiver. Before he could even process what had happened, his father was out of his chair and halfway up the stairs to his third-floor office. Rob stood and raced to the window. Seeing what he thought was smoke coming from the old barn out back, he assumed that some machinery had exploded and started a fire. He was about to call the fire department when his father came down the stairs armed with a rapier.

"Don't ask any questions, stay calm, and follow my lead," he ordered as he hustled past Rob toward the front porch. "We have a problem, and I will handle it. But always remember this. If I fall, there's hope in my office. All you need to know is up there. Your brother, Domenic, and sister, Susan, know everything, and they can guide you. For now, just have faith in me, and do what I tell you to do. No questions asked. Understood?"

Too startled and confused to verbalize a response, Rob nodded his agreement and snatched the pitching wedge that his father tossed to him as they passed the golf bags on the porch.

"You may need something to defend yourself with!"

2

his father yelled over his shoulder as he ran toward the old barn.

A golf club? Defend myself? Rob's thoughts tumbled over each other as he ran behind his father. The cold night air burned his lungs, and he struggled for breath, heart pounding. The moon cast a dim, shadowy light which reminded Rob of his frequent dreams. In those dreams, he needed to run, but his legs wouldn't move fast enough. This situation felt eerily familiar.

As they reached the old barn, his father stopped suddenly and held up his hand for silence. Rob immediately froze but heard nothing except the intense pounding of the blood in his ears.

Without a sound or warning, his father sprang into action. Rob followed but could not immediately see where his father had gone, his vision obscured by the dim moonlight and the smoke that filled the old barn.

Murky moonlight streamed through the damaged places in the old barn roof. Rob made his way cautiously. Suddenly, he caught a glimpse of movement to his left. Before he could shout a warning, two shadowy figures darted to where his father was now standing thirty feet in front of him, sword raised.

The first figure raced toward his father who took a nimble and fluid step to his left. As the figure thrust past him with its arm raised, an unbelievably swift and precise stroke of his father's sword to its throat dispatched it swiftly. A dark cloud of red mist erupted from the gaping wound, and it fell face down at his feet, its throat severed.

His father wheeled around to face the second figure. For several moments, the two combatants stood still and appraised each other.

Finally, his father growled, "Cornelius, we meet again."

3

"Yes," replied the shadow, "only this time, you are alone, much older, and armed with a simple rapier. Without a Sword of Valor, you are as good as dead. Give me the code to the Keeping Room and I may let you live. Refuse, and you will most certainly die tonight."

His father laughed. "The Apostles have been nothing but failures for centuries. You, personally, have been a failure for decades. Did you really think that C4 explosives would work on the titanium, tungsten, and chromium alloy of the Keeping Room? You are a joke, and you will get nothing from me tonight, or ever. However, if you think that fate shines on you tonight, then take your best shot. But I promise you, death is near, and your failure will be final."

Rob tried to shake off the paralysis of fear that had trapped him. It was just like in his nightmares. He gripped the pitching wedge with two hands and tried to shout a warning as the figure fiercely swung a mighty sword, but his voice failed him.

Before Rob could move, he saw his father shoulder-roll under the swinging sword, rise swiftly to one knee, and thrust his sword upward into the heart of his opponent. He watched as the sword of the shadowy figure completed its empty arc, and the figure slumped forward, impaled on the rapier. His father rose up from his knee to his full height, roughly withdrew his now-bloody sword from the heart of the shadowy figure. With one powerful blow, he decapitated his enemy.

"Never on my property, never in my own home. NEVER threaten my family!" his father growled.

Rob stood, feet cemented to the dirt floor of the old barn, gripping his pitching wedge weapon with white knuckles. In that moment, he knew that nothing would ever be the same again.

CHAPTER ONE

DEATH OF A GIANT

Rob's flight home was long, depressing, and uncomfortable. The late departure and the stifling temperature inside the plane were bad enough, but the sense of failure and helplessness made the flight almost unbearable.

His father had always been his staunchest supporter, instilling in him the belief that nothing was impossible, that there was always a solution to any problem, that it was just a matter of time and focus. Right now, it did not feel that way. Time was running out.

He gritted his teeth as he looked out of the window at his own reflection, which seemed to be mocking his efforts. I really should be able to figure this out, he thought. I have the knowledge and the skills, I just need to find the right perspective, and I will have the key to understanding what Dad's issue is.

Once again, he thought through his analysis. Dad's heart was still strong, and his organs were in the appropriate condition for a man his age. He was reasonably fit, and other than that kidney problem a few years back, he'd never had any major surgeries. His appetite was greatly diminished, and he seemed uncharacteristically withdrawn and sullen over the past three months. He had also begun talking cryptically about the future, which wasn't like him at all.

There did not seem to be anything physically wrong with him, yet still he continued to decline. That was when Rob began to focus on his brain. The brain is the control center. It drives and manages everything in the body.

There had to be an issue with his father's brain, and that was something that Rob could deal with. That was his life, his work. Knowing that there were very few brain experts in the world who could match his level of understanding, Rob had identified and contacted a few of his former colleagues and teachers from around the world. They had gathered in Milan for an emergency consultation.

He laid out all the facts, symptoms, medical history, and the research he had already done in the hopes that one of them might see something that he had missed. It had been a wasted effort. They all came to the same ridiculous conclusion. It was obvious to them that his father was willing himself to die.

Around and around his thoughts swirled, tumbling over each other as he drifted into a fitful sleep.

Startled, Rob awoke in a sweat and with his heart beating out of control as the plane made a hard landing. He hated being asleep during landings. As he collected his things to prepare to deplane, he struggled to put his colleagues' diagnosis out his mind and focus on his main objective. He had to get to the hospital before it was too late. He needed more time. He had to speak with his father before...

By the time he reached his car, it had begun to rain. Not just a gentle rain, but a real downpour. It was bad enough that his father was dying but did it have to be cold and stormy too, Rob wondered. Gripping the steering wheel tightly, he fought the weather and the traffic on the Long Island Expressway to get to his father's bedside, fear gripping his heart.

He finally arrived at the hospital, parked the car, and hustled up three flights of stairs to his father's room. Although he was a neurologist, he hated hospitals. There was so much loss, pain, and suffering in such places.

His father's nurse exchanged hellos with him on her way out of the room and said, "The doctor told your father he does not have much time left. We haven't contacted any other family members yet, because he said to call only you." Before she exited the room, she turned and took Rob's hand. "We can't turn back the hands of time. When it is our time to go, we all must answer the call. Destiny is destiny." Then she left him alone with his father.

Rob scanned the darkened room. A soft light above the bed illuminated his father's face. Frequent lightning invaded the gloom through the window, casting brief, shadowy figures on the walls. Those shadows increased the strong sense of foreboding he already felt.

He looked at the man lying in a bed that seemed too big for him. There was a smallness to him now that had never been there before. But there also seemed to be more power. It was as if while his father's physical form diminished, his presence increased.

Rob couldn't help but think back to the night he first found out who his father really was. He would never forget the strength, speed, and agility he had shown in defeating the two shadowy men who had attacked him in the old barn. That was over twenty-five years ago. His father was in his fifties then, but he was still amazingly fit and strong. Rob had always thought his dad would live forever.

He pulled a chair next to the bed and spoke softly. "Dad, it's Rob. I'm here for you. Can you talk?"

His father's eyes opened. He smiled weakly and slowly extended his hand to his son.

"So glad you are here," he said. "I was worried you would not make it back from Milan in time. We have a few things to discuss privately before I go."

"I don't want you to go, Dad," Rob insisted. "We need you now more than ever. You must hang on. I'll find a way to fix this, to make you better."

"I know you want that," his father replied, "and I know you may even believe it, but it is my time. You must let me go."

"But I don't want to do this alone. We have always planned this together. We never intended for me to handle it all by myself. I'm not ready. I need your guidance," Rob implored.

His father replied weakly, "You are ready. You must believe this with all your heart. That is something you must know. You must believe that I would not leave you without hope. Trust is important now. I have given my life to this cause, and now, so must you. Follow the plan. Do the work. Make it happen. Trust in the process."

Father and son discussed many matters in hushed whispers. Several hours later, Rob's father said to him, "Remember, ready or not, they are heroes. They can do this. It is the only way. If failure comes, there is hope in my office. Remember that. I love you all, and I'm proud of you. Now go and do your duty."

"Wait, what about the office? I don't understand. We never got around to discussing the office," implored Rob.

Even as he spoke, he watched as his father's eyes close for the last time and saw him take his final breath. He was gone, and with his passing, he took an entire generation of heroes with him. Now it was up to Rob to raise up a new one. One that could finally secure the victory his father had planned for so long.

"Goodnight, my captain. Rest in peace," he whispered as he sat holding his father's hand.

After a few minutes, he collected himself, rose from his chair, and left the room to notify the nurse. He had a few urgent phone calls to make.

"Billy, it's Uncle Rob. I have bad news; Grandpa is gone. I'll be busy making arrangements for the next day or so. I know you are working hard on a capital raise for our company, but I want you to clear your schedule for the next week."

"Oh, Uncle Rob, I am so sorry," replied Billy. "I know how hard you were working on a cure for him. I suppose the medical team you met with in Milan didn't have any good treatment options, or you would have phoned it in to the hospital."

"That's right Billy, they were as baffled as I was. When they looked at all the data, they couldn't figure out why he had declined so quickly. They said it was almost as if he wanted to die. Will you call Jeffrey for me tomorrow? I don't want to wait too long to let him know, but he won't be reachable until that corporate trial wraps up. Tell him to clear his schedule, too. Finally, make sure you both bring your swords to the funeral. That was one of his last requests."

"Will do, Uncle Rob. And don't worry about the capital raise. I have the initial phases covered, and I think the rest will wait until after the funeral. Just focus on getting through all this."

Rob hung up with Billy and called his sons, Robbie and Ty. He dialed Robbie first, but after a couple of rings remembered that Robbie often worked late on construction jobs and never took his phone with him.

When Ty picked up at his school, Rob said, "Ty, I have sad news; Grandpa passed away just a few minutes ago. I need for you to come home and prepare to be here for about a week. Make sure to bring your sword with you. Grandpa asked that you all have them with you at the funeral."

"Okay, Dad," Ty replied. "I'm so sorry. It must be so hard to lose your father. Did you get to see him before he died?"

"I did, Ty," responded Rob. "It was a blessing to share those last moments with him. I'm also glad that Grandma went first, so she didn't have to bear losing him. At least we don't have her pain to deal with on top of all this."

"I know, Dad, and I'm sorry," replied Ty, "but we will all be together soon. Have you talked to Robbie yet?"

"Not yet," said Rob. "He must be working late trying to finish that renovation job on the Nicholson's farm. He didn't pick up when I called."

"Okay. I will try to reach him, and if I get him before you do, I'll tell him you will fill him in later. Hang in there. I love you. Also, maybe this is insensitive of me, Dad, but finals start in two weeks. I really need to be back in time. Do you think everything will be done by then?"

"I am not sure, Ty." Rob sighed. "All I can say is that I really hope so. If I need to, I will call the school and talk to them. I am sure St. Joe's can make accommodations for family emergencies."

"Okay, Dad," replied Ty. "I'll be there as soon as I can."

After hanging up with Ty, he called Joe and Nick, who were on a hunting trip in the mountains of West Virginia. When they didn't answer, he left a message leaving the same information he had left for the others.

Rob then called his sister, Susan, and his brother, Domenic, and filled them in on the events of the last few hours. All the necessary calls made, he left the hospital, took a deep breath, and walked out into a suddenly much darker and colder world, whose fate he now knew was in his hands.

Joe fidgeted with his cell phone as Nick drove the SUV. Having no cell service for even a few days was nerve-wracking. He didn't like feeling so disconnected while their grandfather lay in the hospital. Everyone knew his time could be close, yet he had protested when Joe had suggested postponing the trip. The trip had been a waste of time, anyway. They hadn't seen a single deer all weekend. So, early this morning, they'd loaded up the tent and gear and headed back to civilization.

As soon as he had service, Joe checked his emails and phone messages. The third message was from his uncle. He listened carefully, then hung up after it ended. Turning to stare out the window, he sat in silence.

After a couple of minutes, he sensed his younger brother's curiosity. Softly, he said, "Nick, that message was from Uncle Rob. Grandpa is gone. We need to head home and clear our schedules for the next week. He said to make sure we pick up our swords before we head up there. Grandpa wanted us to bring them to his funeral."

Nick was silent for a long moment, his expression

11

bleak. "I was hoping that we'd have made it back before he passed. It kills me that we weren't there when he died."

"He did go fast," said Joe, "but he knew we loved him. What's important is that we showed him our love and respect while he was alive."

"I suppose," replied Nick, "but I feel like there was still so much I wanted to talk to him about, to ask him."

"Like what?" asked Joe.

"Life stuff, relationship stuff, things like that," said Nick. "You know that I was up at the vacation home a few months back, right? I had asked permission to spend a few days hunting on the property and Grandpa said it was okay. I was really hoping that he might join me and that we could get some real quality one-on-one time to talk."

"That was a great idea, Nick," replied Joe. "So, how did that work out?"

"Actually, it was really strange. The whole time I was there, Grandpa was really distracted. He spent a lot of time up in his office. When he wasn't in his office, he was running back and forth between the house and the old barn. Some of the time, he was carrying boxes or big duffel bags. When I asked him if I could help, he refused. He barely ate while I was there, even when I bagged a buck and suggested that we cook the back straps for dinner on the grill."

"Wow. That is really weird. He loved grilled back straps." said Joe. "I remember the time he made deer parmigiana and 'forgot' to tell us what meat he used. He thought that was hysterical."

"I remember," Nick said, but didn't smile. "It still bothers me. He acted so strangely, really odd. It gave me a very sick and ominous feeling."

"You know," said Joe, "I had that same feeling three

weeks ago when I talked with him after a round of golf at the country club. He hadn't played well at all. It was if his mind was somewhere else the whole day. You know how good his short game was? Well, that day he could not hit a green from fifty yards and three-putted every hole.

"After we showered and were sitting at the table for dinner, I asked him what was on his mind. He laughed. Seriously, he laughed out loud! It startled me. So, I asked him what was so funny. He looked at me really intensely and said "My mind is a battlefield Joe. It is not a place you want to visit right now."

"Wow!" replied Nick. "Really? That doesn't sound like Grandpa at all. What'd you say after that?"

"I didn't know what to say, so I just started talking about some of my struggles at work. I told him I was getting frustrated about the kind of stories I have to do and how I wished that I could utilize my political science degree more effectively in my journalism. He listened but it was more like he was bursting at the seams to tell me something.

"After I finished, all he said was, 'The world always has a backstory. History has a backstory'. Then he told me that I 'always have to be looking for it,' and soon I 'would see the truth'. He said it would change how I saw life. What do you make of it?"

"I just got goosebumps," said Nick, "and the same sick and ominous feeling. We have a long drive. Let's just call Uncle Rob and maybe we can figure it all out by the time we get home."

Joe called their uncle and gave him their condolences. They spent the next few hours of the drive sharing memories of their grandfather, grateful for how he had influenced their lives, but that nagging feeling never left Joe's mind.

"A humble giant has fallen," said the priest as he began to wrap up his praise for the man lying in the coffin before him. "But his memory, good deeds, and humility will live on after him and bless those who knew and loved him."

He concluded his graveside comments, blessed the coffin and the mourners, and signaled to the workers to lower the casket into the cold, damp earth. Before the workers began, the six cousins, who had been their grandfather's pallbearers, surrounded the grave and raised the swords they had brought with them. They stood in silence, honoring their grandfather in a way that he would have approved. When they finished, flowers were tossed in as each mourner said their last goodbyes under a gray and threatening spring sky.

The cousins and the rest of the family entered their limousines and headed for dinner at their grandfather's favorite Italian restaurant. This gathering wouldn't be anything like the wonderful family dinners he used to host there when he was alive. At least they would be together in a lively environment surrounded by sights, sounds, and smells that reminded them of him. They would make sure to order some Sambuca and drink a toast to his memory.

In the limo that carried the grandsons, Billy, the oldest, spoke first. "I know we all loved him, and we all spent a lot of time with him, but over the past few months, I needed his advice about some deals I have been working on. So, I had dinner with him every week. During those dinners, I kept getting the feeling that there was something on his mind that he wouldn't discuss. He seemed distracted and concerned. I asked him to tell me about it, but you know Grandpa, 'Mr. Better-than-Good'. He would never tell us anything that would worry us or cause us concern."

"I know," said Joe. "I sent him a number of my most recent stories to watch, and all he would say was that I would have a lot more interesting stuff to report on very soon. I thought that was strange, but you know how cryptic he could be, especially near the end."

The limo arrived at the restaurant, and they exited the vehicle and hustled into the building. Jeff's wife, Carol, met them at the door. She reassured him that she and the kids were fine, and he should join the others giving their condolences to Aunt Susan and Uncle Domenic. Then they joined the rest of the family at the bar and ordered shots of Sambuca. Robbie got everyone's attention and raised his glass.

"Let's all raise our glasses and remember the life of a good and honest man. Although he always said he was a dime amongst the pennies, we all know he was a giant of a man. Powerful yet revered, practical yet visionary, tough but kind. We shall never see another like him. Here's to Mr. Better-than-Good!"

With that, everyone saluted the life of their grandfather, then sat down to their soon-to-come feast.

Sitting around the table, it didn't take long for this sad occasion to turn into a joyful commemoration of their grandfather's life. With this family, every opportunity to be together was cause for celebration. Their grandfather had insisted on that. Next to their faith, nothing was more important than family. It was to be honored and celebrated every chance they got.

Joe looked around the room and spotted his sisters, Alexandra and Olivia, sitting together and laughing at something Ty was saying. He was so glad that they had grown up so well, and that none of the issues with their parents' divorce had left any permanent negative impact. In fact, it seemed to have drawn all of them much closer together. It was so much fun visiting at their apartment in Connecticut when he could get time off. He said a silent prayer to God in thanksgiving and lifted the glass of wine to his lips.

Nick nudged him as he was taking his sip, almost spilling it on his new, white shirt. "Sorry, Joe. I didn't mean to startle you," said Nick. "How are you holding up?"

"I'm okay," Joe acknowledged, "but I am worried about Aunt Susan. She idolized Grandpa. They were so close, and she was his princess. She looks broken to me. I think she's devastated by how quickly grandpa passed. She was there almost every day, and I'm sure it kills her that she wasn't there when he died. I hope Uncle Rob and Dad can help her through all of this."

Just then, they heard their father, Domenic, tapping his glass for everyone's attention.

"I know this has been a tough day for everyone," he began, "and I know the upcoming days and months may be even worse as we all deal in our own ways with the loss of our beloved father and grandfather. Just remember, the one thing we can do to honor his memory is to love each other and carry on as a loving and united family. He would be most proud of that legacy.

"I also want to read a poem that he once read to Susan, Robert, and me when we were small. It is sad, but there is a wonderful lesson to be learned about life and death, legacy and perseverance. It is called 'Lament', written by Edna St. Vincent Millay.

"Listen, children: Your father is dead.
From his old coats, I'll make you little jackets;
I'll make you little trousers from his old pants.
There'll be in his pockets
Things he used to put there,
Keys and pennies covered with tobacco;
Dan shall have the pennies
To save in his bank;
Anne shall have the keys
To make a pretty noise with.
Life must go on,
And the dead be forgotten;
Life must go on,
Though good men die;
Anne, eat your breakfast;
Dan, take your medicine;
Life must go on;
I forget just why."

"A good man has died. Yes, we lament his loss, but we must remember, he has left something for each of us to remember him by. His love, his laughter, his advice, and his counsel. The legacy of his hard work and his example of strength and humility. Always remember that he loved each and every one of you. Honor him with your lives and be brave when trials come, for come they will. Remember, you have worthy blood in your veins. Be strong and courageous and never let anything come between you and family." Domenic sat down and put his arm around his younger brother, Robert, whose eyes had begun to tear up.

As Joe looked around the table, he saw that everyone was doing the same. Robbie and Ty had their arms around their sister, Ellie; Billy and Jeffrey were hugging their

17

sisters, Colleen and Kate; his and Nick's sisters, Alex and Olivia, were weeping in each other's arms; and Aunt Susan and Aunt Carolyn, Uncle Rob's wife, were holding hands and wiping their tears.

Joe put his arm around Nick's shoulders and said, "Now this is what family is all about."

After dinner was complete, Joe watched as the family began saying their goodbyes. *In our family, this could take another hour,* Joe thought, chuckling to himself.

Uncle Rob tapped Joe on the arm.

"Would you meet me at the bar when you're ready to go?" he asked.

"Sure, Uncle Rob. What's up?" Joe asked.

"I'll tell you when you're all together," his uncle said enigmatically.

Joe shrugged, finished his goodbyes, and headed to the bar. Nick, Billy, Jeff, Robbie, and Ty were already there.

Uncle Rob didn't waste any time. "I have something for each of you from Grandpa," he started, "but I can't give it to you now. I need for you all to meet me at the family vacation home in the Catskills tomorrow morning. I will tell you all about it there. Leave early enough to avoid the Friday traffic, bring your swords, and don't stay out too late drinking. I need you alert and focused."

He turned, gathered up his coat, and left them there.

Joe felt bewildered.

"What was that all about?" asked Nick. "I know Uncle Rob just lost his father, but he seemed extra serious just now. Do you guys think this is something bad?"

"No," replied Jeff, the lawyer of the family. "Probably just some paperwork we need to review or sign. Grandpa had a lot of investments and properties he owned, and he probably wants Billy and me to look at them from a legal and financial perspective. I wouldn't worry about it too much. Let's go up there with the idea that we are going to help him sort this all out and help the family. It's the least we can do."

They all agreed.

Joe and Nick found their father, Domenic, as he was saying goodbye to his sister, Susan.

"Sorry to interrupt," said Joe as he and Nick approached, "but we wanted to say goodbye before we left."

Domenic kissed his older sister on the cheek. "We will talk soon. Remember, I love you, and we will get through this together." They hugged one last time, and then he turned to his sons.

"Are you guys leaving, too?" he asked. "What are your plans for the next few days? Are we going to have any time together before you head out?"

"I thought so," Joe replied, "but Uncle Rob wants us all to meet him up at the family vacation home tomorrow to talk about some things. If that goes quickly, we will head back to Long Island and maybe grab dinner. How does that sound?"

"Sounds good to me," replied his father. "Just be careful driving."

"We will," replied Nick, "but Dad, do you have any idea what Uncle Rob wants to discuss? Are you in the loop?"

"I have an idea," he replied, "but I will let him discuss it with you. He has some decisions to make, and he needs your input. I guess he feels it needs to happen right away, and it is his call. Just listen carefully and let him lay it all out." Then he grabbed them, hugged them both, and said, "Make me and your sisters proud."

Before leaving, Jeff spent a few minutes talking with Carol to make sure she and the kids would be all right while he headed north to the family home. She seemed to understand the importance of what he needed to do and said that she would spend the time with her parents on Long Island, not to worry, and to take all the time he needed.

Jeff kissed her and the children. "Thanks honey, I don't know what Uncle Rob has to tell us, but it must be important. I appreciate your understanding, and I will be back as soon as I can. Don't let the kids grow up too much while I'm gone. You know how I hate to miss anything."

He then joined the others as they headed out for what they intended to be a quick drink and an early night. They didn't often have the opportunity to be together, since they were scattered around the country these days with careers and schools separating them, and Joe truly enjoyed himself when they did. They found a quiet tavern within walking distance of the restaurant and settled into a large booth where they could talk and catch up.

"So, Joe, how is the life of an up-and-coming TV star going for you?" asked Ty, a little tongue-in-cheek.

Ty liked ribbing his older cousin, because he knew that although Joe had done well and was in a broader market, he was getting impatient waiting for his big break.

"Cut me some slack, Ty," moaned Joe. "I'm working my butt off every day covering stories that no one else wants. I'm the new guy, so I have to pay my dues. It gets old sometimes."

"I can imagine," Ty replied, switching from teasing to supportive when he saw how frustrated his cousin was. "Hang in there. Your dreams of being a top correspondent for a major network will happen, because you are an energetic, fiercely hard-working, and precise reporter."

"Thanks for the vote of confidence." Joe sighed, "but patience isn't my strong suit, so I feel like I always have to push myself to be better every day. What about you, 'Dr. Frankenstein'? You're just as dedicated and hard-working in your studies. Neurology can't be easy!" His voice turned teasing. "Dissect any rotting cadaver brains this week?"

Ty grinned. "I love the science of it all. In fact, I would like to have the opportunity to study your brain, Joe. Now that would be interesting. It could win me a Nobel prize!"

Joe laughed. That was one of the things Joe loved about this family. They always knew that they could be real and honest with each other and that no one in the group was ever going to escape being the brunt of a joke.

"Ty," said Joe, "for you, my buddy, I would gladly give my brain to science, just let me finish with it first. That is, if it doesn't turn to mush from all the reporting I'm doing about school board meetings, bridge openings, and free flu shots at the clinic."

Nick jumped in. "Hey, Ty, I can give you the brain of the next deer I shoot, if it will help your studies any, but I get to keep the rack."

Ty responded, "Thanks a ton, Nick, but I'm not allowed to keep brains in my dorm. Although, it might make a good present to leave for my roommate. Let me think about it and get back to you."

"Well, don't take too long," Nick said. "I will probably have one for you by the end of the day tomorrow. That forty acres of Grandpa's is crawling with deer, and I intend to get one of them for us to have for supper Saturday night."

Ty laughed. "That's mighty ambitious, Nick. Typical of you, though. Big heart, big dreams, and big talk."

"Hey!" Nick pretended to be offended. "You have to admit that most of the time, I back up my big talk with big results. I'm a crack shot!"

"Great," said Billy, "just what we need, Nick's deer casserole. Sounds like an incredibly bad idea, count me out."

Nick slapped him on the shoulder. "You're missing out, cousin. Just because you've already graduated from Wharton Business School…"

"…with honors while playing varsity lacrosse," Billy added.

"…with honors," Nick mimicked with a grin. "Just because you drive yourself as hard as any of us, doesn't mean you get to snub your nose at my delicious deer casserole."

"Why don't we just stop on the way up there tomorrow and pick up some civilized meat, like a few filet mignons?" Billy suggested. "We'll fire up the huge grill Grandpa has and have us a real feast."

They all agreed that that was a better plan, but Nick added, "Whatever, I'm still gonna kill me some deer!"

"Atta boy, Nick," chimed Robbie, "don't let them stop you from being you. Go out there and do your thing. Grandpa's house could sure use some animal heads on the walls. In fact, I'm creating a new sculpture that would look great in the family room next to the fireplace. Between you and me, we will bring some character to that old house."

The cousins moaned dramatically.

"The artist speaks!" Ty cried. "I wonder if he can top the sculpture of old vines he made for Aunt Susan last year."

"Or the mountain scene he painted on the shovel for Uncle Domenic two years ago," Billy added.

"Hey, that was a real a showpiece," Robbie protested. "Know what, Nick? I may even take the rack from the deer you kill and use it in my piece!"

"I don't think so," said Nick. "You can have any other part, but the rack is mine."

While the others bantered, Jeff sat quietly. Joe noticed his silence and watched him for a few minutes. Jeff wasn't an overly-talkative person, but when he did speak, he was funny and quick-witted. Always thoughtful and measured, he had a habit of rolling things over and over in his mind. This seemed to be one of those times, but something felt different about his silence tonight.

Finally, Joe asked, "Jeff, what's going on? You seem extra quiet tonight. Are you okay, or are you just dreading Nick's deer casserole?"

"Just thinking about what Uncle Rob said to us tonight," Jeff responded. "I can't figure out why he would need us to help him with anything regarding Grandpa's estate. Grandpa had a ton of lawyers and accountants, and I know he would have had everything relating to his estate all wrapped up years ago. Knowing Grandpa, he would never leave any loose ends."

"I know," added Billy. "I was thinking the same thing, but no use worrying about it tonight. We need to get some sleep and deal with it tomorrow. I'll run to Grandpa's condominium and get the SUV. I will pick you guys up at 7:30 a.m. sharp, and we will be at the vacation house by 10:00 a.m."

The cousins agreed and headed to their hotels and homes. Joe searched each of their faces as he said good-bye. He noticed a variety of emotions in their expressions and in their eyes. It made sense. His own emotions were a mixture of concern, curiosity, and even dread as he contemplated returning to the family vacation home tomorrow. It just wouldn't be the same without Grandpa.

CHAPTER TWO

MEETING WITH
THE PROPHET

The cousins arrived at the vacation house at 10:15 a.m. Uncle Rob was waiting for them on the front porch with a cup of coffee in his hand.

"Uh-oh," Nick said. "We're in for it now."

"Nah," Billy assured him. "I got this. Watch the master at work."

As they got out of the car, Uncle Rob greeted them, but not with a smile. "Nice of you guys to make it up here before noon. Stay out too late last night?"

"No," replied Billy, "we had to wait for Fabio over there to make sure his 'he-hive' was perfect." He grinned at Robbie, who was much more handsome than Fabio.

"It's not a 'he-hive,' fool. It's a man-bun. If you knew anything about fashion, you would understand. Keep wearing your 1987 Gordon Gekko power suits and wondering why you can't get a date with anyone under fifty," countered Robbie.

Rob, who had just taken a mouthful of coffee, laughed, spewing it everywhere. The cousins laughed with him. When the laughter died down, their uncle grew serious again.

"Now that you're here, let's get down to business. Give me your swords, put your bags in the bedrooms, and meet me in the family room in ten minutes."

Exactly ten minutes later, they gathered around the fireplace in the family room. Nick glanced around and realized that his brother and cousins were just as anxious as he was to find out what was going on. Except Billy. His expression was pure anticipation. Interesting.

Uncle Rob didn't waste any time. "I'm sure you are puzzled about why I summoned you here. I know this seems odd and out of character for me, but what I have to share with you today is serious family business. It will affect not only our family but everyone in the nation and the world. There are things you need to know and understand that can't wait. History has taken a turn and only our family, actually only you six, can do what needs to be done to prevent disaster."

Ty laughed. "Okay, Dad, good one! You really had us going for a minutes. I know we love to play pranks on each other, but this one takes the cake. Couldn't you have at least scheduled this for a more convenient time of day, like late afternoon, so that we could have slept in?"

His father just glared at him.

Ty's eyebrows raised, and he stopped laughing.

"I'm not joking here, Ty, and this is no prank. As I said, this is serious business, and I need your focus and attention. I only have a few hours to get you guys up to speed and ready for action. If you fail in what I'm about to lay out for you, there will be no tomorrow, no returning to school, no 'Dr. Ty', only devastation and chaos. So, get serious and listen."

The cousins looked at each other with profound surprise, then refocused on him.

Silently, Uncle Rob looked each one in the eye

before he continued. "I will start by telling you who your grandfather really was. You know that he was the son of immigrants, a great athlete, and a highly decorated World War II hero. You know he was a successful banker and investor. What you don't know is that he was also The Meglio di Buono of the Cincinnatus family and was the international head of the most powerful family of the Guardians of the Swords of Valor."

"Okay, stop right there," insisted Joe. "Are you telling us that Grandpa was a mobster? That he was the head of some crazy crime family?"

"No, Joe, that is not what I'm telling you. Just listen, and you will soon understand," said Uncle Rob with a hint of frustration in his voice.

Joe raised his hands in surrender and nodded his agreement, so Uncle Rob continued, "The Guardians of the Swords of Valor are a group of five families who have been chosen throughout history to be the guardians and protectors of the most powerful swords in existence. Each family was charged with the protection and keeping of two swords that originally belonged to some of the greatest people in history. We are part of, and descendants of, the Cincinnatus family."

He handed them each a piece of paper, then asked Nick to read it aloud.

Nick cleared his throat, then began.

Lucius Quinctius Cincinnatus - Cincinnatus was a Roman patrician, statesman, and military leader of the early Republic who, by the time of the Empire, became a legendary figure of Roman virtues, specifically Roman masculinity and civic duty. Despite his old age, he worked his small farm until an invasion prompted his fellow citizens to call for his leadership. He came from his plough to assume complete control over the state, but upon achieving a swift victory, relinquished all his power and returned to his farm.

Nick looked up, puzzled. "This reads like an article from Wikipedia or something. Is that where this came from?"

Rob frowned. "Does it matter? The information is accurate and important for you to know. Please keep reading."

"Yes, sir," Nick responded, then continued.

His success and the subsequent resignation of his near-absolute authority immediately after the crisis ended has often been cited as an example of outstanding leadership, service to the greater good, civic duty, lack of personal ambition, and modesty. As a result, he has inspired many organizations and other entities, some named in his honor.

Cincinnatus served as consul in 460 BC and as dictator in 458 BC and again in 439 BC when the patricians called on him to suppress a feared uprising.

He was an inspiration to George Washington, and there is a statue of him at Washington's home in Mount Vernon. Washington resigned from public life after the war, when he could have used his influence to become very powerful. Instead, he moved to his "villa" in the country, a term Washington used only after his retirement, probably alluding to his desire to be like Cincinnatus.

"Thank you, Nick. As you can see," Uncle Rob continued, "our ancestor was a well-respected and important historical figure. Every one of you is a direct descendant of Lucius Quinctius Cincinnatus. You have the blood of a warrior of valor and virtue running through your veins. That is why, during the centuries that followed, our family was chosen to be one of the Guardian families. Since that time, it has been our duty to protect and keep safe two of the Swords of Valor; the Sword of Roland called Durandal, and Braveheart, the Sword of William Wallace."

Billy spoke up. "Uncle Rob, we know about them, because Grandpa gave us replicas of those swords when we turned twelve years old at the initiation ceremonies. He gave me the replica of Durandal, the Sword of Roland. We understand Grandpa's fascination with swords. Are you telling us that those swords are replicas of the true originals?"

"No, that is not what I'm saying," Robert answered. "What I'm trying to tell you is that those are the originals; the real thing."

"No way!" Nick exclaimed. "I've been carrying the actual Sword of Michael the Archangel all these years? That's unreal!"

"How is that possible?" Jeff asked. "And why are you telling us about it now?"

"Wait," Joe spoke up, "how is it that our family was assigned to guard two of the swords, but all six of us have original Swords of Valor? Where did the other four come from?"

Uncle Rob held up a hand to forestall further questions. "I will get into all of that shortly. May I continue?" The cousins nodded, and Rob resumed.

"Your grandfather knew that we were entering a time in history when the swords would be the key to the survival and freedom of mankind. There is a group of men who want their power for themselves. They are the Apostles of Azazel. They are increasing their efforts to get their hands on the swords we were protecting, so he determined that the best place to hide them was in plain sight. The enemy would never suspect that he would give the most valuable and powerful swords in the world to young children.

"He kept the copies here on this property, so that even if the enemy were to discover this place and ransack it, all they would get would be useless copies. For years now, you have possessed the actual Swords of Valor. Now you will be required to use them."

Shocked, Nick looked at the others, seeing similar emotions on their faces. He turned back and asked, "What are you talking about, Uncle Rob? Are we going to war, or something?"

"That can't be it," Billy scoffed. "Nobody uses swords in battle anymore."

"Don't be too sure, Billy," Uncle Rob warned. "Each of you was given a sword based on the personal characteristics, qualities, and virtues Grandpa observed in you while you were growing up. Do you remember the qualities of the swords you possess?"

Again, Billy spoke first. "I have Durandal. It represents the qualities of temperance and diligence."

"That's right, Billy," Rob nodded. "What about the rest of you? What qualities do your swords represent?"

"I have Braveheart, which was the sword of William Wallace. It represents persistence and fortitude," Robbie replied.

"Good. Who's next?"

Joe, looking thoughtful, answered, "He gave me Excalibur, the Sword of Melchizedek. It was later used by King Arthur and represents benevolence and love."

"I bear Joyeuse, the Sword of Charlemagne," Ty replied. "Are you telling me that Grandpa thought I was generous and had ethics?" He started to grin, then wiped

30

the smile from his face as his father just stared at him. "Sorry, Dad. It's just that Grandpa never really talked about this except at our initiation ceremonies. Did he really think we have these qualities?"

"He felt you had the beginnings of those qualities, Ty. He knew that you'd need time and experience to develop them fully. Jeff?" Rob asked.

"Mine is the Sword of Solomon, representing wisdom and faith," Jeff answered.

"And I have the Sword of Michael the Archangel," Nick offered before Rob could ask. "It represents justice and courage."

"Excellent. But you all need to understand that the swords in your possession don't just represent those qualities, they possess them. Your grandfather chose them carefully, with great understanding and insight. You can see what he believed about each of you. You need to believe these things about yourselves and each other. Your lives will depend on it in a few hours.

"As I stated, our family is part of a greater group of five Guardian families. Jeff, you asked if our family only had responsibility for two swords, Durandal and Braveheart, how was he able to give you the other swords? The answer to that lies in the recent history of the swords.

"Since the end of World War II, the Apostles of Azazel have successfully captured four of the ten Swords of Valor; the Sword of Tristan, the Sword of Leonidas, the Sword of St. Peter, and the Sword of Joan of Arc."

"Who was responsible for those swords?" Nick asked.

"If you're asking who's to blame," Uncle Rob looked stern, "remember what Grandpa used to tell you about that?"

Nick ducked his head, "Fix the problem, not the blame." He looked up. "But I'm not wanting to blame anyone. I was just curious which families had responsibility for which swords."

Uncle Rob looked at him for a moment. "I apologize if I was quick to judge you, Nick. I'll answer your questions. The family of Cincinnatus was given charge of Durandal and Braveheart. The family of Joseph of Arimathea safeguarded Excalibur but lost the Sword of St. Peter. The family of David the King kept the Sword of Solomon and the Sword of St. Michael the Archangel safe. The family of Richard the Lionhearted lost Curtana, the Sword of Tristan, but secured Joyeuse, the Sword of Charlemagne. The family of Christopher Columbus lost both the Sword of Joan of Arc and the Sword of Leonidas. Any questions?"

When no one spoke, he continued. "World War II was tough on the Guardian families. The family of David the King was almost wiped out by the Nazis. The family of Richard the Lionhearted was also decimated by the war in Europe. The Columbus family had already lost the Sword of Leonidas when the Santa Maria sunk, and they lost the Sword of Joan of Arc before D-Day. After the war was over, the families of the Guardians had a great conclave where they decided that the two remaining intact families, those of Cincinnatus and Joseph of Arimathea, would protect the remaining Swords of Valor.

"Excuse me, Uncle Rob," Nick asked. "Would you explain what qualities the lost swords had?"

"Certainly. Curtana, the Sword of Tristan possesses mercy and meekness. The Sword of Leonidas bears bravery and prudence. The Sword of St. Peter embodies reverence and brotherly love. And the Sword of Joan of Arc exemplifies self-control and chastity. These swords must be returned to our family. Many good people have given their lives to protect them over the years.

"The remaining swords, the ones that were presented to you by your grandfather, were given over to the Meglio and his family after the great conclave, as were all the assets from the other families. These assets were to be used for the building of a safe place to keep the swords and the security systems needed to protect them. The other decimated Guardian families also handed over all their libraries and historical research documents relating to the swords.

Ty turned to Billy. "Did you notice that our family was the only one that never lost a sword?"

Uncle Rob frowned at him. "Not true, Ty. The family of David the King did not lose any swords while they possessed them. But remember, that family was nearly wiped out by the Nazis. I'll tell you more about their story later. You also need to know that while the family of Cincinnatus has not lost either of the two swords assigned to them, we are part of a family who has."

"What?" Nick asked, confused. "You just said..."

Uncle Rob held up a hand to stop him. "Once again, I will state that we are of the family of Cincinnatus, but we are also part of the family of Joseph of Arimathea, who did lose one sword, the Sword of St. Peter."

At this revelation, Nick's jaw dropped. He stared at his uncle in disbelief. After a moment, he found his voice. "Excuse my lack of understanding, Uncle Rob, but how is that so? Was Joseph of Arimathea a distant relative of Grandpa too?"

"No, Nick, he wasn't, but he was a distant relative of your grandmother."

"Come on, Dad, seriously?" exclaimed Robbie.

"You can't be serious with all this stuff! This is all just way too hard to believe. How is it possible, assuming any of this is true, that we never heard anything about this from anyone? I have been on every ancestry website out there and looked up our family history and genealogies and have never seen anything even close to this kind of news."

His father just glared at him and went on. "I will just say that certain genealogical records have been 'managed' over the years. Also, this kind of information is not something that you share until the time is right. It is not something that can be entrusted to kids who don't know when or how to keep their mouths shut."

"Oh, but we can be entrusted with six of the most powerful swords in the universe when we are only twelve years old," Ty commented. There was no mistaking the sarcasm in his voice.

Nick shook his head at his cousin's lack of tact. He glanced at Uncle Rob, whose face was growing redder by the moment. Nick recognized that look. It was one of disappointment and anger. Ducking his head, Nick wondered if he should say something to try and smooth the situation. He didn't have a chance, however.

Uncle Rob exploded. "You know what? Maybe this was a big mistake. I told my father you might not be ready for this when the time came, but he had faith in all of you. I'm not sure that I do. Nothing in your reactions indicates to me that you have any sense of the seriousness or gravity of this situation. I'm going to get myself some coffee. When I get back, there will be some decisions to make." With that, he turned and left the room.

After a moment of silence, Nick spoke up. "I don't get you guys. This is all great information. Hard to take in all at once, I know, but really cool stuff! If any of this is even close to being true, then we need to shut up and listen."

"I agree with Nick," Joe concurred. "I want to hear Uncle Rob out and learn more."

"Look," said Robbie, "you guys don't know our dad like Ty and I do. He goes off sometimes. He gets this whole Wizard of Oz attitude. 'I am Rob, the Great and Powerful. Why do you seek me?'" His voice sounded deep and resonating, effectively imitating the wizard in the movie they remembered so well. "Look, he talks a lot about destiny and mission statements and life plans. I'm not sure this isn't part of some attempt to inspire us, to make us want to get focused on our lives and make something better of ourselves."

Ty agreed. "Yeah, it's like we can never live up to his expectations. Sure, he tells us he is proud of us or that he thinks we have put in a good effort every so often, but I always have this feeling that I can never live up to his example, or Grandpa's for that matter. He can be a tough guy to live up to. He has so many people who think he is a genius, and I think to myself, how am I ever going to get there?"

Billy jumped in. "I hear you guys, but think about it. Think about the documents he showed us. Think about the information he just shared. Do you know how much time and effort it would have taken for him to put all of this together? Grandpa died less than a week ago. Do you think he just threw all this together in that time, while he was dealing with his father's death and making all the funeral arrangements, so that he could 'make a point' with us? I don't think so. I think the smart thing for us to do right now is to listen and learn. When he comes back in here, I'm going to tell him we are ready to shut up and listen and won't interrupt again, agreed?"

One by one, the cousins agreed.

Five minutes later, Uncle Rob walked back into the family room with a fresh cup of coffee and looked at each of them. "So, what is the knucklehead committee's decision?" he asked them.

"We are all in agreement that we will shut up and listen to Mr. Wizard," said Billy. Ty and Billy chuckled a bit, but everyone nodded their heads in agreement.

"Good, then let me continue," said Uncle Rob. He sat down, took a sip of his coffee, then set it on the side table. "Where was I? Oh, yes, your grandma. As I said, we are part of the family of Joseph of Arimathea, in addition to the family of Cincinnatus. Our family has bloodlines from Cincinnatus on the Italian side, and Joseph of Arimathea on the Celtic side.

"I have told you about the life of Cincinnatus. Now let me tell you about the life of Joseph of Arimathea and some of what you may not have learned about him from the Bible or the history books." He handed each of them another document, then began reading aloud.

Joseph of Arimathea: First Head of the Arimathea Family of Guardians - Joseph was a wealthy merchant and high-ranking member of the Sanhedrin in the time of Christ. He was present at the crucifixion where scholars say that he caught the streaming blood of Christ in the cup that was used at the last supper. He, along with Nicodemus, begged Pilate for the body of Christ so that they could bury him according to Jewish Law. Joseph buried Jesus in a tomb that he had dug for himself.

Upon the resurrection of Jesus, he renounced his membership in the Sanhedrin. He and a group of followers departed for what are now the British Isles to spread the gospel message, bringing with them the sword and the sacred chalice, known now as the Holy Grail. Before landing there, they journeyed via his merchant ships to Gallia, the region that is now France.

During their travels, they spread the gospel of Jesus and became well known. While in Gallia, he was met by a group of men who asked if he was a member of the family of David the King. He told them that although Jewish, he wasn't of the House of David. Upon further conversation, they said that they had heard rumors that he was in possession of the Sword of Peter and that they had another sword that needed protection, the Sword of Melchizedek. Given his close association with the Lord Jesus and his heritage as a devout Jew, they felt that he was a trustworthy and holy man. They believed that the swords would be safe in his keeping.

Thus, he became the leader of the Arimathea family of the Guardians of the Swords of Valor. He agreed and took the swords with him to Britannia and kept them safe in an abbey he built at what is now known as Glastonbury. When Joseph arrived in Britannia, he is said to have landed on the island of Avalon and climbed up to Wearyall Hill.

Exhausted, he thrust his staff into the ground and rested. By morning, his staff had taken root. He believed this was confirmation that this was the place where he should protect the treasures he had brought with him. With his twelve followers, he established the first monastery at Glastonbury. He secured both the swords and the chalice in a secret place, said to have been at the entrance to the underworld, just below the Tor. The spring at what is known as Chalice Well is believed to flow from there.

Joseph established and grew his family of Guardians, all the while spreading the gospel and making converts to Christianity. Over the millennium, the Sword of St. Peter was lost to the Apostles of Azazel.

The Sword of Melchizedek is now known to the world as the sword Excalibur. It was given to Arthur by a member of the

Arimathea family, known in legend as the Lady of the Lake. She presented it to him in his time of need, to carry out his God-ordained plans to institute a better way of leading people. The sword was then returned to the Lady of the Lake upon Arthur's death and remains in the Arimathea family of Guardians until this day.

He set his paper aside. "As you know, the stories of the quest for the Holy Grail also originated about this time. Over time, through intermarriage, the Arimathea family line ran through the Royal Stewart Clan. Your ancestors on your grandmother's side are members of that clan. Eventually, the leadership, of both the clan and the Arimathea family was given to the head of your grandmother's family. Any questions at this point, gentlemen?"

The cousins shifted positions, and looked at each other with varying degrees of interest, bewilderment and amazement. But no one responded with a question, so Uncle Rob went on.

"Now I will connect the dots for you about how the two families came together, why we are the most powerful and respected family of Guardians, and why the other families felt that they needed to put their swords in our hands for safekeeping. First, about your grandfather. Here is his official Guardian dossier." He handed them another document and again began reading aloud.

Joseph Melillo: the Meglio Di Buono of the International Guardian Families of the Swords of Valor

Personality: Gregarious, intelligent, and brash.

Accomplishments: Joined the Marines in WWII to do his duty and see the world. Attained the rank of master sergeant. Sharpshooter. Decorated for bravery in combat.

Civilian Occupation: Banker

Family: Son of Domenico Melillo, an immigrant from Naples, Italy, previous Meglio of the Cincinnatus family of Italy assigned to guard two of the Swords of Valor.

Husband of Catherine Petrie, daughter of Robert Ogilvie Petrie, the previous Meglio of the Joseph of Arimathea family of the British Isles assigned to guard two of the Swords of Valor

Father of two sons, Domenic and Robert, of the Guardians of the Swords of Valor, and daughter, Susan.

History: After returning from his honeymoon, he met with his father and his new father-in-law. They told him that his marriage to Catherine was the intertwining of the two greatest Guardian families, and he became a soldier in the effort. He was briefed on the history of the Guardians, of the families themselves, and was given his first assignment.

Over the years, he performed many secret assignments for the Guardians and earned their respect and admiration as a tireless and fearless operative. He moved up the ranks of this international organization. Upon the death of his father-in-law, Robert Ogilvie Petrie, he was elevated to the position of Meglio di Buono of the International Guardian Families by unanimous acclamation.

During this time, he moved the family headquarters to the Catskill Mountains of New York and bought a two-hundred-year-old 'vacation home' on forty acres. On this land, he built a fallout shelter beneath the old barn behind the house. This became the Keeping Room for the Swords of Valor and has been expanded and upgraded many times over the years. This room is now one of the most secure places on earth.

In the Keeping Room, there is a library of select books, scrolls, and maps relating to the swords, including facts and legends about the most notable events in the lives of the heroes who used them.

Joseph constantly prepared and awaited the time of crisis that he knew would be coming during the time of his grandchildren. He prepared letters of explanation and instructions for each of them when they were born. He carefully observed each one as they grew to determine their best qualities, abilities, and flaws. On their twelfth birthdays, they each were given one of the Swords of Valor. They were told were replicas of famous swords from history and were reflective of their best qualities.

He knew that when the time of crisis came, he might not be around. So, he instructed his son, Robert, that upon his death, when the crisis came, to convene a meeting of the grandsons at the family headquarters and reveal to them the family history and give them the letters of instructions.

"Any questions?"

There were none once again, so he continued. "I will now tell you about your great-grandfather." He handed them yet another dossier, reading it aloud, as well.

Robert Ogilvie Petrie: Previous Meglio Di Buono of The Guardians of the Swords of Valor and Head of the Royal Stewart Clan

Personality: Quiet, strong, and daring.

Accomplishments: Graduated from the University of Edinburgh. Joined the British Army, Black Watch, 51st Highland Division. Fought in France on the Western Front during WWI from 1915 to 1918.

Accompanied General Edmund Allenby on December 11th, 1917, during his respectful entry on foot into Jerusalem for the reading of the martial law proclamation.

Participated with the honor guard at the Jaffa Gate. That guard was composed of English, Welsh, Scottish, Indian,

Australian, and troops from New Zealand, with twenty soldiers each from Italy and France.

Family: Son of Andrew Ogilvie Petrie, former Meglio of the Arimathea Family of Edinburgh, Scotland, assigned to guard two of the Swords of Valor, former head of the Royal Stewart Clan

Husband of Susan McKenna of Glasgow, father of Catherine Petrie.

History: His father called him into his study after he returned from Scotland and told him the history of the Guardians of the Swords of Valor and the history of the family of Joseph of Arimathea.

He then received his first assignment. He traveled widely in the service of the Guardians and fulfilled many assignments. He met with then-Princess Elizabeth prior to the Battle of Britain in 1940 when she was relocated for safety reasons to Windsor.

After his marriage, he immigrated to the United States where most of his assignments were taking him. He eventually was selected as the Meglio di Buono of the International Guardians, a position he held for over twenty years. Upon his death, Joseph, his son-in-law, was acclaimed the new Meglio di Buono.

As he finished the reading of the resumes of their grandfather and great-grandfather, Uncle Rob looked around the room. He asked again, "Any questions? Any thoughts?"

Jeff responded to his question. "Okay, so now we understand the history and how it all ties together. Grandpa and both Great-Grandpas were Meglios. What exactly does that mean?"

Rob replied, "Meglio di Buono translates in English to 'better than good'. Now you know why he always responded 'better than good' when anyone asked him how he was. It was another way for him to hide something vital in plain sight. Everyone thought he was just an affable old banker, a fierce golfer, and a faithful family man, but they never knew the half of it. That was the way he wanted and needed it to be.

"It is an ancient title of authority that reflects the idea that all the heads of the families of Guardians were good men. But this family, your grandfather and great-grandfathers, were even better. They were better than good, the best of the best."

Ty spoke up. "I always wondered when we were all up here at the old house why Grandpa would spend so much time in that old fallout shelter under the barn. We were never allowed to play back there. I always thought that he was just a little too paranoid about nuclear war or something. Now I understand. Will you show us what's in the fallout shelter?"

"Yes, I will, but not yet. I still have several things to tell you before that can happen," his father replied. "There are still some details you need to know."

Joe spoke next. "My question is about the assignments they went on. In both of their dossiers, it said that after being told about the history of the swords and the families, they were sent on their first assignments. What exactly does that mean?"

Uncle Rob replied, "Everyone selected to be a soldier of the family is given an assignment immediately after everything is revealed to them. It may seem presumptuous to put someone in a dangerous situation with very little time to adapt to the new reality, but both your grandfather and great-grandfather were highly decorated soldiers and had experience in war. It was an easy call for the families to put them out there. The assignments themselves involved thwarting the plans of the Apostles of Azazel to capture any Sword of Valor they could get their hands on.

"These are ruthless people who will use any means necessary to gain control over the swords and the world itself. Many times, our intelligence group will get wind of an impending attempt on a sword. Our soldiers are sent out to stop it. Both men were capable and never knew defeat. They operated mostly in their own timeline. However, there were occasionally situations which required them to travel back in time to accomplish an assignment."

"Back in time?" blurted Nick. "Did you just say that they traveled back in time for these assignments? Seriously, how? I mean that's cool and all, but how?"

Uncle Rob answered, "As I stated, it rarely happened. It is not foolproof and requires a lot of concentration and focus, but yes, it is what they did. The swords themselves contain the power for time travel. Each one individually can do it, but it is limited to the timeframe in which the sword existed. To go back further than that requires multiple swords; the more swords, the further back they could go.

"The process involves the crossing of the swords while the rightful users hold them. These rightful users have the qualities that resonate with the virtues of the swords. The users then need to focus in unity on one place and time in history, while standing around a fire. The swords then take them to where they have agreed to go."

"Uncle Rob," began Billy, "you keep mentioning the Apostles of Azazel, and obviously they are the evil counterpart to the Guardians of the Swords of Valor. Can you tell us more about them and their history? What swords do they have? What powers might we have to face?"

"Certainly," Rob agreed. "Here is another document that Grandpa put together for all of you. Study it well. Know your enemy and always be on guard. Joe, would you read this one?" He asked as he handed them the documents.

"Sure," Joe nodded, taking the paper and glancing at it for a moment before he began.

There have been five families who, through the centuries, were chosen to keep and preserve the Swords of Valor given to men to defeat evil, to implement freedom, to establish righteousness, and to protect the virtuous.

There have also been five families that, over the centuries, were chosen to gather and utilize the Swords of Terror to enslave humanity and to eventually eradicate all virtue from the face of the earth. These families are known as the Apostles of Azazel. They now have all ten Swords of Terror and four of the Swords of Valor. They have become strong enough to challenge the last remaining intact Guardian family.

If they capture even one more Sword of Valor, they will begin to initiate the processes that will eventually enslave humanity. In fact, we are now in a crisis period and have been since 2008.

While the Guardian families were in possession of the ten Swords of Valor, the people of the world had access to all the good and heroic qualities inherent in the swords. But if the swords fall into the hands of evil, then evil will become recognized as good, and all people will be blinded to the truth.

The people of the world will become enslaved to evil, be divided one against the other, and they will destroy themselves from within. This will begin by dividing the Guardian families and setting them against each other. Then every family of the earth will become divided. Civil wars will arise, and then a final world war. Valor, virtue, and unity will vanish. This process must be stopped at all costs.

The following is a list of the ten Swords of Terror along with the qualities of each.

> *The Sword of Cain - envy and murder*
> *The Sword of Goliath - blasphemy and pride*
> *The Sword of Attila the Hun - cruelty and anger*
> *The Sword of Nero - fear and corruption*
> *The Sword of the Prince of Persia - perdition and confusion*
> *The Sword of Midas - ambition and greed*
> *The Sword of Nebuchadnezzar - idolatry and gluttony*
> *The Sword of Genghis Khan - wrath and licentiousness*
> *The Sword of Ivan the Terrible - depravity and lust*
> *The Sword of Herod the Great - bloodlust and sloth*

"As I told you earlier, we are the only fully-operational family left, and our duty is to stop the progress of evil." Uncle Rob said.

"I have a follow-up question," said Joe. "Who chose the families of the Apostles of Azazel and why?"

"Another great question, Joseph, and I have the answer right here. You can see that your grandfather was well prepared for the questions you might ask. He prepared another document for your study. Jeff, would you read?"

Jeff nodded and began.

The families of the Apostles of Azazel have been chosen for their ferocity, ambition, and willingness to use terror and cruelty to accomplish the will of Azazel, who taught men to make swords, knives, shields, breastplates, and all the weapons of war so that the world became altered. Azazel was one of the most powerful of the Watchers named in the Book of Enoch and has been around since the time of the Garden of Eden. Assigned the ancient task of causing division and strife among the human population, Azazel's ultimate plan is to enslave and then destroy mankind.

Azazel is the one who taught Cain to kill Abel. He is the one who gave Nimrod, the first king, the Sword of Cain. The first metalworker, Tubal-Cain, had fashioned that sword for his grandfather, Cain, who feared for his life.

Before the flood of Noah's time, which scholars believe happened in 2304 B.C., Azazel hid the sword in a chamber buried beneath the paws of the Sphinx, built somewhere between 2603 B.C. and 2578 B.C.

Later, Azazel empowered the Sword of Goliath of Gath, a descendant of the Nephilim. He fought against Michael the Archangel as the Prince of Persia and was the spiritual guide for Nebuchadnezzar in the time of Daniel the prophet.

He incited Herod the Great to order the killing of the children in an attempt to murder the Christ-child. He has gifted empowered swords to Attila the Hun, Genghis Khan, King Midas, and Nero. He has been the instigator of many evil episodes in history, such as the Spanish Inquisition, the Salem witch trials, the Holocaust, and the Bolshevik Revolution. Josef Stalin, Hitler, Muammar Gaddafi, and Saddam Hussein were all under his influence.

His final plan is to gather the Swords of Terror together along with as many Swords of Valor as he can claim, then use the ten Swords of Terror to destroy the Swords of Valor he has obtained, thereby crippling the effectiveness of the Swords of Valor to counterbalance the evil in the world.

"Dad, are you saying that the Watchers are real? Will

we have to fight demons to get the swords back?" asked Robbie.

"The answer to your first question is yes, Robbie, the Watchers are real. There has been, from the beginning of time, spiritual warfare taking place all around the people of the world. The objective is to prove to God that His creation of humans was a mistake, and they are not worthy to exist. They intend to finally confirm this to God by stripping us of the virtues he has instilled in us and letting Him see us as the evil creatures that the Watchers believe us to be. With only our basest natures left as our guide, we will destroy ourselves.

"The answer to your second question is, I don't know. No one can predict the actions of the Watchers. They don't often directly involve themselves with mortal men; they prefer to utilize their human minions to do the work and fight the battles, but they will empower and influence the Apostles of Azazel to resist your efforts," he finished.

"Wow!" exclaimed Nick. "It looks like we are going to have some real obstacles to fight through; Watchers, time travel, and the Apostles of Azazel. Are you sure we are up for this challenge? Seriously, I know we are all cocky and full of ourselves when we are together, but none of us has even imagined anything like this. Why did Grandpa think we could handle it?"

"Honestly, I don't know if you are up for this," Uncle Rob replied uncertainly. "Your grandfather believed you were all capable, and that even if you were not entirely ready, you would adapt and be ready when it counted. He also not only believed in you individually but as a team. You each have been members of athletic teams your whole lives and have learned how to work together.

"He was at every game you guys played, and he

wasn't just watching for fun or to support you. He was observing how you played, how you interacted with your teammates, and how well you took coaching and criticism. All of this went into his decision to put the family's fate in your hands. If he believed in you, then who am I to disagree?"

He shrugged, then looked at his watch and added, "We have been at this for a couple of hours. Let's take a break, get something to eat, and then start up again in the Keeping Room. When we resume your indoctrination, you will learn why you guys are heroes and why I'm the prophet."

"Wait!" Nick called after his uncle's retreating back. "You're a prophet? A real…" His voice faded when Uncle Rob didn't turn around.

CHAPTER THREE

THE KEEPING ROOM

———❧———

"What shall we eat?" Joe asked, his stomach growling. He looked in the refrigerator as his cousins checked the cupboards in the spacious kitchen.

"Hey," Jeff snapped his fingers. "Grandpa always had plenty of sauce, meatballs, sausage, and peppers in the freezer. Somebody start the pasta." He retrieved enough for all of them and set it to cook on the gas range.

Robbie pulled the plates and utensils from cupboards and drawers, then set places at the table.

Joe found the key to their grandpa's wine cellar and returned with a bottle of good red for them to share.

As dinner was reheating, he poured the wine and remarked, "I don't know about you guys, but I'm starting to get pretty pumped about this. Don't get me wrong, I'm still a bit confused and concerned, but just hearing about how much faith Grandpa had in us gives me courage and a real incentive to not disappoint him, or Uncle Rob for that matter."

"I know," agreed Billy. "It feels like he has been planning this our whole lives, preparing us for it behind the scenes in ways that we could never imagine.

Observing us, teaching us, directing us all along the way, and we never knew. He obviously believed that not only could we do this, but that we could succeed."

Ty jumped into the conversation. "Okay, I get the fact that he believed in us individually and together, but I'm still confused about all the hero and crisis stuff. Since when are we heroes? We are just regular guys. None of us has done anything heroic. Except for that time we were all playing tag in the dark, and Alexandra split her forehead open. It still amazes me that Billy carried her up the stairs from the basement all by himself! And what was that comment Dad made about him being a prophet? I think there is more coming that we need to prepare ourselves for."

Joe took a deep breath as the scent of sizzling meatballs filled the air. Grabbing a large spoon, he stirred the now-bubbling sauce.

Billy drained the pasta and announced, "Dinner is served!"

As he took his first bite, Joe felt a twinge of sadness that Grandpa wasn't eating with them. He'd loved a good pasta and meatballs meal. "I miss Grandpa," he said quietly.

Robbie nodded. "Me too."

Each cousin nodded, and silence descended on the room. Joe remembered many meals in this spacious kitchen. Grandpa and Grandma always made them feel welcome and loved. He remembered stories Grandma told them, and lessons Grandpa taught about life and being a man, about honor and virtue. Joe never dreamed that those lessons meant anything more than regular life lessons, the kind any grandfather would teach his grandsons.

Now… now it seemed those lessons were going to

mean much more, maybe even life and death. That thought made his heart beat faster. This is ridiculous, he thought. I'm not even in a life or death situation yet and I'm already acting like a silly child. Get a hold of yourself, Joe. Grandpa thought you could do this, so step up and get to work.

Looking at the others, their expressions told him their thoughts mirrored his own. Excitement, fear, disbelief, and doubt were written on their faces.

"Hey, guys," he said, "Let's just remember that Grandpa had faith in us. We've got this, especially if we work as a team."

Jeff nodded. "You're right, Joe. We're family, we're a team, and we can do this!"

Ty looked at the empty dishes and quipped, "Okay, team, let's get these dishes done and get back to it!"

The tension broken, they laughed and worked together to clean up, then reassembled in the family room. After a few minutes, Uncle Rob entered the room. He started, "I hope you guys enjoyed your meal. I'm not sure how much time you will have to eat in the next twenty-four hours, so I hope you ate enough."

Robbie replied, "Absolutely, Dad. We ate all the meatballs, sausage, and peppers. Maybe we should have broken out the chicken cutlet parmigiana too."

"No, those are mine." Uncle Rob grinned, then grew sober again. "I want you to go to the Keeping Room under the old barn, and I will meet you there."

Joe looked at his watch. 2:30 p.m. Briefly, he wondered why they might not have time to eat in the next twenty-four hours. He frowned, feeling more and more troubled by all this.

As they approached the old barn, he had to smile. Their grandfather had left the barn in a moderate state of disrepair. He had always said that he liked the worn look of it and that it gave him comfort. Grandpa thought the symbol of the old and weathered barn standing out there despite years of wind and rain and snow reflected his own life. Even when he restored the two-hundred-year-old farmhouse that was now the family vacation home, he left the barn to age. Just like Grandpa, Joe thought. While he embraced new things, he still wanted to hold onto the old, as well.

Joe and the others were aware that he had built what he said was a fallout shelter beneath the barn back in the mid-1960s. He and some of his "friends" dug it out very carefully so as not to damage or disturb the footings of the barn. They always wondered why, as Ty had pointed out earlier, they were never allowed to play in or near the barn. But with forty other acres to rollick on, they hadn't given it too much thought. Their grandfather spent a lot of time there, though.

Sometimes, he and the cousins would make up stories about what was down there. Maybe a treasure, or a map to a treasure, or a huge freezer full of ice cream that Grandpa didn't want to share! Now they would know the truth. Now it was their turn. Now they would finally see the Keeping Room.

As they entered the barn, Joe saw that their uncle had left the lights on and the trap door open for them. The heavy metal door was six inches thick and wired with all sorts of electronic and digital devices. It also had a manual lock that could be shut and opened from the inside.

The cousins carefully approached, and Jeff was first to look down into the hole in the ground.

"Well, here we are gentlemen, at the entrance to Wonderland," he said. "Who wants to go in first?"

"I'll go first," said Billy. "As the oldest, I should do it. Everyone agree?" They all nodded in agreement. "And the rest of you should go down in order of age and position in the family. Jeff will follow me, then Joe, then Nick, then Robbie and lastly Ty. That is what Grandpa would have wanted."

They all agreed once again, and Billy slowly descended the long stairway down into the Keeping Room. As Joe followed Jeff, he was impressed with the sturdiness of the stairs; so different than the outside of the barn. When he arrived at the bottom, he stopped and stared. This was not at all what he'd expected!

"Hey!" Nick poked him in the shoulder. "Keep moving! There are others here who want to see, too."

"Sorry," mumbled Joe, moving further into the room.

The Keeping Room was huge, with thick walls lined with bookcases made of mahogany and filled to overflowing with leather volumes. What appeared to be ancient Persian carpets covered the floors. Right there, in the middle of it all, stood a square, glass case made of four-inch-thick, bulletproof glass, brightly lit from the top. Inside the case rested the six Swords of Valor. In this setting, the swords were even more impressive. Joe had always appreciated the craftsmanship and beauty of the swords even when he thought they were just copies. Now, seeing them in the Keeping Room hanging inside that brightly-lit glass case, they were magnificent.

Beyond the sword case stood a group of long, wooden tables. On them lay all manner of maps, charts, and documents. Surrounding these long tables was a half-wall, comprised of cubbyholes filled with ancient scrolls and rolled-up maps.

Further into the Keeping Room, past the tables, was

an enormous wooden door. Billy tried the handle. It opened easily, allowing passage into another room filled with an amazing array of electronic equipment and communication devices covering three walls. There were enormous viewing monitors like those used in corporate boardrooms for holding international virtual meetings.

In the middle of it all, was a huge round table, about ten feet in diameter, made of black marble with a glowing circle in the center approximately four feet across. Around the table were ten high-backed chairs of diverse sizes and designs.

The cousins hadn't said anything while they explored the Keeping Room. Joe was sure they felt as he did, so overwhelmed and in awe of the construction and contents of this impressive place that they were unable and unwilling to speak. Joe also felt a mixture of wonder, reverence, and safety.

Billy finally broke the silence. "Can you believe this place? I have seen a lot of corporate boardrooms and strategy centers around the world, but nothing like this. This looks like it has the most up-to-date data and communication equipment available today. I just finished upgrading my company's security and data analysis systems and thought we had utilized the best of the best, but this is in a completely different class. I recognize some of it and can't believe what I'm seeing. Those are quantum computers!"

Jeff gawked at him, "Billy, seriously? I thought quantum computers were just theoretical. I have read several articles on the development efforts, and according to them, no one has solved the problem of translating the data input into a quantum language. If and when they can do that, we would all have access to technology that is a million times more powerful than current systems. If this is truly a quantum computer, then it will make our research efforts much easier. How can we confirm that, and can we figure out how to use it and access whatever data it contains?"

Billy stood silent for a moment, then he spoke again.

"From the research I've done, the magic of quantum computers will be their ease of use. When fully developed, there will be no keyboards, no user interface to speak of. The computer would interact with the users via voice only. It will be able to anticipate the next question and have an answer ready before you ask, based on the tone of your voice, body language, eye movements and brain waves. It will be able to identify a person as an authorized user based on a bio-electrical signature unique to every person. It will, in effect, recognize you.

"Quantum computers only run probabilistic algorithms. This means that they can analyze the most difficult multidimensional problems much faster than what we have now. Quantum computers may be able to solve problems, and solve them efficiently, which are not practically feasible on classical computers."

"Sounds like HAL from 2001," Joe remarked.

"You're exactly right, Joe," responded Billy. "That was the concept and theory that HAL was based on. The same goes for the computer systems in Star Trek. Mankind has been searching for this type of system for decades, and if I'm correct, that's what we have underneath this old barn."

"Okay," said Nick, "that's great, but how do we turn the thing on?"

"Not sure," replied Billy, "but my guess is that it already knows we are here and is waiting for the right time to interact with us. I think it knows we are trying to understand and is giving us time to absorb it all."

"You are correct," came a voice from nowhere. It seemed to surround them and come from both inside their heads and outside their bodies at the same time. "Who are you?" the voice asked.

Bewildered, Joe turned to Billy. "How do we answer that?"

Billy shrugged at Joe, then spoke to the air. "I don't understand the question."

The voice responded, "This is a question you have been asked many times in your lives, you should be able to answer it easily, if you are truly the sons of the Meglio di Buono. I ask again, who are you?"

Jeff, looking serious, spoke up. "That question sounds familiar. It's simple enough, but it seems critical that we respond correctly."

"I agree." Billy nodded. "It must be a test. Let's put our heads together and figure this out."

Robbie began. "Let's think about this creatively. Obviously, the simple answer is that we are people, or guys, or a team of cousins or something like that, but that can't be correct. This thing probably already knows that. So, we need to think outside the box. Remember that Grandpa built all this, and he spent a lot of time here. He probably interacted with this computer every day. Maybe this is some sort of password-type thing. What would Grandpa have used or set up as an initial password?"

"Great thinking, Robbie," said Ty. "I'm sure Grandpa would have used something that we all would know but that only our family would understand. From my study of neurology, I know that Grandpa was a strong right-brained person. He was creative and always saw the big picture. He would never have used numbers or dates to create the password; he would have used something familiar and personal, like a nickname or a phrase or something like that. Let's think about our interactions with him. Think about what he would say to us each time we would see him."

"Well," said Jeff, "sometimes he would bust our chops about not calling Grandma enough. Or he would tell us to get a haircut or stuff like that. Would any of that work?"

"No," said Billy. "If Ty is right, that's not personal enough."

At this point, Joe interjected. "Don't you remember that whenever we would see him the first thing he did was quiz us? He would ask us, 'Who are you?' And we would have to answer, 'The best!' Then he would ask again, 'What are you?' And we would have to answer, 'better than good!' Could that work?"

"Light bulb moment!" Ty crowed. "That must be the right answer."

Billy said, "Okay, let me use that and see what happens, but be prepared to get out of here if we are wrong. This thing is extremely powerful, and I have no idea what sort of security Grandpa built into it. It could get ugly."

Billy looked around at the equipment, took a deep breath and began. "Computer, we have the answer. May I speak?"

"Yes," came the reply.

Speaking loudly, so as not to be misunderstood, Billy replied, "The answer to who we are is: The best!"

The computer responded, "And what are you?"

Billy replied, "Better than good!"

A quiet, deep hum began to resonate throughout the room. Joe felt the vibrations throughout his body. He whispered, "Do you think we answered incorrectly? Maybe security systems have been activated that will trap us here, or who knows what else."

Robbie took a step backward. "Should we make a run for it?"

Suddenly, a loud, familiar voice spoke out. "Nice to see that you knuckleheads were able to pass your first test!"

They recognized their grandfather's voice! How was that possible? They turned to where the voice originated, and there, in the middle of the large round table, stood an almost life-sized holographic image of their grandfather. Smiling, he looked directly at them. He wore his usual attire of black slacks and a crisp, white shirt.

"What are you guys staring at? Sit down and let's get down to business," the image commanded. "We don't have time to waste."

The cousins, complied quickly. Once they were seated around the table, Joe spoke up. "Grandpa, this is amazing. What is going on, and how is this possible?"

The image replied, "What you are seeing and interacting with is a holographic image generated by the quantum computer. As Billy pointed out in his discussion with you earlier, it is an immensely powerful system, capable of interacting with humans in a human-like manner. The artificial intelligence advancements of recent years, combined with the exponential increase of processing speeds available with quantum computing, will make your interaction with the system feel like you are working with a human being. I wanted to make the experience more user-friendly, so I had our scientists input all my personality traits into the programs. What you see and hear is a very accurate representation of me. Impressive, isn't it?"

"Yes, it is," replied Jeff, "but a bit overwhelming. Why didn't Uncle Rob tell us all this and prepare us for it before he sent us down here?"

"Inquisitive as always, I see," replied the image of his grandfather, smiling at Jeff. "I understand that you must feel overwhelmed with all of the information and new concepts that have been revealed to you. I'm sure you understand that the importance of this situation can't be overstated. It will require a precise process and several critical steps. None of what your uncle told you will work if you are not thinking clearly, creatively, and in unity. The first test was to see if you could figure out how to get past the initial password process to access the quantum computer. We knew it would require some creative and collective thought. You worked together, came to an agreement, and acted as one. That will be the basis of your success in the assignments to come. Remember it!"

Joe hesitantly raised his hand. "May we call you Grandpa? It sounds so much better than saying 'computer'."

"Yes, Joe, interact with me just as if you are speaking with your grandfather. That will make your interactions and my responses more accurate. It also means you don't have to raise your hand. This isn't a classroom, although it will feel like one at times," the image replied.

Joe chuckled, then continued. "I get that we need to do this, and even why, but how do you know this will work? I mean none of us has ever done anything like it before. Why did Uncle Rob say we were heroes and that he was the prophet? What does that all mean?"

At that point, their Uncle Rob entered the room. "I see you have passed the first test and have met 'Grandpa'. Good, now we can get down to business." He took a seat at the table. "Please begin," he said to the image.

The hologram began. "As you all know, your grandpa was a voracious reader and an avid student of history. Not only was he interested in it, but he knew it was the key to understanding the future. One of the concepts he discovered is that history is not linear. It goes in cycles. Not that it repeats itself exactly, but that the events and circumstances of society tend to be dependent on the characteristics and behaviors of the people they are happening to. So, the events themselves do not determine the results, but the way people respond to them does. The moods and attitudes of the particular generation dealing with the issue or problem are what drives the outcome.

"For our purposes, I will say that a generation is a twenty-five-year period in which a group of people is born. Many things influence each generation, creating their collective mindset; their parents, society, and their peers. This mixture is unique to each generation and creates generational personality types. However, these influences always result in one of four archetypes. They never vary, and they always follow in the same order over the course of every one hundred years. Please, give your attention to the monitors around the room, and I will display the information you need to understand all of this."

The monitors around the room winked to life. Great setup, Grandpa, Joe thought, noticing that each one of them could view a monitor easily without craning his neck. He looked at the screen directly across from him, scanning the information quickly.

The Prophets - born during a High
The Nomads   - born during an Awakening
The Heroes   - born during an Unraveling
The Artists   - born during a Crisis

After giving them a moment to read the screen, the

image continued. "You six, as well as your siblings, were born during the most recent 'Unraveling' period of history, which started in 1984 and ended in 2008. That puts you all squarely in the hero generation. Your Uncle Robert, along with his siblings, Susan and Domenic, was born between 1954 and 1960. That identifies them with the prophet generation. Your grandpa was born in 1925, putting him in the hero generation of his cycle. So, you can see how it goes; we arc a family of heroes and prophets. Each prophet generation builds the skills and character of the next generation of heroes, preparing them to face the next crisis.

"For the missions you will participate in over the next thirty-six hours, Robert will be your Prophet. He will educate you, guide you, and remind you who you are. He will inspire you and try to bring out the best in you. It is his job to awaken the hero in each of you and to get you to do the same for each other. That is his role. That is what he was born to do. He is your commander in all of this.

"Your Aunt Susan and Uncle Domenic are also Prophets of the family, but they have different roles. Susan is the Prophet of Administration. She is responsible for managing the family business and communication with the other Guardian families and is the backup to Robert. In the event that he cannot perform his duties, she will step in. Domenic is the Prophet of Remembrance. It is his duty to keep records of the family's history, our victories and defeats, and to always remind us of who we are and what is most important.

"As I said, history goes in cycles lasting about one hundred years. This has been observed as far back as the Etruscans in pre-Roman days. They referred to it as a saeculum, roughly equating to the length of a very long human life and to our concept of centuries today. In each century, the world repeatedly turns through four seasons, each following the other without fail and without delay.

"Each season plants the seeds of the next. A High is the result of the resolution of the Crisis. It is like the springtime of the world. It is when, after a long, hard winter, the warmth returns, and things begin to grow. The seeds that were planted in the fall begin to sprout, and it becomes a time of plenty. People come together, and isolation starts to end.

"Eventually, the High period evolves into an Awakening period. This equates to summertime. There is plenty, but it is being consumed. There is leisure time for reflection. There is freedom from want, and the world is not oppressed. People gather together. During this time, people examine themselves and their world and begin to yearn to change things for the better.

"This is followed by an Unraveling. This equates to the fall. The Awakening starts to run out of steam, and things begin to wither and die. The world gets colder day by day. People withdraw from each other, spending time in their homes and with their close relations. Isolation and fragmentation occur. Seeds are scattered to the winds to fall where they may. People gather up the fruits of the harvest. They start preparing for the winter to come.

"This winter is the Crisis season. It is a colder and darker period. The world is dead and hard. People are in maximum isolation mode. Resources are scarce and must be used for survival. Things die. The beautiful things of the world have either died, fled, or have gone into hibernation, like flowers, birds, and bears. All that remains are predators and scavengers. We are now in that Crisis period. We have been since 2008. It will last until sometime in the late 2020s."

Ty cleared his throat. "Um, Grandpa, this is all interesting information, but what does it all have to do with us right now?"

"I was wondering the same thing," Billy added. "And where do the swords come in?"

Joe chewed his lip, wondering if he should answer Billy's question. As a reporter, he could well believe that the world was in crisis! "Can I try to answer that, Grandpa?"

"Please do, Joe," the image nodded.

Joe faced his cousins, looking them each in the eye. "I've seen a lot of current events in my job."

"Like school board meetings?" Nick quipped.

"Well, yes. But it's not the meetings themselves that are important. It's what's happening in those meetings. There's arguing, blaming, name-calling. Everyone's pitted against each other. No one's working together. On a larger scale, we are dealing with a fragile economy, terrorism, bigotry, rising crime, and governments that seem to look out only for the politicians' pocketbooks instead of the people they are supposed to be serving."

Robbie chimed in, "I think I understand. It pervades everything and everyone, doesn't it? My own art is much darker now than when I started. Sometimes, I feel a hopelessness as I paint or sculpt, and that comes out in my work."

"I can relate to the fragile economy," Billy said. "It's getting harder to raise capital for expanding the business, and we're not seeing the returns that we did even a few years ago."

"Rising crime rates, yes," Jeff spoke somberly. "I see it in my practice, and in my neighborhood. We've experienced more thefts and vandalism in the past few years, and I thought I was raising my kids in a safe community! We don't even allow them to walk the two blocks to school without us anymore."

"I think you are beginning to see the problems," Uncle Rob said. "Your grandpa was right. We are well into a new Crisis season. That is why you were born. Your generation must take up the cause just as the GI generation did during World War II. They put their own self-interests aside, answered the call, and did the hard fighting that resulted in freedom from evil and oppression. They were no more prepared than you for the mission they faced. They only had their collective courage, a can-do attitude, and trust in each other to get them through. They were unified.

"Today, we know them as the 'Greatest Generation' because of their heroism and fortitude. You can be the 'Next Greatest Generation', if you so choose. The world needs you, and you must rise to the challenge. Though you are all heroes, you all possess different skills, perspectives, and character traits. These differences could easily cause friction, confusion, and defeat. If you choose to accept this challenge, you must put aside any differences and work in unity, or we will fail.

"The first great battle of this current crisis season starts today," Uncle Rob finished.

"Today?" Ty squeaked. "But…"

"Today," his father interrupted. "There have been skirmishes over the past few decades, but those were only brushfires compared to the conflagration you will be facing if we don't succeed."

"So, what say you all? Are you in?" asked the image of their grandfather.

There was silence in the room. The tension filled the open space where they gathered.

Joe was the first to speak. "Uncle Rob, I can't speak

for the others, but despite my concern and apprehension about what is to come, count me in. I will do whatever it takes to make Grandpa proud of us."

"This sounds like a crazy idea," Robbie said. "It sounds incredibly stupid, profoundly irresponsible, and wild." He paused, then grinned. "I love that! I'm in, too!"

Billy spoke, his expression more somber than usual. "Despite my nagging concerns, I agree with Joe and Robbie. Let's do this."

Nick simply said, "Let's go get us some swords."

Jeff nodded and added, "And some apostles."

Finally, Ty finished with, "As Grandpa used to say, 'Can you smell what the cousins are cooking?' Here we come!"

The prophet breathed an audible sigh of relief. "You have all made me proud. You are my sons and my nephews, my flesh and blood, and my responsibility. I love each and every one of you. Truthfully, I have dreaded this day for years. I'd hoped it would never come." He looked at the faces of the cousins scattered around the room. When he spoke again, his voice hitched a little. "As much pride as I feel in you, I feel that much dread for your safety. You are strong and have just committed to the fight of your lives... for all our lives. That makes you true heroes, no matter the outcome."

He took a deep breath, then observed, "Now that we have a consensus, I need to fill in some additional information. We need to discuss the details of the assignments. The computer will lay them out for you one at a time. It will reveal the situations, the swords that are in play, and the framework you must operate within. But you must decide on the exact date and place you need to travel to.

"Unless you listen to the research and understand

the facts for yourselves, there will always be a bit of doubt that could creep into your minds during the initiation of the time travel process. The quantum computer will provide all the research you need. It will also monitor each of you while you are on your assignments.

"You remember the Sword Initiation ceremonies we had on your twelfth birthdays? I'm sure you recall that part of the ceremony where Grandpa pricked your finger, and you placed the drop of blood on a specific part of the handle. That may have seemed like a small part of it all, but it was critically important.

"You see, Grandpa had embedded in each of the swords a quantum diagnostic and interface device. By placing your blood into that device, you and the swords effectively became bonded for life. Your DNA was imprinted within the very molecular structure of the sword and became part of it. It became attuned to your thoughts, feelings, and emotions on a quantum level. It can monitor you and feed information back to the quantum computer for analysis and evaluation. That is why the swords have such an influence on you, and why you feel like they are a part of you.

"This had nothing to do with Grandpa spying on you or knowing if you were speeding or anything trivial like that. It had to do with your development of the qualities and characteristics that would be needed to address the crisis that he knew was coming. It had to do with ensuring your understanding of virtue and valor, on the most basic level.

"As you travel to your assignments, the swords will still be able to feed quantum data to the computer. The computer will be able to interpret your brainwave patterns, and combined with the physiological, environmental, and emotional diagnostic information, be able to create a representative 3D holographic image for us to follow. We will have a sense of your situation, environment, and stress levels. We can, in effect, witness your assignment as it happens."

"You'll be able to see us?" Joe asked, shocked.

"We'll see a representation of you," the prophet clarified. "We won't be able to hear you or see what's happening around you. We can't interact or assist you in any way, but we will be aware of your progress."

Joe thought back to his initiation ceremony where he'd received his sword. That ceremony was a cherished highlight in his life. He, his brother, and their cousins were invited to spend the weekend with their grandfather at the family vacation home. All six cousins went, and it was just them and their grandfather. He took them golfing at Sunnyhill, they had a cookout, and then at dusk, they headed down to the fire pit by the river. Their grandfather built a roaring fire, and they took seats around the blaze.

He began by telling them all about the sacredness of becoming a man and what that meant. He read to them about initiation traditions from many diverse cultures. Then he began the ceremony. He talked about the sword he had chosen, the history and meaning behind it. He told stories of the hero who had wielded it and why he had decided on that specific sword to present that night. Then he'd taken out his pocket knife and pricked Joe's finger. Grandpa instructed him to apply the blood to a specific part of the handle and hold it there while he recited:

> "Today you are a man.
> Many trials you will face.
> You must always stand for truth
> And run an honest race.

Many times, you'll fall,
But never fail to rise.
Hold fast unto your virtue
A man's most precious prize.

This sword is but a symbol
Given on this day,
To remind you of your valor
And to always show the way."

When the verses had been spoken, there was silence for a few moments, and then each cousin rose and shook the hand of their closest cousin. Joe had felt so special, respected, and loved.

After the ceremony, their grandfather read poetry to them from one of his favorite anthologies. He shared "Opportunity" and "The Fool's Prayer" by Edwin Rowland Sill, "El Dorado" by Edgar Allen Poe, "Silence" by Edgar Lee Masters, "Lament" by Edna St. Vincent Millay, "Miniver Cheevy" by Edwin Arlington Robinson, and many others. Each one contained a lesson to be learned.

Joe remembered listening with rapt attention as Grandpa explained the poetry and gave his own perspective of the poem's meaning and life application. It was a truly magical occasion; not just because of the atmosphere, but because of the closeness it created between them. It was a lifelong bond that could never be broken, even by death.

Each cousin celebrated their twelfth birthdays the same way. At the time, neither Joe nor the others had any idea that it was their preparation for the future.

"Joe?" the prophet spoke again.

"Hm?" he answered, pulling himself from his reverie. "What?"

Frowning, the prophet repeated, "Do you understand?"

"I'm sorry, Uncle Rob. I was remembering the initiation ceremonies and didn't hear what you said."

The prophet sighed. "You need to pay attention. This is important, and you need to focus."

Joe looked down at his hands. "I'm sorry."

His expression softening, Uncle Rob replied, "I know this is hard. It's a lot of information all at once, but it's critical that you understand what's happening and what's expected of you."

Looking up, Joe locked eyes with the prophet. "I understand, sir. I'll stay focused."

"Good, let's begin." The prophet smiled, turning his attention to the image of his father.

The image spoke. "Here is the outline of your assignments. You must travel back in time to recover each of the four Swords of Valor that have been stolen by the Apostles of Azazel. To do this, you must go back to a time before the swords were captured when they were at the height of their power.

"When they are in our possession, Robert will, as family Prophet, perform the designated process, utilizing all ten Swords of Valor to nullify and extinguish the power of the Swords of Terror. If the Apostles of Azazel succeed in their plans to bring the ten Swords of Terror together and destroy the four swords they have already captured before we have all ten Swords of Valor, it will forever tip the scales of evil versus virtue in their favor. The Apostles of Azazel would have enough power to cause chaos and enslave the world.

"You must complete each of the four assignments

69

and bring the swords back to the prophet. When all the Swords of Valor are together, he will recite the 'Initiation Protocol' and fully activate the virtuous powers of the swords. One by one, they will cancel out all the evil Swords of Terror.

"You must complete each assignment before sunrise following the day you arrive. This is an absolute. If you don't, you won't be able to return, and all will be lost. You and the swords will be trapped in the past, and evil will prevail.

"Additionally, the swords will grant you the gift of tongues. They will enable anyone you encounter to understand you just as if you were speaking their native language or dialect, and you will know what they are saying as if they were using modern English.

"The swords will also cloak you. That is, they will make you appear as if you are dressed appropriately for the historical date and time you have returned to. As I said earlier, the swords are powerful, especially when used together. Most importantly, don't do anything to change history materially!

"Remember, you are there for one thing only, to obtain the specific sword and return as quickly as possible. Nothing else, got it?"

The six young men nodded.

"Your first assignment will be to travel back to the time of World War II, specifically to the time just before the Battle of Britain. You must find and obtain, with the willing agreement of its rightful owner, the Sword of Tristan, also known as Curtana, the Sword of Mercy. When you obtain the sword, you will repeat the process that sent you there and return to the area the prophet will show you. The prophet will be waiting for you.

"It is for you to determine the exact date, place, and

time to target for your arrival. You need to be as precise as possible, because you only have until sunrise the following morning. If you arrive too far away from your target and need to travel a great distance to get to your objective, you will waste time. If you choose the wrong date, you will fail."

"Wait a minute," Ty spoke, lifting a hand to interrupt. "Why do we have to decide? Wouldn't the quantum computer be, I don't know, a gazillion times better at estimating that?"

"It's part of the process," the prophet said. "If the computer told you where and when, you wouldn't be as invested in the destination. If all of you discuss and decide together, that date and time will hold meaning for you, giving power to the time travel ritual."

The image nodded. "Exactly. You have received your assignment. Now you must decide on where and when to arrive. Choose wisely and carefully."

Jeff spoke, his voice filled with concern. "Grandpa, we all have some understanding of history and have all been on teams before, but none of us are soldiers or historians. You have told us we have to determine the exact dates and places to travel to in the past to obtain the swords at a time of their maximum power. There are so many variables involved and so many unknown aspects that we could easily make the wrong choice. How can we be sure that we make the wise decision?"

"Jeff, as always, you seek wisdom. You won't find wisdom here. What I can give you is information. The computer will provide you with facts and perspective gathered throughout the centuries to help you make your best decision.

"The information available to you has been collected by teams of scholars from every Guardian family

throughout history. It includes the writings of Plato and
Socrates and all the other scholars and writers of ancient
Greece, the political and sociological insights of Marcus
Tullius Cicero, the extrapolations of the Midrash of the
ancient Jews, all the oldest versions of both the Torah and
the Bible. It contains a vast amount of literature and
reference information recovered from ancient scrolls
thought to have been lost forever when the library of
Alexandria burned down.

"It also includes all the legends and fables from the
past and has been able to sort through and isolate fact
from fiction in all cases. You will have available to you the
true stories represented by these legends and fables and
the real circumstances and the historical people involved.

"Finally, your grandpa programmed in all the
information about every assignment you will receive and
all the facts that we know about the times, places, and
people involved. I will present those facts to you before
each assignment. You and your cousins will need to make
the final, unified decision about where and when to travel
to by utilizing your knowledge, understanding, and
common sense. You will have to go with your gut
instincts in some instances.

"The bottom line is that you will have to take the
information, combined with your instincts, and then rely
on yourselves to make a wise choice. I don't sense any
more relevant questions, so let us begin."

Ty interrupted. "Sorry, Grandpa, but I do have a
question."

"What is it, Ty?" the image responded, actually
looking a little annoyed, if that was possible for a
holographic image.

Ty looked sheepish. "You have all this high-tech
equipment down here, and all this historical

documentation and stuff, which is great, but what I need to know right now is…" he hesitated, then continued apologetically. "Do you have a bathroom down here?"

The image just stared at Ty for five seconds, put his head in his hands and said, "Yes, Ty, there is a bathroom. Just past the case that holds the scrolls and to the right. Can you figure out how to use it?"

Looking relieved, Ty responded, "Sure thing, Gramps, not a problem. I'll be back in a few minutes." He took off and left the rest of them there to wait.

"I see nothing has changed," said the image. "I hope that is a good thing. Does anyone else need to use the restroom before we go on?"

They all chuckled and answered, "No, sir."

When Ty returned, the image of their grandfather began. "The first assignment should be the easiest, but that is not to say that it won't be dangerous or challenging. You will be returning to World War II England, so the environment and circumstances won't be too far outside of your frame of reference. I have explained about the powers that the swords have regarding tongues and cloaking, but that is less critical on this mission than it will be in the ones to come.

"You need to determine the whereabouts of Curtana. A member of the Apostles of Azazel infiltrated the royal security force during the preparations for the wedding of Prince Charles and Diana and stole it. At that time, Curtana was replaced with a replica. You must return to a time before the sword was taken and when it was at the height of its power.

"You will convince the rightful owner of the sword to give it to you or to allow you to take it. This is critical. You can't take it back here without their consent and agreement. You may also tell them that if we are successful, that the sword will return to its rightful owner and its proper place in history. If it does not, they will know that we failed, and all is lost.

"Most critically, you must not do anything that materially changes history. If you do, the effects will be unpredictable and may disrupt both the timeline and the ability of the quantum computer to provide you with the accurate information you need to complete your assignments. Are we clear?"

Most of the cousins answered, "Yes, sir!"

But Nick asked a point of clarification. "Grandpa, how would you define 'materially'? Can you give us some examples?"

"Love your attention to detail, Nick," responded the image. "As with all things that relate to time travel and history, I can't predict the impact even the smallest changes will have on the timeline. Think of it as throwing a pebble in a pond. The bigger the stone, the more ripples it creates and the wider it spreads. That is how it is with timeline changes.

"If you change anything, there will be an impact, but some changes fade away and are absorbed easily by the timeline, others will echo throughout history and will have far-reaching effects. All I can tell you is do what you must do, but don't be cavalier about it. Try not to change anything, if possible. Always make sure to tell your uncle about anything you might have done that would impact the timeline when you return from your assignments. He can work with me to make any necessary adjustments.

"Okay, we are nearing the point of decision. I will lay out all the facts we know about the situation you are traveling into, and then at the end, I need a unified decision from you six as to the time and place you intend to start.

"The last time the Sword of Tristan was at its height of power was just before and during the Battle of Britain in July through the end of October of 1940 during World War II. England was facing its most serious threat to its existence, and the influence of the sword was needed desperately. The country had begun to experience the fury of the V2 rockets the Nazis had developed. It was being bombed daily. The people were becoming discouraged and panicked.

"During this time, they began to fear an imminent invasion, so they hid many of the country's most valuable objects. These included the Crown Jewels. Curtana is part of that collection. It is one of the three swords used during the coronation of every monarch of the British Empire since before the Middle Ages. It is representative of the qualities of mercy and kindness that every ruler needs to govern appropriately. It is said to have been the sword of the legendary knight, Tristan. Its end is blunt and squared-off, symbolizing mercy. This is how you will recognize it.

"In addition to hiding the majority of their most valuable historical artifacts, the British also moved their most important citizens to safer locations. This is the case with the then-Princess Elizabeth and her sister Princess Margaret.

"They had been evacuated for safety reasons in May of 1940 to Windsor Castle, away from the worst bombings. They remained there for the next five years. As you may know, the future Queen Elizabeth was only fourteen years old at the time of the Battle of Britain, and it wasn't yet known that she would someday ascend to the throne.

"We know she was taken to Windsor Castle to wait out the bombing there under heavy security. What wasn't known until recently, and even now there is some doubt, is that the Tower of London vaults were emptied in 1940, and their contents were also stored in the bowels of Windsor Castle. Recently uncovered research implies that the Crown Jewels were hidden at Windsor Castle in a place that the Nazis would never look for them. Although the precise hiding place has never been officially confirmed, our analysis points to a wooden trapdoor in the castle basement where the servants who tended the fireplaces had their quarters.

"So, our best information tells us that Curtana was most likely at Windsor Castle and at the height of its power in mid-October of 1940. I will print out schematics of the castle for you to take with you. Now it is decision time. What date do you choose and what location will you travel to?"

Billy spoke first. "It seems to me the obvious choice is Windsor Castle sometime in October of 1940. Am I missing something?"

Joe responded, "No, probably not, but we need to be more precise. We apparently need to decide on a day, maybe even a time of day. Remember, we only have until sunrise the following day to complete the assignment. So, I suggest we buy ourselves as much time as possible and plan to arrive in the morning. But we still need to identify a specific day in May."

"Why don't we split the difference and go back to October 15th, 1940?" said Robbie.

The image of their grandfather spoke up. "We know that when she was just fourteen, the princess gave an address to the nation from Windsor Castle during the BBC's Children's Hour radio program. This took place at 5:00 p.m. on October 13th, 1940."

"Okay," said Nick, "then if we go back there at 6:00

a.m., maybe we can get access to the castle while it is still early enough to avoid too much activity, find the princess, and convince her to take us to the basement without too much trouble. We will be working mostly in daylight and should have plenty of time. When I go hunting, I like to get an early start."

"Sounds good to me," said Ty. "Let's do that."

Finally, Jeff agreed, "Okay, so the plan is to go back to October 13th, 1940, to Windsor Castle at 6:00 a.m., local time. Is everyone in agreement?"

They all agreed and looked at the image of their grandfather for validation. He just nodded and said, "So be it. Go and take up your swords, and use them well and with honor. Godspeed." His image disappeared.

They rose from their chairs around the round table, picked up the printout of the castle schematics, collected their swords, left the Keeping Room, and exited the barn.

As Joe placed his sword in the sheath around his waist, he felt comforted. The cousins had enjoyed messing around with them, but they had always felt heavy and unwieldy. Now, his sword felt weightless on his hip. It felt as if it was part of him, and now he knew why. This all felt so right.

They arrived at the house, and the prophet asked them, "Are you ready to do your duty for the family and for the Guardians?"

"Yes," was their unified response.

"Good, let us begin," he said, "but first, does anyone have to go to the bathroom?"

He looked directly at Ty.

"What?" Ty feigned surprise and responded, "why are you looking at me, Dad? I already went in the Keeping Room."

"Okay, then," the prophet said. "If you are all

prepared, we will gather next to the river, in the clearing near the picnic area, and will perform the departure. Let's go."

CHAPTER FOUR

THE SWORD OF
TRISTAN

———— ❧ ————

"Now it begins," said the prophet to the heroes. "Clear your minds of distractions and pay close attention to what I direct you to do.

"Stand in a circle around the fire. When I tell you, lift your swords in unison, very slowly, using your right arms. Don't cross swords or touch them together until you are instructed to do so. When I give you the word, gently cross your swords so that they are all touching each other. When that happens, there will be a bright flash of light, and you will depart. You must be thinking about the date, place, and time you have decided on. You must focus on that only, or this won't work. When you are ready to return, you must repeat the same process in the same manner around some kind of fire. Understood?"

"Got it, Dad," said Robbie. "Right hands, fire, concentration. Simple."

His father erupted. "It is not so simple! It is complex and dangerous! This can easily go wrong. Stop with the cavalier attitude and show some respect for the magnitude of all this. You guys are not going into some paintball game. It is a matter of life and death for millions of people, for the survival of this family and the nation, and it will have eternal consequences! If you don't go into this with humility and respect, you will fail. That can't happen. What you do today on these assignments will resonate throughout history. So, straighten up and get serious."

"Yes, sir," said Robbie, taken aback by his father's reaction.

The prophet refocused and commanded, "Gentlemen, raise your Swords of Valor."

The cousins unsheathed their swords and raised them high.

For a moment, the prophet was mesmerized by the sight. His sons and nephews stood tall, their swords reflected the firelight. They really look like the heroes the world needs, he thought. It was magical and inspiring.

Blinking back the tears that filled his eyes, the prophet spoke again. "Now gently bring the swords together. Godspeed!"

The young men did as instructed… but nothing happened.

"Are we there yet?" asked Nick.

So much for heroes, the prophet thought. He sighed and answered, "No, you are not there yet, Nick. Something has gone wrong. Were you all focused on October 13th, 1940, Windsor Castle at 6 a.m. local time?"

"October 13th? I thought it was October 19th," said Jeff.

"I was focused on six in the evening," said Joe.

"No!" shouted the prophet. "You must all have the same objective! Remember, October 13th, 1940, six in the morning, Windsor Castle. Let's try this again. Gentlemen, raise your Swords of Valor."

They obeyed.

"Now, bring your swords together. Godspeed."

This time, a bright flash of light momentarily blinded the prophet, obscuring the six young men from his view. When he could once again see, he was startled. He saw three of the cousins standing there with their swords held high. Not zero, not six, but three. Something must have gone awry. He could only hope that the three who were not standing here now were safely back in 1940 and that one of them had the schematics of Windsor Castle.

"Well, that was certainly less interesting than I had hoped," remarked Jeff.

"Yeah," agreed Nick, "a lot less fun than riding my dirt bike, for sure. What happened?"

As the prophet approached, Ty called out. "Dad! Why didn't we go, and where are the others?"

"I don't know," he replied. "I have a theory, but I need to check with the quantum computer. Let's head back to the Keeping Room."

The prophet's mind was spinning with questions and worry. He hoped the computer would have answers he could live with. He prayed the three heroes who went would be able to return safely.

As they stepped into the Keeping Room, the image of his father appeared without being summoned. "I see you have a problem you need to discuss. It obviously has to do with the fact that three of the six of our heroes are still here with us and not on their first assignment with their cousins. Ask your question."

"Yes, we have a problem and a question," the prophet replied. "What happened? I have never heard of this happening before, and I need answers. Were you aware of this?"

"Of course, I was aware. I have quantum capabilities. But being aware is not the same thing as knowing. When dealing with the twin variables of the quantum mechanics of time travel and the mystical qualities of the swords, the probabilities become unpredictable. The chaos aspect always comes into play and can result in widely varying outcomes.

"What happened this time is that the swords chose only the swords and heroes with the powers and virtues necessary to accomplish the task. Remember, each sword only has the power to return as far back as its own time. Any further than that is outside of their individual reach. The combined power of multiple swords increases that reach, but it can drain them for a brief time. So, the swords choose only as much power as is needed to get there and back, never more.

"Apparently, we were sending too much firepower. The swords always choose correctly. Since this was a short trip back in time, all the swords were not needed. Additionally, Billy, Joe, and Robbie, who are in possession of the swords, must have the right qualities to complete the assignment, or they would not have been chosen for the task. As I said, I was aware, but didn't know what the outcome would be."

"Well, 'Dad'," protested the prophet, a bit of sarcasm in his voice, "I don't find that very comforting. I'm responsible for all their lives. Sending them out there without knowing which team members will be participating in the assignment is troublesome."

"Robert," the image replied, "you have always had a bit of a problem with trust. You, too, will learn something from this experience." Then, without another word, the image disappeared.

The prophet sighed. He was still troubled by the turn of events and had learned nothing helpful from the computer. There were three young men out there on an assignment that were in danger, and they were his responsibility. He had to figure out how to be more certain about who the swords would choose and why, and he had to make sure that they would have the right information and resources to help them succeed.

Not having the schematics could be a big problem for the team that had gone to Windsor Castle. Maybe he could figure this all out by the time they returned. If they returned.

"So, what are we supposed to do while we are waiting for the team?" Nick asked after he'd hung his sword in the case.

"Nothing. Just sit here and pay attention to the quantum diagnostics. Make sure your cousins are staying alive and moving."

Nick's eyebrows rose at his uncle's tone, but he wisely remained quiet as he joined the others at the table.

Billy, Joe, and Robbie suddenly found themselves standing not on their grandfather's land next to a river, but in an open meadow about a hundred yards from what they recognized as Windsor Castle. The sun was barely peeking over the horizon. They sheathed their swords and looked around.

"Wow, that was intense," Robbie remarked, "a real rush! Why are there only three of us? Where are Jeff, Nick, and Ty?"

"I don't know," replied Billy. "Maybe we got separated in the time stream."

"Or maybe they forgot the right date and time," said Robbie.

"No," Joe shook his head. "We saw back at the house that the whole thing would not work if any of us weren't clear on the date or time. Something else must have happened; I hope they're okay."

"Let's take a quick look around and see if they landed somewhere nearby. If we don't find them in about twenty minutes, let's meet back here and start the assignment ourselves. Agreed?" asked Billy.

"Sounds like a plan," Joe concurred. "I'll head toward the trees over there, Robbie can go toward the outbuildings in that direction, and Billy, you check out what's over those hills opposite the castle. Twenty minutes and then back here. Let's go!"

The three of them sped off in different directions, hoping to locate their missing cousins. After twenty minutes of searching and finding no trace of their other three cousins, the young men met back at the appointed spot.

"No one spotted the others?" asked Billy.

"No sign of them," Joe replied.

Robbie shook his head. "Well, we can't wait for them or delay anymore. Let's plan how we are going to get into that castle. Who has the schematics? Maybe we should check them for a drainage pipe or a sewer entrance that leads to the basement."

"I don't have the schematics," Joe said, looking at Robbie. "Do you?"

"Nope," Robbie replied, then he added, "I think Jeff had them."

Billy frowned. "Great. Just great. We have to improvise already. I'm good at plans and strategy, but I get uncomfortable just winging it."

"No problem, Billy," said Joe. "I always have to change plans on the fly. Every day some crisis hits the newsroom, and my day changes on a dime. We also have 'Mr. Creative' with us, Robbie. He is always thinking outside the box and can see things no one else does. We'll be all right. We can do this."

"Agreed," Robbie nodded. "In fact, when I was checking the outbuildings, I noticed a truck filled with boxes of fresh fish on ice. It had a flat tire that was being repaired. My outside-the-box brain tells me that they were probably making a delivery to the castle when they got a flat. After it's fixed, they will be bringing it in. If we can get to the truck, that could very well be our way in."

"I like it," said Billy.

Joe added, "And because of the cloaking and tongues abilities of the swords, we should look and sound like real English delivery men! Perfect! Way to go, Robbie! You can even keep the 'he-hive'."

Robbie glared at him and said, "It's a man-bun! How many times do I have to tell you two barbarians? That's it! I'm taking it down!" He undid his man-bun and let his long, dark brown hair fall around his face. "Happy now?"

"Better," said Joe. "Now you look like Mel Gibson in Braveheart. Matches your sword perfectly!"

"Let's go," said Billy. "Robbie, you lead the way."

They took off at a trot for the outbuildings.

Hiding behind a shed, Joe peeked around the corner, then pulled back to whisper, "There are only two of them, but I'm not sure how we're going to distract them long enough to get the truck. Any ideas?"

Robbie nodded. "Let's rush them. There are three of us and only two of them. We can take them!"

Joe shook his head. "That would attract too much attention. We need to be subtle about this."

Billy jabbed Robbie with his elbow. "Yeah. Subtle, like your 'man-bun'."

Robbie glared at him, but before he could respond, Joe interrupted. "Get a grip, guys. How can we draw them away from the truck without drawing attention from anyone else?"

"What if I run up and steal something, then run away?" Robbie offered. "They would follow me, and you two could take the truck. Would that work?"

"Not bad," Joe nodded. "If we time it right, they could have the tire mostly replaced so the truck is drivable. We'll grab the truck after you've drawn them away. When you're far enough away, find a place to hide. After they pass you, double back and we'll pick you up before we reach the unloading area."

"I can do that," Robbie nodded.

"Sounds workable," Billy agreed.

When the delivery men had the new tire on and most of the lug nuts finger-tight, Robbie raced out, tapped them both on the shoulder, grabbed the lug wrench and ran like the wind. As they'd predicted, both men chased him, yelling for him to stop.

"I wish they'd yell quieter," Billy complained. "That's going to attract too much attention."

"Then we'd better work fast," Joe stated, already moving towards the truck.

Their plan worked like a charm. Billy slid into the driver's seat, found the keys in the ignition, started the truck, and pulled away slowly in first gear.

Joe glanced back to see Robbie far ahead of the delivery men, dodging between buildings and piles of supplies. "I hope he can double back soon, or we're going to be too far ahead for him to catch us."

He needn't have worried. Within a few moments, Joe glanced back again and saw Robbie overtaking them.

"Stop the truck, he's almost here," he ordered. Joe

opened his door, then slid into the middle of the bench seat.

Robbie jumped in and tried to shut the door behind himself, but his sheathed sword caught near the floorboard, keeping it from closing. Growling under his breath, he pulled the sheath close to his leg and slammed the door shut.

"Go! Go!" he yelled. "Let's get out of here."

"You got it!" Billy exclaimed reaching for the gear shift.

"Nice work," Joe grinned, but his grin turned to a scowl when Billy ground the gears, released the clutch too fast, killing the engine.

"Why didn't you tell us that you didn't know how to drive a stick shift?" Joe asked him. "That's kind of a key thing to know, don't you think?"

"I do know how to do it; I just haven't done it in a long time," replied Billy, restarting the motor.

"It looks like the last time you did it was when you were twelve," responded Robbie.

Looking back, he breathed a sigh of relief when he didn't see any sign of the delivery men. This time, Billy released the clutch more carefully. He drove slowly and cautiously, only engaging the clutch too fast three times.

A few minutes later, he hissed, "We are almost at the service entrance, so keep your mouths shut and let me do the talking."

A guard reading the newspaper lazily looked up, wrinkled his nose at the smelly truckload of fish, and waved them in.

"That certainly went well," said Robbie with a smile.

"Maybe, but we still have a long way to go, so don't start patting yourself on the back too soon," warned Billy.

With that, they pulled into the loading dock area of

the castle. Billy said, "Robbie and I will start to unload some of this fish. Joe, you head into the castle and figure out where we are. Try to find the servants' quarters if you can. Any information will be helpful."

The cousins exited the truck, taking care to be sure the sheaths were secure around their waists. Billy and Robbie began unloading the fish, taking care to move as slowly as they could without seeming to dawdle too much.

Joe headed through the loading dock bay doors and into the warehouse itself. It was vast and cluttered and had many workers, but they were all focused on their tasks and ignored him, even with his sword. He wondered about it at first; then he remembered that the cloaking works to make the swords invisible to the people around them.

Working his way from the warehouse area to the first hallway, he noticed a stairway leading down. He took it and found himself descending much further than he had imagined. "Castles must have very deep cellars," he said to himself and continued his descent.

Reaching the bottom of the stairs, it didn't take him long to find the servant's quarters, but there were so many people around, he didn't dare explore any further. He didn't want to inadvertently wander into an area where he'd arouse suspicion. After glancing around, he headed back up the stairs and outside.

He was walking toward them and saw a man approach Robbie asking if he had a light. Robbie checked the truck, found some matches, and lit his cigarette.

Coming closer, Joe heard Billy say, "Excuse me, old chap, could you by chance tell us from where the princess will be making her address to the children tonight? My daughter is so looking forward to hearing her, and I think she would enjoy the experience more if I could describe the setting to her."

The man replied, "Certainly, my good man, but everyone knows that all addresses to the nation from Windsor Castle originate from the East Sitting Room, closest to the bedrooms. It is the most convenient location for the children and is easily accessible from the Great Hall. I can take you to the Great Hall, if you like."

"That would be great! I mean, that would be capital, my good man," replied Billy.

The man nodded, then wrinkled his nose. "I'll finish my cigarette over there while you finish unloading the fish."

Billy laughed. "They are a bit smellier than usual today, aren't they, old chap?"

As the man walked a distance away, Robbie looked at Billy like he was crazy and whispered, "What are you doing? You don't have to use that awful fake British accent here! We have the gift of tongues from the swords, remember?"

"Oh, yeah," replied Billy. "I forgot."

Joe rejoined them shaking his head. "It's no good, guys," he said. "I couldn't find where the sword is. Too many people."

"No worries, Joe," Billy reassured him. "That nice gentleman over there is going to take us to the Great Hall. From there, we can look for the East Sitting Room where the princess will make her address tonight. We need to find her and convince her to help us persuade her father, whom I assume is the rightful owner of the sword, to let us take the sword back to our time."

When the last fish was unloaded, they locked the truck and looked for the worker. He'd just finished his cigarette and was ambling towards them. Seeing them coming his way, he nodded, then led the way inside.

As the three cousins entered the Great Hall, Joe glanced at his watch. It was a little after 2:00. It had taken a long time to borrow the truck, make their plans, and accomplish everything up to this point, but now they were in the heart of the castle and had plenty of time, he hoped.

The Great Hall was alive with people. There was an excited buzz in the air. The worker who had accompanied them apparently knew everything about the princess's address to the children of the nation. It was like having their own personal tour guide.

They moved to the center of the Great Hall, stepping around people and cables.

"This reminds me of many of the press conferences I've covered over the years," Joe remarked. Spotting a cameraman who looked friendly, he said to their guide, "Excuse me a moment. I think that's someone I know."

Joe came up behind the cameraman and tapped him on the shoulder. "Excuse me, is that a Bell & Howell Eyemoe camera?"

"Why, yes it is," the cameraman grinned. "They are the very best for shooting documentary films like the one we are producing here today. They really show well on the big movie screens. Are you a cameraman?"

"No, actually I'm a reporter," Joe replied, thinking quickly. "From America."

"Welcome to England," he said, shaking Joe's hand.

They spent the next few minutes talking about the camera, the sound equipment and what the focus of the documentary would be.

When he finished, Joe returned to the others. "Wow," he said, "that was interesting."

"Why?" asked Billy.

"Seeing the type of equipment they have to work

with really put what I do in perspective. I don't know how these guys can deal with this antiquated stuff and still put out quality work. He asked me what kind of equipment I used, so I tried to explain, but he couldn't understand the concept of television news and digital cameras, and I think he thought I was lying."

"Joe!" exclaimed Billy, "We're not supposed to do anything that could change history! Talking about digital cameras and TV could screw things up."

"Calm down, Billy," said Joe. "He had no idea what I was talking about. Anyway, what is he going to do? Go back to some workbench somewhere and create a digital TV camera out of vacuum tubes and copper wire? I don't think so."

"Just be careful," Billy finished and turned to speak to the worker.

"You mentioned that the East Sitting Room is upstairs near the bedrooms. Do you believe that is where the princess will be waiting until broadcast time?"

"Yes, for a while, but she always takes afternoon tea at 4:00 p.m. Tea will last until just before 5:00 p.m. That's when she will address the children of the nation," replied the worker.

Billy turned to Joe and Robbie and quietly said, "We have to get to her before she takes her afternoon tea. There will be far too many people around for us to speak with her then, so we need to do it as soon as possible. I'm going to ask our tour guide if he can get us closer to her bedroom."

He turned back to the worker and said, "I would love to see the East Sitting Room so that I can describe it in detail to my daughter. She would be so thrilled to know that I was in the same room that the princess will be in. It would mean so much to her. Could you possibly escort us up there?"

"I don't know," said the worker, "they are pretty fussy about who goes wandering through the castle, but with all these strangers here today, I think we could get by as BBC people. So, I'm game if you are! Just don't speak with anyone and don't touch anything."

With that, they ascended the long, elaborate staircase. They reached the top of the stairs and saw that the bedroom wing was off to the left and the East Sitting Room to the right.

The worker pointed them in that direction and said, "I have to use the loo. Enjoy your visit to the East Sitting Room." He left them standing alone as he went in search of the bathroom.

Billy, Joe, and Robbie stood there for a moment, taking it all in. They walked toward the sitting room to get a better look and think about their next move.

"We have to get to the princess right away," Billy said.

"Right. So, why are we looking at this room?" Robbie asked.

Joe replied, "Because we need to understand the whole layout. If we have to make a run for it, we need to know the lay of the land."

Billy added, "And we need some time to plan this out. Right now, we only have one plan, without a plan B. So, let's look around, find another way down, and then head to the bedrooms and figure out which one belongs to the princess."

The cousins did their recon work and identified an elevator that would take them to the basement. As they were making their way back toward the staircase to head down the hall to the bedrooms, Joe was startled by a voice. Looking around, they saw a butler carrying a tray.

"I say, good man, what are you doing up here?" the butler asked them as he approached. "No one is supposed to be in this area until tea time."

Joe responded, "Sorry old chap, we are with the BBC, and we were trying to figure out the best sound configuration for the newscast, excuse me, I mean the radio broadcast tonight. You wouldn't want the princess's voice to be over-modulated, would you?"

"My good man, I don't believe our princess's voice could ever be, as you say, over-modulated." With a little sniff, the butler turned and resumed his duties.

Robbie praised Joe. "That was pretty slick, Joe, but what is it with you guys and the horrible accents? We have the gift of tongues, remember?"

When the coast was clear and headed down the hall to the bedrooms. They listened at each door to see if they could hear any sounds that might indicate that the princess was in one of them. As they reached the fifth door on the right, they heard a muffled cry. It sounded like a young girl's voice, and she was in distress.

Billy opened the door, and there, in the grasp of the worker who had been so helpful to them, was Princess Elizabeth. They entered, and Robbie closed and locked the door behind them.

Then they turned to the worker, and Joe demanded, "Let her go!"

The worker laughed. "Seriously? You think I'm going to let her go just because you idiots tell me to? You have got to have something better than that up your sleeve. If not, you had better turn and leave now before you get hurt."

With that, all three unsheathed and raised their swords, which instantly became visible. "Are the swords Excalibur, Durandal, and Braveheart enough to convince you?"

The worker laughed again and raised his right arm. Instantly, a sword appeared in his hand. "I know all about cloaking, and your silly fake accent was a real giveaway too. You should have stuck with the gift of tongues! In my hand, I hold the Sword of Herod the Great, known for spilling the blood of innocent children. Appropriate, don't you think? After this innocent child reveals the location of the Sword of Tristan to me, I will kill her and be gone. So, stay out of my way."

Just then, the princess ducked her head and bit her captor viciously on his sword arm. He yowled and released her, holding the wound with his free hand. Quick as a flash, she was standing behind the three cousins.

"I guess the princess was the one to draw first blood," grinned Joe. "Should we see who is second?"

At that point, they heard a key opening the door. It was the butler they had seen before. He turned, relocked the door, and joined the three cousins and the princess. He raised his right hand, and a sword appeared.

"Simeon, so good to see you again," he said to the apostle disguised as a worker. "But once again, you will fail. You always do. When will you stop trying?"

"When I have your head on a silver platter, Robert," was his quick reply.

"Do you two guys know each other?" Robbie asked.

"Certainly," Robert replied. "We have done battle many times over many swords. What we have here is a serial failure. He always falls short just when the prize is close. I'm so happy to be able to witness it once again."

Without warning, Robert charged Simeon, and with a lightning swift move, smashed him in the teeth with the pommel of his sword, sending Simeon staggering backward.

The cousins rushed forward to enter the fray.

Robert drew his arm back to strike a stabbing blow to the apostle, but his elbow caught Joe's jaw, knocking him to the floor. Excalibur fell from his now-limp hand, clattering to the floor near the princess's feet.

Looking startled, Billy hesitated.

Robbie shouted to him, "Help Joe! I'll help Robert."

Billy's expression changing from startled to confused. "What?" he asked.

Then, instead of following Robbie's order, he ran towards Robert, bumping into Robbie on the way. The two tripped over one another, tumbling to the floor.

As they struggled to disentangle themselves from one another, the princess snatched Excalibur from the floor. She looked at the guardian and the apostle struggling on the other side of the room.

Robert had the apostle by the throat with his left hand and was using his own sword to keep the Sword of Herod from piercing his side.

Joe struggled to clear the sparks from his vision. Out of the corner of his eye, he caught a flash of silver, and saw the princess slide the sword past Robert's arm and into the chest of the apostle. The eyes of the apostle grew wide for a moment, then glazed over as breath fled from his lungs and a fountain of blood erupted from his chest, covering Robert's face.

Releasing his grip, Robert stood, blinked several times, then wiped the blood from his eyes with his sleeve.

Joe turned his head to see the princess, partially covered in the blood of the apostle, standing tall, straight, and defiant.

Robert approached her and asked gently, "Are you well, Princess?"

"Yes," she replied, her voice cold and angry. "I did

what I had to do. This is my home. I will not tolerate invaders and usurpers fouling it with their evil."

"I thank you for your assistance," said Robert as he bowed slightly.

Joe, still groggy, struggled to stand. Robbie and Billy reached down to help him to his feet.

The princess reached down, withdrew Excalibur from the chest of the dead apostle, turned, and handed it to Joe.

"Thank you for the use of your sword," she said, her tone respectful.

"Certainly," replied Joe sheepishly as he grasped the hilt. "I'm sorry I wasn't able to use it myself."

"What are we going to do with the body?" asked Robbie.

"I have people who can take care of that," replied Robert as he reached down to collect the Sword of Herod from the fallen apostle. As he took hold of the sword, it vanished from his hand.

"It is always the same; the Swords of Terror cannot abide in the hand of virtue," he stated as he turned to the cousins and the princess.

"Well," said Robert, "I think introductions are in order. If I may, Your Highness, I'm Robert Ogilvie Petrie, and I'm honored to have been of service." He bowed deeply and courteously.

Then he turned to the cousins and said, "Gentlemen, who might you be? It is obvious that you are soldiers of one of our five families of Guardians, albeit inexperienced ones," he said with a wink. "What are your names, and what family do you belong to?"

Joe was stunned by the revelation and realization that standing there before them, speaking to them, was their great-grandfather. Looking at his cousins, he saw they were awestruck, as well.

Finally, Billy responded to his inquiry. "We are Billy, Joe, and Robbie. We are with the Cincinnatus family, and as you guessed, this is our first mission."

"How wonderful! I know many other members of that family, and they are about the best we have. Well done, sirs! Please, would you bow before the princess to show her the respect due?" their great-grandfather encouraged.

The cousins bowed.

The princess nodded her head in acknowledgement, then paused, brushing at the blood on her gown. She grew pale, then took a shaky breath.

"Perhaps you should sit, Your Highness," Robert suggested, gesturing to a nearby chair.

She looked at the chair and took a wobbly step forward. Robert caught her elbow and helped her sit. Once she was seated, she addressed the cousins, her tone tight.

"You spoke of a mission. Please tell me of the object of your assignment."

"Your Highness," replied Billy, "we have an extraordinary story to tell and an even stranger request to make of you."

Elizabeth gestured to other chairs around the room. "Please sit and continue your tale."

They all took seats and Billy began to speak.

"We are here today on a critical, and as you surmised, urgent assignment. It is imperative that we obtain the Sword of Tristan and return with it to our own land. For this, we desperately need your cooperation and agreement."

Elizabeth looked stunned. "The Sword of Tristan? The coronation sword? The very one mentioned by the apostle I just dispatched? It is one of the Crown Jewels of the realm. I will do no such thing!"

"Your Highness, please, I implore you to listen to these young men," their great-grandfather encouraged. "They fought valiantly despite their inexperience. I believe they speak the truth. Let us hear them out and consider what they have to say."

After a moment's thought, she agreed to let them continue.

Joe took it from here. "Until six hours ago, the three of us were just ordinary cousins. Upon the death of our grandfather, we were told about our secret family history. Our family is one of the five families that have been chosen over the centuries to be the Guardians of the Swords of Valor. The Swords of Valor are ten of the most powerful and influential swords in history, and they must be protected and kept out of the hands of evil.

"As you heard from his own mouth, the apostle you dispatched earlier was here to steal the Sword of Tristan. It is one of the ten Swords of Valor. Where we come from, it has fallen into the hands of evil and is being used for destructive purposes."

At this point, the princess interrupted him. "Excuse me, a point of clarification, please. How is it possible that the sword has fallen into the hands of this evil group? I know for a fact that it is here in Windsor Castle at this moment. Please clarify for me where you come from?"

Joe responded after looking at Robbie and Billy for permission to reveal the truth. "To be clear, Your Highness, we are from the United States, but we are also travelers in time. We are from the year 2016 and have been sent back to 1940 to recover the Sword of Tristan at the height of its power before it falls into the hands of evil. In our time, the world has entered a Crisis season, and after gaining the permission of the rightful owner of the sword to return with it to our own time, we will use it to avert a worldwide disaster. Please know that upon the completion of our mission and the successful resolution of the crisis, the sword will return to its rightful owner and its rightful place in history. Please consider helping us."

The princess looked surprised but seemed less shocked than Joe expected. He thought that her recent experience killing the apostle may have had an impact, but he also felt certain that she was wise beyond her years and highly intelligent.

She responded. "As you may know, our country is facing a crisis of our own. We are bombed every day. We have evacuated our precious children to places of safety to protect them and our future. We fear imminent invasion and need all the power we possess to survive this threat. How can you ask me to give you a sword that contains so much power, at a time such as this when it is most needed?"

It was an intelligent and mature question, thought Joe. He responded, "Your Highness, you are right. It is a dangerous time for Britain, but I can tell you that all will be well. The nation and the world will survive and prosper in freedom. Your countrymen will exhibit the bravery and courage that inspires other nations to rally to your cause, and together you defeat the enemy.

"We, on the other hand, have no such assurance. If we fail in our time, all the lives lost fighting this current war will be for naught. As we said, the sword will return to you after we use it to stop the crisis in our time. It will seem to you as if it were gone for only a few minutes and will return with even more power than before. Trust me. Your nation will need that increased strength in a couple of months. Please believe us on this point, and consider our request."

The princess turned and addressed their great-grandfather. "Sir, are you also from this future time?"

"No, Your Highness. I'm part of the same organization of Guardians, but I'm from our time. I was here on an assignment to prevent the sword from being stolen today. If any of the Swords of Valor have fallen into the hands of the apostles of Azazel, then there is truly a crisis of epic proportions. I urge you to help them."

"So, you advise that I consider their request?" asked the princess.

"I do," replied Robert.

She was silent for a moment, then replied. "You have all fought valiantly for my safety. I believe your story, and I will help you. Please, tell me what I need to do."

Joe explained that she needed to convince her father, the king, of all that she had been told since he was the rightful owner. She needed to convince him to release the sword into their keeping.

The princess stopped them. "The King is in Scotland and won't be back for two days. I suppose we can wait until then. I will make arrangements for you to stay in the castle as our official guests."

The cousins looked at each other, their expressions devastated. They hadn't counted on the absence of the King.

Their great-grandfather spoke up. "Excuse me, gentlemen, but you have assumed that only the King is the owner of the Crown Jewels and the sword. That is not technically true. The jewels and the sword belong to the entire royal family. Therefore, the princess is one of the rightful owners of the Sword of Tristan!"

Joe heaved a sigh of relief as Billy pumped his fist.

"Yes!" he exclaimed.

"Wonderful!" exclaimed Robbie. "That solves that problem, now all we need to do is figure out how to get it from the cellar before the princess makes her address to the children of the nation."

"Your Highness," said Billy, "we know that the Crown Jewels and the Sword of Tristan have been brought here for their protection and safety. It is our understanding that they are hidden in the castle beneath a wooden trapdoor in the basement where the servants' quarters are. Do you know where that is?"

"I certainly do," responded the princess. "I enjoy the company of those servants and play with their children often. I will go there now, request entrance to where the sword is hidden, and bring it back here. I will tell them that I want to examine the sword and take inspiration from it before I address the children tonight. If what you say is true, and you are successful, it will be back in my hands before I make my address. No one will be the wiser. Will that work?"

"Yes!" they exclaimed in unison, then Joe added, "Thank you, Your Highness."

The men rose to their feet as the princess stood. They bowed in gratitude.

The princess grabbed a bathrobe from her wardrobe, covering the blood stains on her gown, and departed to accomplish the task, leaving the cousins alone in the room with their great-grandfather.

Robbie turned to Robert and said, "We have the same name, you and I. In fact, my father is also named Robert. It is a family tradition to name the second son after the mother's father. Do you have a similar tradition?"

"Why, yes we do, my young man. How interesting.

101

It is good to see that such traditions survive into the future," his great-grandfather replied.

He continued addressing all three cousins. "I see you have three of the most powerful swords, and you must learn to use them well. It is apparent that you have not had much training in battle strategy or tactics, but you must be quality individuals to have been given the swords you bear. Make sure to learn all you can as quickly as possible, so you may wield them with honor. Regardless of your inexperience, I'm proud to have made your acquaintance and to have fought by your side."

"We feel the same, sir," said Joe. "In fact, in our time, you are something of a legend. Not only to our family, but also to the International Guardian Families. Your heroism and bravery are recognized and celebrated. We three are especially in your debt, for we would not be here today if it were not for you. I can say that without reservation." He then observed a strange look cross the face of his great-grandfather.

After a brief moment, his great-grandfather smiled. "Well, I'm humbled by your appreciation and very proud that I had something to do with your service. When you return, please give my wishes for success to your family."

They turned as the door opened. It was the princess, and in her hands was the Sword of Tristan. They recognized it from the flat tip of the blade.

"Quickly," she urged, "we don't have much time. I was required to be a trifle more stern than I usually am in order to convince the servants to comply with my demands. I fear they will alert security." She handed the sword to Billy and said, "Good sir, please be careful with it and know that my blessings and faith are with you in your efforts."

Billy replied, "Thank you, Your Highness, but

before we leave, please allow us to honor you by touching you with our swords. You have a tough road ahead, and the swords will empower you with their strength and give you the courage and fortitude you need to lead this great nation."

Frowning, the princess answered, "This is most unusual. Typically, only a monarch can dub someone with the sword."

Joe tried to reassure her. "We do not presume to confer a knighthood, Your Highness. We only wish to grant you the gift of the swords' power."

After a moment's hesitation, she agreed.

The cousins stretched forth their swords. "Your Highness, these are the swords Excalibur, Durandal, and Braveheart. May their powers and strength enable you to rule benevolently, ethically, bravely, generously, and worthily all your long life."

The cousins gently touched the princess's bowed head with Excalibur, her right shoulder with Braveheart, and her left shoulder with Durandal. They observed a faint glow emanating from her face, and when she looked up at them, her eyes reflected determination and strength.

"Thank you for that gift, my fine and handsome gentlemen," the princess said. "Now we must hurry. How are you to return to your proper time?"

Robbie replied, "We must stand around a fire, lift our swords, and gently touch them together, crossing the blades. We will then go back to our own time and place. Or so we hope. This is our first solo attempt. Where can we find a fire?"

"I have a fireplace in the bedroom, but it is not large enough for you to stand around and lift your swords. Perhaps you could build a small fire in the ash bucket and stand around that. Will that suffice?" suggested the princess.

"It will suffice," responded their great-grandfather. "I speak from experience."

The three cousins and their great-grandfather set about collecting the items needed and lit a fire in the large ash bucket. As it started to burn, they turned and thanked the princess for her gift of the Sword of Tristan.

Joe added, "Your Highness, remember to be strong and courageous. The evacuated children of the realm need you now more than ever. Encourage them in their time of need and be the example of courage they need. It will all be well."

With that said, the cousins took their place around the fire, Robbie holding his sword in his right hand, and the Sword of Tristan in his left. They lifted their swords, gently touching them together as they crossed, and disappeared.

As the flash of bright, white light faded, the princess whispered, "Godspeed."

Turning to Robert, she cocked her head, examining his face. She excused herself, disappeared into her bathroom, then returned with a wet washcloth. As she began to gently wipe the blood from Roberts face, she commented, "Such handsome young men! I do hope I get to meet them again. That young Robbie was quite fetching. He would make a wonderful consort to some fortunate queen someday." Then she blushed.

Robert Ogilvie Petrie just smiled and responded, "Yes, Your Highness, he has the blood of heroes in his veins. They all do. I am very proud of them."

CHAPTER FIVE

THE FIRST RETURN

———— ∿ ————

A flash of bright, white light eclipsed the light of the fire where the prophet and three heroes sat. When they could see clearly once again, they saw three young men standing around the fire, arms upraised, swords outstretched before them.

"Wow, still a rush," said Robbie.

The three cousins who had been left behind rushed to their returned cousins. They exchanged hugs, pats on the back, and fist bumps. The prophet breathed a sigh of relief and said a quick prayer of thanks.

"Do you have the Sword of Tristan?" he asked the returned team.

"Yes," Robbie replied. He walked to where his father stood, knelt, and extended the sword, handle first. "Prophet, I present to you the Sword of Tristan, given to us by the hand of Princess Elizabeth of Britain, the rightful owner of the sword."

After reciting the words, he shook his head and mumbled, "I don't know why I just did that." Then he turned to his father. "Hi, Dad! What a great trip!"

His father shook his head and replied, "The

influence of the swords. While you are using them for their purposes, they can influence your behavior. Come quickly. We must go to the Keeping Room and debrief. Head back to the house, wash up, and I will meet you there in fifteen minutes." He turned and walked away.

Once everyone had gathered in the Keeping Room, he said, "Gentlemen, well done! Not only did you complete the assignment quickly, but you did it without the schematics and the rest of the team. I'm very proud of you all."

Robbie replied, "Thanks, Dad. But it didn't feel quick to us. It took us around ten hours. What time is it here?"

"By our reckoning, you left three hours ago," the prophet answered. "Apparently, you experience some form of time dilatation effect during the time travel. It's good to know. Are you feeling all right? Any unexpected effects from the time travel?"

The cousins who'd gone looked at each other, then Joe spoke for the three of them. "No ill effects, except a bit tired."

Uncle Rob nodded. "That makes sense. You've had several more hours of activity than the rest of us. I'm hoping that the swords will help you rejuvenate quickly, because there is still much work to do. Let's move on. Are there any questions before we start?"

Ty asked the returned cousins, "How was it? Was it fun, dangerous, and exciting?"

Almost in unison, they replied, "Yes!"

Billy asked, "So, what happened to you guys? When we got there, we looked for you and then just had to push on with the assignment. We were kind of concerned about you."

Jeff replied, "The swords did not choose us for this

assignment. After we were left here, we all came back to the Keeping Room to ask Grandpa about it and to monitor you guys. He said that the swords only choose the specific people and swords needed for the task and time selected. Apparently, that's what will happen each time. We will never know who will be chosen. Uncle Rob was pretty freaked out that the schematics of the castle were left behind, weren't you, Uncle Rob?"

"It did concern me, but I think we have a solution to the problem," he replied. "I'll get into that later. We were able to monitor your general activities, movements, mindset, and health while you were on assignment. We did not observe anything negative, but we need details. Who wants to start?"

Robbie was the first to speak and explained how they got in with a delivery truck. He reported everything up to the point where they met their great-grandfather, Robert Ogilvie Petrie.

"Of course, he knew we were Guardians, but I don't think he knew we were related to him. Anyway, what a stud he was! He smashed the apostle in the teeth with the butt of his sword. We all tried to help him, but Joe got knocked out and Billy and I tripped over each other trying to join the fight. It was kind of a mess, but it turned out okay after the princess killed the apostle while great-grandpa held him down."

The image spoke, "That would explain the additional biometric impulses we observed as we were monitoring you. We assumed that there was just some echo in the quantum field. Now we know that the quantum computer was picking up the essence of your great-grandfather. That is excellent information, boys. But please clarify your comment about the princess actually dealing the death blow to the apostle."

Joe began, "With all of us out of the fight for the moment, the princess picked up Excalibur, which had fallen from my hand, and used it the kill the apostle. I guess I am pretty surprised that a fourteen-year-old girl was brave enough to actually do that."

The image of their grandfather replied "It is not surprising. She was and is a woman of virtue and valor. She would not have been able to use the sword if that were not so. Please continue."

Robbie resumed the story. "After that, we introduced ourselves to the princess and to Great-Grandpa, never letting on that we were related to him. We convinced her to get the sword for us, and she did. When she got back, we built a fire in the ash bucket near the fireplace in her bedroom and performed the time travel process. Next thing we knew, we were standing around the fire back by the river. That's about it."

The prophet nodded. "Well done, it sounds like an efficient mission, but I have some additional questions. First, did any of you interact with anyone other than the apostle, the princess, and your great-grandfather?"

Billy replied, "Well, Joe had a conversation with a cameraman, but that is all."

"Joe," said the prophet, "tell me about this conversation."

"It wasn't anything really; I just was interested in his equipment and the focus of the documentary they were shooting. I wanted to get a feel for the technology of the times and the old-time approach to the news, especially during wartime. He showed me his equipment. I may have mentioned something about television and digital cameras, but he didn't understand, so I dropped it," Joe finished.

"I see," said the prophet. "I will have to run that

through the quantum computer to test the probabilities of impact on the timeline. There shouldn't be an issue, since television was invented in 1929. It remained experimental until 1939 when Franklin Delano Roosevelt used it to address the nation, but it didn't become commonplace until 1946. That could explain his ignorance of it, but still, we need to be sure. It is just one example of why you must avoid extraneous contact and avoid doing anything that will change the timeline. Anything else?"

Robbie spoke up. "Before we left, we did an odd thing. Without thinking about it or having discussed it beforehand, we asked the princess if we could touch her with the swords. We told her that the swords would empower her and strengthen her for the tough years to come. Joe touched her head with Excalibur, I touched her right shoulder with Braveheart, and Billy touched her left shoulder with Durandal. As we touched her, we saw a slight glow surround her face, and she thanked us. I, for one, have no idea why we did that. Does anyone else?"

"I think I understand," replied the prophet. "As I said earlier when Robbie knelt and presented the Sword of Tristan to me, while you are using the swords in the right way, for the right purposes, you are under their influence. Remember, these are Swords of Valor and are empowered by virtue. So, while under their influence, you will act virtuously. The swords will influence you to do the right thing in any situation.

"If you keep any selfishness or personal gain out of your minds, you will be free to act without having to think about it too much. You will be free from worry and self-doubt and can be assured your actions will always be virtuous. This goes for your speech and behavior also. Hence, Robbie's presentation of the sword and your blessing of the princess. Both virtuous and chivalrous acts."

The image broke in, "That also explains the flux we observed in the power of the swords. You must be careful about sharing that power when you are on assignment. Having done that so close to the leaving process could have drained the power of the swords enough to have prevented you from leaving until they recharged themselves. You should always trust the leading of the swords, but you must also be aware of the possible consequences. Take a quick break, and when you return, we can begin discussing the second assignment."

As they left, the prophet noticed Nick touch Joe's shoulder.

"Hey, Joe, you okay? You seemed a million miles away during that last bit."

Joe chuckled. "Not that far. I was just wondering what my station manager would say if I came back and told him what we'd just done. How would I begin? It's too fantastic! No one would believe me. Yet, I personally experienced all of it, and there's nothing more compelling than a first-hand witness."

Nick's eyebrows raised for a moment, then he laughed. "First-hand witness or not, brother, he'd have you put away!"

"Yeah," Joe agreed. "That's what I thought, too."

When they were gone, Rob turned back to the image. "They are so young, Dad. They managed to accomplish this assignment, but what about the rest? This one was only the tip of the iceberg!"

The image nodded. "Yes, but they are intelligent and resourceful young men. They have the ability to grow and adapt to unusual situations. I believe they will succeed, Robert. Have faith in them."

"You're right," Rob agreed. "It's just that what's to come is so monumental, I have moments of doubt."

The image laughed. "You wouldn't be human if you didn't, son."

Ten minutes later, the cousins re-seated themselves around the table. The computer began. "Now let's get ready for the next assignment. You will be required to obtain the Sword of Joan of Arc, the Maid of Orléans. Here are the details.

"It was stolen by the Nazis right before D-Day. The allies were bombing the Normandy area prior to the invasion, and some of the bombs fell on a church. Apparently, the sword was there. It was later given to the Apostles of Azazel. We don't have any information to tell us where it was found or where it was hidden at the time.

"So, you need to return to a time before the Maid was burned at the stake to get her permission to bring the sword back here, just as you did before. Convince her of the need and get her to tell you its location. When you have finished, return with the sword and present it to the prophet."

Nick asked a question. "Can you fill us in on the date, time, and location that we need to focus on?"

"Yes, Nicholas," responded the image. "As you know, I can't give you the exact details. I can provide you with facts, but you must decide. Here is all we know.

"The trial of Joan of Arc took place in May of 1431 AD in Rouen, Normandy. She was imprisoned for about a month while the trials took place. Most people think that they imprisoned her in the keep of the castle of Rouen, the only surviving remnant of the fortress.

"Since then, it has been called the Joan of Arc Tower. But it housed only one of the sessions of her trial on May 9th, 1431. That was the one where they showed her the instruments of torture. When she saw them, she replied, 'Truly, if you have to pull my members and my soul from my body, I shall say nothing else; and if I say something to you, I would always say to you afterward that you made me say it by force'. She wasn't imprisoned there all the time. She was mostly kept in the now-lost Tower of the Maid.

"During her trial, she stated that at the age of twelve or thirteen, she 'heard a voice from God to help and guide me', but that at first she 'was much afraid'. She added that the voice was 'seldom heard without a light' and that she 'often heard the voice' when she came to France. Joan stated that the voices had spoken to her many times since the previous session. They were the voices of St. Catherine and St. Margaret, who had guided her for seven years. The first time she heard a voice, however, was when she was about twelve. It was that of St. Michael.

"When asked about where she got her sword, she replied, 'When I was at Tours or Chinon, I was sent to the church of St. Catherine of Fierbois to seek a sword hidden behind the altar. It was found all covered with rust. This sword was in the earth, all rusty, and there were upon it five crosses, and I knew it by my voices. After this sword was found, the prelates of the place had it rubbed, and at once, the rust fell from it without difficulty'.

"The story of how Joan found her sword is perhaps the most intriguing connection to it. According to her own words, her voices told her it was behind that altar. Joan had a great devotion to Saint Catherine, so it's no surprise that the sword came from a church dedicated to her.

"The fact that it was found buried behind the altar is not altogether unusual. Soldiers in that day often left their swords or armor as an offering of thanksgiving after battle. There have been many legends about who might have placed this sword behind the altar. One is that it belonged to Charles Martel, grandfather of Charlemagne, who halted the Muslim invasion in Europe. Charles Martel founded the church of Saint Catherine de Fierbois, and he secretly buried his sword for whomever God would choose to find it and use it to save France.

"When her judges questioned her about the location of the sword from St. Catherine of Fierbois, because they certainly didn't want any relics floating around, she refused to provide an answer, saying it didn't concern the case. The only information she would give was that it was lost in battle and that her brothers had the rest of her goods.

"After her trial, she was burned at the stake on May 30th, 1431 AD, in the marketplace of Rouen just before sunrise. That, gentlemen, should give you enough information to choose the time and place of your next assignment. Agreed?" asked the image.

"So, let me see if I have all the facts," said Jeff. "The trial of Joan of Arc took place in May of 1431 AD in Rouen, Normandy. She really was imprisoned in the now-lost Tower of the Maid. Her sword was lost in battle, and her brothers had the rest of her goods. After her trial, she was burned at the stake on May 30th, 1431 AD, in the marketplace of Rouen. Her sword apparently was in a church in Rouen until the Nazis stole it right before D-Day on June 6th, 1944. Do I have it all correct?"

"Yes" replied the image of their grandfather.

"So," asked Jeff, "why don't we just go back to a time just before D-Day and get the sword from the church?"

The image replied, "Because we need the sword at the height of its virtuous power, and the permission of its rightful owner. It was never more powerful than when the Maid of Orléans was facing death. It gave her all the strength and valor she needed to face her fate. That is the time you must return to."

"Can I make an observation?" asked Joe.

"Certainly," the image replied.

"When we arrived at Windsor Castle, we were about a hundred yards away in a field and had to figure out how to get inside. Is there any way to make us appear inside the building we are targeting when we go back in time? It would be much easier to start from the inside. We will need to find the Maid, and she very well may be in a cell or a dungeon. That will be hard enough without having to fight our way into the castle."

"Now you are thinking and learning," the image responded. "The swords will take you anywhere you are thinking of with precise accuracy, but you must hold that exact location in all your minds along with the date and time while you are performing the leaving process. All of you appeared around the fire pit by the river when you returned from Windsor Castle. That was because that exact location was already embedded in your minds, and you knew that was where you would return. It works the same way when you are leaving to go on an assignment."

"Okay," said Robbie, "but we were familiar with the fire pit and the river. How can we do the same thing with a place we have never been to before and that doesn't even exist today?"

The image replied, "Obviously, we need to rectify that somehow. As I told you, there is a massive amount of information in the quantum computer. We have ancient maps, diagrams, and architectural plans of many buildings and locations.

"I will pull up the plans for Rouen Castle during the

time that Joan of Arc was imprisoned there. The quantum computer can create a realistic 3D holographic image right here in this room. You can wander through the building to experience and familiarize yourself with the rooms and hallways. Will that work for you?"

"Absolutely!" was Nick's reply. "But why didn't you offer that to us for the first assignment? I'm sure that the others would have appreciated knowing that before having to depend on Robbie to get them in."

"Yes, you are correct, Nick," the image confirmed. "However, this is a learning process, and you all must use your brains and work together. You should have asked that question before heading out blindly on the first mission. Did any of you have any idea where you were going to land when you arrived at Windsor Castle? A couple of you had probably seen pictures of it in the past. The swords just searched your minds for that image and placed you safely in the field you had seen.

"Now you have thought critically about the assignment and asked the right questions and have received a great answer. This assignment will be easier now than it would have been. The holographic rendering of Rouen Castle is ready; would you like to begin your immersion?"

The cousins agreed and stood. They looked surprised when Uncle Rob stood, as well.

"I've never experienced a holographic rendering," he smiled. "May I join you?"

The cousins grinned at each other, then nodded.

"The images will surround you and move for you," said the image. "You don't have to walk through it, although it will feel so realistic that you will want to. Resist the urge and stand still. The immersion will start at the entrance and will take you through every part of the castle.

We will now begin!"

The lights in the room faded, and the cousins were immediately surrounded by and immersed in the 3D holographic image of Rouen Castle. They stood in a large entryway. They could look all around and see everything. The quantum computer even filled in the details, such as carpets, wall hangings, and windows.

Without taking a step, they began to move through the room and around a corner. They went down a hallway, taking the opportunity to study each room. They saw the great dining hall, the meeting rooms, and the kitchen area, along with many other, smaller quarters.

After examining the first floor, they ascended the staircase to the second floor. Another grand room was ahead of them at the top of the stairway. The hallway was circular, and as the cousins moved, they observed bedrooms, libraries, and servants' quarters.

As they returned to the top of the stairway, they advanced into the grand room they had seen earlier at the top of the stairs. Through the huge, stained-glass windows, they spotted two towers. The immersion took them out a door at the side of the room and across the top of the outer wall of the castle toward the towers. They came to the first tower, went in and up a set of narrow, winding steps to the uppermost room.

Upon entering, they saw a prison cell with a sturdy door, iron bars on the narrow window, and straw strewn on the smooth, stone floor for bedding. There were two stone benches built into the walls on either side of the window.

The image then led them to the lowest level of the castle. This housed more servants' quarters, massive fireplaces, and the muster room for the castle guards. Surprisingly, the muster room had a doorway leading to a small stable. The roughness of the opening suggested that this stable wasn't originally part of the castle, but was added later, allowing the guards on duty quick access to their horses.

They returned to the grand entrance, the lights in the room came on, and the immersion ended.

Everyone returned to the table as the image appeared once more.

"Amazing!" said Ty. "That was crazy! Way better than any virtual reality I have ever experienced. It felt so real."

"Remember the castle as you experienced it," instructed the image of their grandfather. "Think about the rooms and passageways. Fix it all in your minds and use it to determine your place of arrival. You now have all the information and experience you need to come to a decision. Do it now."

The cousins huddled together and discussed the facts and the immersion experience in the Castle of Rouen. After ten minutes of vigorous discussion, they came to a decision.

"Grandpa, we have made our choice," announced Billy.

"Speak it now," said the image.

"We choose to return to Castle Rouen on May 29th, 1431. We wish to arrive just before sunrise in the stables on the lowest level of the castle," said Billy.

"You are all in agreement?" asked the image.

"We are," they replied.

Billy added, "It makes the most sense. We're less likely to run into someone if we appear in the stable, but we'll have ready access to the castle through the door in the muster room."

"So be it. Godspeed," the image stated before it

faded away.

The prophet rose from his chairs around the table. The cousins followed, gathered their swords once again from the glass case, climbed the stairs into the barn, and exited. Not a word was said between them on the way to the fire pit. The prophet observed their grave expressions and knew that they had learned well that these assignments were deadly serious. There was plenty to think about.

As they stood around the fire, he gave them final instructions. "The immersion has shown you the castle, and you know where Joan of Arc was kept. The one thing it didn't show you is people. This is a variable we can't really prepare for, because people tend to be unpredictable. As you know now, it's possible that not all of you will go on this assignment. That's another variable that can't be accounted for. Try not to worry about it. Just be aware. Keep all the arrival information running through your minds so there will be no mistakes this time."

CHAPTER SIX

THE SWORD OF JOAN OF ARC

Arriving at the fire pit, the prophet stood staring at the now furiously roaring blaze. His thoughts twisted and swirled with the flames. He knew that shortly the cousins would be speaking with a saint who was burned to death by a fire much larger than this, and the idea left him in awe.

As he stood there lost in thought, he felt a hand touch him on the shoulder.

"Dad," asked Robbie, "are you okay?"

"Yes, Robbie," he replied, "just thinking."

The prophet turned and faced the cousins. He said to them, "It begins again. Clear your minds of distractions and assume your positions around the fire. Fix the date, time, and location clearly in your minds. Fix it there! Now raise your swords slowly, and gently bring them together."

The young heroes complied with the prophet's commands, and immediately a flash of pure, white light enveloped them. When he could once again see clearly, he saw Joe, Billy, and Robbie standing there with swords held high. Once again, the swords had only chosen three of them. But now he understood why.

Jeff, Ty, and Nick found themselves in the bowels of the Castle of Rouen and heard the neighing of panicked horses. They ducked into an empty stall and crouched behind the wall.

A moment later, they heard two guards enter the stable. "What's all the noise about?" one asked the other.

"Could be anything… or nothing," the other answered. "Let's just get them calmed down. It's almost time for drills."

Their boots thudded softly on the hard-packed earth as they stopped at each stall, calming the horses. As the guards approached their hiding place, the cousins held their breath, praying they'd pass by the supposedly-empty stall.

Surprisingly, the guards didn't even glance their way. After checking each horse, they exited through a side door into the courtyard, grumbling about spooked horses, wasted time, and being late for drill. After their footsteps faded away, Nick peeked around the stall wall. Seeing no one, he nodded at the others and stood up.

"The swords must have influenced them," Jeff observed, watching the open doorway where the guards had disappeared. "They didn't even glance at this stall."

"I'm glad they left quickly," Nick commented. "Do you think the swords influenced the horses, too? They were pretty panicked when we appeared. We could never have calmed them that fast ourselves."

"Maybe," Jeff agreed.

"What is that awful smell?" asked Ty looking at his cousin Nick.

"If you ever spent any time around horses, you

would know, Ty," replied Nick. He pointed down. The three cousins were standing in manure. "The quantum computer's immersion program was great, but it left out a few pungent details!"

A quick scan of the area didn't reveal any people around, so they quickly hid in an empty stall to make plans.

"Okay," said Jeff, "it looks like the swords selected only us three for this assignment. Fortunately, we didn't need a schematic for this one, since we all experienced the immersion. Our objective is that tower the program showed us. Given that Joan of Arc is scheduled to be burned tomorrow before sunrise, we have a lot to accomplish before then. Any ideas on how we're going to meet up with her?"

"Well, when we saw the tower during the immersion, I noticed that there was straw used for bedding on the floor. Maybe we can gather some and make like we are going to replace the stuff on her floor?" suggested Ty.

"Or we could go to the kitchen and get some food to bring up to her for her last meal?" Nick proposed.

"Both of those sound good," agreed Jeff. "The kitchen is on the main level, and we also saw the muster area for the castle guard down here with uniforms hanging on the walls. What I propose is simple.

"Ty, you gather up as much straw as you can carry. I will go to the kitchen and gather up some food. Nick, you head to the muster room and put on a castle guard uniform. When you're dressed, go up and relieve the guard standing watch over Joan of Arc. When you are set, we will follow you to the tower with the straw and the food. We can then talk with the Maid and try to convince her. Ty, let's plan to give Nick about fifteen minutes to get dressed and up there."

Nick asked, "Why do I have to put on a uniform? Won't the cloaking work for me?"

"Probably," said Jeff, "but I don't want to take any chances. We are not sure what kind of clothes the people we encounter will see us wearing. It may be that they are appropriate for the common people of the period, but we can't be sure they'd see you in a specific uniform. I'm just trying to make sure that we cover all our bases. You are the critical element here, Nick, and we have to be sure."

"Got it," replied Nick. "I'll change and meet you in fifteen minutes."

Jeff turned to Ty and said, "I'm going to the main level to get some food from the kitchen. Are you all set here? You know what you are supposed to do and when?"

Ty looked at Jeff with disdain. "Seriously? All I have to do is get straw and wait fifteen minutes, how could I screw that up?"

Jeff returned his look. "I hope you're right." Then he and Nick headed for the doorway leading to the muster room.

As they moved away, Ty mumbled to himself, "I hate being the youngest one. I'm studying to be a neurologist, and they still don't give me any respect." He shook his head and began gathering straw.

Approaching the doorway, Nick slid to one side of the opening, as Jeff moved to the opposite side. He glanced into the muster room and saw a few guards getting dressed and motioned for Jeff to wait. After a few moments, the room was clear. Jeff headed for the stairs while Nick made his way to the few uniforms left on the wall.

He took one down and pulled it on. It was large enough to fit over his clothes, but there were no uniform boots to go with it. He hoped the cloaking would cover that noticeable difference. He checked himself against what he had seen of the other guards' uniforms and felt confident that he would pass for one of them. Then he climbed to the tower.

As he approached the cell, he saw that two guards stood watch outside the door. He would have to figure out how to get them to leave, and he only had a few minutes before his cousins would arrive. He stood up straight and marched up to them.

"I'm here to relieve you," he informed them.

Puzzled, they looked at him and said, "It is not time yet for our relief. Why this change in plans?"

Nick responded, "The final sentencing of the prisoner is taking place in a few hours, and the commander believes there may be trouble. He needs all the experienced men he has to control the crowd."

They looked him up and down and commented. "Well, it is obvious that you are new. You don't even have the right uniform boots. You know the rules include wearing the full uniform when you show up for duty. Next time you show up for work without your boots, I hope the commander has your head." Then they left him there alone.

Releasing the longest breath he'd ever held, he checked the door. It was locked. He had forgotten to get the keys. Running after the two retreating guards, he called out. "Sorry, guys, I forgot to get the keys from you!"

The biggest one of them threw the keys back over his shoulder without turning around and scoffed, "New recruits are all the same!"

Nick retrieved the keys just as Jeff arrived with the food. He asked Nick, "Any trouble?"

"No," replied Nick, "just had to get a little creative with my story. I have no idea when they might return, but let's not waste any time. What about you? Any trouble?"

Jeff made a face. "Not really. They were cleaning up from breakfast. I saw a woman directing the others and thought she'd be my best bet. I got creative, too. Told her the prisoner needed food. She said it wasn't time. That's when I made a mistake, I think."

Nick looked surprised. "You? You made a mistake?"

"Can it," Jeff grimaced. "I'm human, too, you know. I told her that whatever she had was fine, that the prisoner was not long for this world and was an enemy of the people."

"How'd she react?"

"She spat at me."

"What? Spat at you?"

Jeff nodded. "She told me to watch what I say. She said this country, maybe all of us, will pay the price for what we do with her tomorrow. She said we've condemned a good woman, and God will judge us! Then she gave me the best food she could find, warned me to deliver all of it, and said, 'God forgive us' as she pushed me out of the kitchen."

"Well, she got that right," Nick nodded. "God forgive us!"

Jeff asked, "Has Ty shown up yet?"

Just then, Ty came running up with an arm-load of straw. "Sorry," he said. "I tried to find as much clean straw as I could, but there really wasn't any. Thanks for giving me the worst job, Jeff. As I was making my way through the castle, everyone ran away from me because of the smell!"

Their own noses told them he was telling the truth.

Nick replied, "Are you sure it wasn't your face they

SEASON OF THE SWORDS

were running from?" He and Jeff laughed.

"Shut up, and let's get this thing going," Ty responded, annoyed.

The cousins approached the door and tried several keys before they found the right one. They unlocked the door, and what they saw surprised them.

A young girl about nineteen years old and dressed in man's clothing sat on the floor of the cell between the stone benches they'd seen in the immersion. Her legs were bound together tightly with cloth strips from her ankles to above her knees, but her arms and hands were free. Her light brown hair was shorn short. She had a calm, yet determined, look on her face.

When they entered the room, she didn't move. She just asked them, "Is it time?"

Jeff replied, "No, Maid, it is not time, but soon. Please, don't be afraid of us, we are here on a special mission to ask for your help in a worthy cause."

She replied, "I fear no mortal man. I fear only God, as He can destroy both body and soul. Unless your request is from Him, I will refuse."

Nick then asked, "Dear Maid, may we release you from your bonds?"

She replied, "First, I'm a soldier. Speak to me as such. Second, you may not release me from my bonds, as they are of my own making. They are for the protection of my chastity and virtue against the evil men of this castle. Speak to me of your mission, and I will decide if I shall assist you."

Jeff started. "We have come here from a time far in the future, many centuries from now. We are the Guardians, the protectors of the Swords of Valor. The sword that was given to you by St. Catherine is one of these. In our time, it has fallen into the hands of evil and will be used to destroy all that is virtuous in the world. We need to obtain the sword and bring it back to our time so that we may thwart the plans of evil. We can only do this if you tell us where the sword is and give us your permission to take it. Will you help us?"

She looked at him skeptically. "How do I know this is not some ruse by the English to get me to reveal the location of the sword? They have asked me about it many times during the trial, and I have always told them truthfully that it was lost during the battle, and that my brothers have the rest of my belongings. I don't know where it is. Even if I did know, I would not tell you unless my voices gave me leave to do so."

At that point, Ty spoke up. "We are aware of your voices. We know that St. Catherine, St. Margaret, and St. Michael the Archangel guide you. If you ask them for confirmation, they will affirm that all we say is true."

Joan growled at him, "Be very careful what you ask for, boy, the consequences will have an eternal impact. You are risking your souls by calling upon the holy saints to give their testimony! I will ask them, but if I were you, I would be prepared to meet my maker."

Then she closed her eyes and entered a deep state of prayer.

Nick stood quietly with his brother and cousin. He had a bit of trepidation in his heart. He didn't know what to expect. Their cause was righteous, but still, would the saints confirm it, or would they be left on their own?

After a few minutes, Joan spoke. "My voices tell me that you will give me a sign. It will be a sign that I will recognize. I won't tell you what it is. If I see the correct sign, I will give you my permission and tell you all you need to know. If not, I will pray for your destruction. Proceed."

Startled, the cousins looked at each other. They hadn't realized they would be required to produce a sign, and they were unprepared.

Ty spoke first. "Well, our grandmother is named after St. Catherine. Is that what you were looking for?"

"No, that is not it," Joan replied, fixing him with a steely glare.

Jeff responded, "We have with us the swords of Solomon, Charlemagne, and St. Michael the Archangel. Is that the sign?"

At that, the Maid's expression changed. She demanded, "Show them to me at once!"

Immediately, the three cousins pulled the swords from their sheaths, raised their right arms, and the swords appeared. As they held them outstretched in the air in front of them for her to see, the Sword of St. Michael the Archangel burst into flame. It was a flame without heat. It was bright, white, and pure. It filled the room with a sense of power and absolute safety. Nick almost dropped it as the sudden burst of flame startled him.

Joan cried out, "Thank you, my protector! Thank you, St. Michael. Thank you for your sign! Thank you for your love! I'm unworthy of your faith in me. I will give these young men what they need." Then she put her face in her hands and wept.

The flame died, and the cousins lowered their swords. Nick felt encouraged and joyful, but mostly humbled. What they had just witnessed was beyond anything he had expected. The heroes quickly went to the Maid, knelt, and surrounded her. Nick put his strong arms around her and whispered, "Come with us. Let us rescue you. We can take you away from here, and you won't have to face the fire. The swords will protect us all."

The Maid looked at him with love and appreciation.

"I can't go with you. I tried to escape earlier in the month by leaping from the other tower where I was held for a short while. I landed on some soft ground but was found the next day unconscious. The following day, my voices admonished me. They told me that the greater purposes of God would be served by my fulfilling the Lord's will for my life. I am to wait here until I am called. I will obey, and I fully accept the will of God. May He do as He wills with my life and my legacy."

Nick gently kissed her forehead and said, "Dear Maid, take comfort that, in time, you will become a saint, and your legacy will be one of courage, fortitude, and faith. You will become an inspiration to fighting men everywhere and to the women of the world. You will have won your greatest battle."

Jeff spoke softly. "Now it is time for you to tell us where we may find the sword. The guards may be back soon, and if we are to succeed, we must be gone before they arrive."

Joan responded, "I always speak the truth. I don't know its whereabouts. It is possible that my brothers may know, since they have always accompanied me and have all my other worldly belongings. They will attend my final sentencing hearing today in the courtyard of the castle. You will know them by the banner they carry. It is the same one I carried into every battle.

"The field of it is sown with lilies, and therein is our Lord holding the world, with two angels, one on either hand. It is white, and upon it is written the names Jesus and Mary, and it is fringed with silk. Speak with them and tell them that I and St. Michael sent you. Show them the swords. Tell Pierre and Jean you have my permission to retrieve the sword that St. Catherine gave me."

The three cousins stood to leave. Jeff gave her the

food he had brought from the kitchen. One last time, Nick asked her to escape with them. Her final response to his offer was, "I was born for this."

Ty reached under his shirt, removed a cross and chain he was wearing around his neck, kissed it, and placed it in her hands. "For comfort and strength in facing your trials, dear Maid," he said, and then he and his cousins departed.

Joan of Arc sat there awaiting her fate, comforted by the knowledge that her last moments were spent for a worthy cause. She would now face her final fate knowing that she had persevered and accomplished the will of God.

"Give them success," she whispered. Then she bowed her head in prayer.

The cousins made their way back to the stable area to talk about their next move. Nick reflected on their encounter with Joan of Arc. She was so much more powerful and inspiring than the history books could ever convey. They were now more committed than ever to completing the assignment.

"What should we do next?" Ty asked his older cousins when they were safely hidden in the empty stall.

Jeff responded. "I think our next move must be to stay out of sight in the stables until the crowd in the courtyard gets bigger. Then we can slip out the side door and mingle with the people. They are all going to be so focused on the verdict they won't bother with us. We can scan the area until we spot Joan's banner and identify her brothers. We speak with them, tell them what Joan told us to tell them, and ask them to assist us. Are we in agreement?"

The others nodded. They waited for an hour or so until the crowds grew large and boisterous before exiting the stable into the courtyard. It was now almost noon, and the sentencing was about to begin. They walked around the edges of the throng, looking for the banner that the Maid had described to them.

"I think I see it," said Nick, "over there, next to the well in the center of the courtyard." He squinted a little, then added, "I can barely make out the words. I think they say '*Jhésus*' and '*Maria*'. That's not exactly what the Maid told us."

Jeff responded, "Those are the French translations of 'Jesus' and 'Mary'. We heard the English, but apparently, you're seeing them in French. Ty and I will make our way over to them, but Nick, you hang back and keep us in sight while scanning the crowd for any threats. If you see any guards coming our way, distract them."

"Got it," replied Nick.

He watched Jeff and Ty approached the imposing brothers. Both were broad-shouldered, had stout chests, and were more than six feet tall. They had the bearing of military men who had seen many battles. When Jeff and Ty got close to them, the brothers shot them a wary look.

"Stop where you are, strangers," the taller one ordered. "Come no closer. State your business, or we will drop you where you stand."

Ty and Jeff stopped immediately, and Jeff answered their demand. "We have come with word from the Maid. She has a message for you. It is she who alerted us to your presence here today and charged us with a message for you. Please let us approach so that we may deliver it."

The brothers beckoned them closer. "If you speak falsely, my brother and I will slit your throats before you can take another breath. Speak!"

"Your sister has a request," replied Jeff. "She told us to tell you that St. Michael the Archangel has sent us. She instructed us to show you our swords and to tell you that we have her permission to retrieve the sword that St. Catherine gave her. She believes that you may know where it is."

The taller brother stiffened, his mouth tight with anger. His eyes narrowed, and he quickly turned to his brother and said, "Brother, we may have some killing to do. Let's take these two behind the guard tower and have a look at these swords. I suspect they are spies sent to steal the last remaining worldly possessions our sister has. Quickly! Before the sentencing is completed."

They grabbed Ty and Jeff by the arms and hustled them back behind the nearest guard tower.

"Now," said the taller brother, "reveal your swords!"

Nick didn't hesitate. He raced towards the tower, rounding the corner just in time to hear the taller brother order them to reveal their swords.

Jeff and Ty unsheathed their swords, raised their right arms, and their swords became visible to the brothers.

"Trickery and witchcraft!" accused the shorter brother. "They are of the devil! Let us slit their lying throats."

"Not so fast, tubby!" Nick shouted. He removed the Sword of Michael the Archangel from its sheath and immediately, it burst into flame.

Awestruck, the brothers dropped to their knees and hid their faces in their hands.

"Don't be afraid," said Nick. "Obey the final commands of your brave sister. She has given her life for righteous causes. Today you will help her aid us in another. Come! Take us to your home, and we can discuss this together."

The taller brother hesitantly lifted his face from his

hands and asked, "May we stay until the sentencing is complete? We need to see her one last time before they sentence her. We need her to know that we love and honor her, and we will never betray her trust."

"So be it," replied Jeff. "We will stand with you."

The five men returned to the area beside the well and watched as the Maid was led onto the platform for her sentencing. Still dressed in men's military attire, she stood tall and defiant, appearing serene, yet determined. Her eyes sought the heavens in prayer.

"Here are the charges for which we have found the defendant guilty!" shouted the magistrate.

"First, she is guilty of using magic to conjure the voices of demons. These demon voices drove her to take up arms and dress as a man.

"Second, her actions were inappropriate as a woman in the church. She dressed as a man, fought in war, and took communion as a male.

"Finally, she does not submit herself to the judgment of the Church, or to that of living men, but to God alone, whom, she has said, she claimed to know through her diabolical voices. She is found guilty on all counts. On the morrow before dawn, she will be burned to death at the stake in the marketplace for all to take heed!"

With that, he rolled up the scroll he read from, and they took the Maid back to her prison in the tower.

The brothers stood with their jaws set in anger. "We have to do something!" the shorter brother cried. He took a step forward, but his brother held him back.

"We can't help her now," he growled, holding him tightly.

Nick stepped around to look the shorter brother in the eye. His voice was stern. "All we can do for her, all she wants of us, is to complete the assignment set before us this day. It is her final wish and her final command. She is in the hands of God from this moment on."

Finally, the shorter brother relaxed with a sigh of resignation.

Knowing they could do no more for the Maid, the five men departed for the brothers' home. When they arrived, they gathered around a rough wooden table. The brothers shuttered the windows, produced wine and cheese, then sat and began to talk in hushed tones.

"Now may be a good time to make formal introductions," said the taller brother. "I am Pierre, and my brother's name is Jean. Our sister is correct in suspecting that we know the hiding place of the sword given to her by St. Catherine. When she was taken in battle by the English, she was pulled from her horse and lost her grip on the sword. We were nearby, and while they were binding her, we grabbed the sword as it lay on the ground. We took it back with us when we retreated and eventually brought it here."

"Is it here now?" asked Jeff.

"No," replied Jean, "We knew they would come looking for it, so we hid it with the dead. We must wait until long after dark. It will be dangerous, and if caught, we could very well be joining our sister at the stake!"

"Great!" said Nick, "Dead people, midnight, and being burned at the stake. Sounds like a few redneck parties I've attended. Can't wait. Let's hear the details."

The cousins filled Pierre and Jean in on their mission and purpose. Jean, after recovering from his shock and disbelief, told the cousins about the sword's hiding place and how they could retrieve it.

"After we returned home with the sword, we knew that it could never resurface, or it would fall into the hands of the English. We had worked on the Cathedral of Notre-Dame de Rouen a few years back. With our masonry skills, we helped to expand the windows in the choir area. While working in the church, we saw that the tomb which contains the heart of Richard the Lionhearted was just off to the side of the place we were working.

"When we were thinking of a place to hide the sword, we thought that would be the best place. The English would never look for a French sword in the tomb of one of their most revered kings. Since we worked on the church building, we knew all the secret entrances. We took the sword there and placed it in the tomb next to the heart of Richard the Lionhearted. That is where it is to this day."

"I assume you still know the way in and can take us there tonight?" asked Jeff.

"Yes," Jean replied, "but we must be careful. Getting it back here without being seen may be the most difficult part. We will leave here after midnight when there will be fewer people in the streets."

"Agreed," said the cousins. They settled in for a long evening of waiting.

The brothers took turns explaining the plan and how to gain entrance to the cathedral. When the time was right, they gathered their things and headed out to recover the Sword of Joan of Arc. They made their way through the dark and mostly-deserted village streets to the cathedral. The brothers brought them to the church cemetery.

There, they opened the door to an elaborate above-ground mausoleum. Entering the small building, the brothers lifted the carpet covering the floor, revealing a trap door and stairs. They all lit their torches and descended.

"Wow, this is intense," said Nick. "How far is it to the cathedral?"

"It is a short walk," said Pierre. "We must remain quiet from this point on. So please, no talking, or we could be discovered."

The group silently made their way through the long, dark tunnel and emerged in the basement of the cathedral. The brothers led them up a set of stone stairs in the back of the church underneath the choir loft. They then made their way quietly to the sarcophagus. It was a stone box, approximately seven feet long, four feet high, with an elaborately carved image of Richard the Lionhearted on the stone lid.

Surrounding the tomb of Richard the Lionhearted, they worked together to lift the heavy lid. They moved it only enough to be able to access the sword. Peering into the open tomb, they felt relieved to see that the sword they sought was still there. It lay next to a small, lead box containing the heart of Richard the Lionhearted.

Nick's heart quickened. The Sword of Joan of Arc lay before their eyes; the very one that was given to her by St. Catherine. The five crosses were clearly engraved into the blade, confirming for him that it was the sword they were seeking. I am in the presence of the very heart of the great King Richard the Lionhearted, Nick thought. What an inspirational moment!

As awed as they were, they didn't waste time. Nick reached in and grabbed the sword. He took time to briefly touch the lead box containing the entombed king's heart. He felt a slight spark as he withdrew his hand, and he noticed that the Sword of St. Michael the Archangel glowed softly for a few seconds.

They replaced the top of the tomb and quickly

retreated the way they had come. Soon, they were back at the mausoleum. Gathering themselves, they began the journey back to the home of the brothers of Joan of Arc.

They hadn't gone far when someone called out. "Halt, who goes there?" It was one of the castle guards that Nick had replaced earlier at the tower where the Maid was imprisoned. "Halt!" he ordered. "What are you doing in this area at this time of night?"

Then a look of recognition crossed his face. "I know you!" he growled. "The new recruit with the wrong boots. I have a bone to pick with you. When we arrived at the courtyard to report to the commander, he said that he hadn't told anyone to relieve us and reprimanded us for leaving our post. He made us go to the stables and clean up after the horses as punishment. I have been looking for you all day!"

"I'm sorry, sir, I had the wrong tower! My mistake. It won't happen again," said Nick. "I'm just taking these guys to the marketplace. They have been conscripted to help prepare for the burning of the prisoner. After I return from the marketplace, I'll meet you back here. Then we can settle this like men, agreed?"

The castle guard replied, "They have almost completed the preparation work. They will be burning her in five minutes. They didn't want to delay because the crowds are getting rowdy. So, they have decided they are going to do it immediately, before sunrise. If you are not back here in ten minutes after the burning, I will find you and beat some sense into you." Then he stormed off to wait next to the blacksmith's shop.

Nick rejoined the group and said to Ty, "He smelled like you!"

"Cut it out," objected Ty. "I have been making myself sick all day with the smell of that manure. Let's get back to the house before that guard changes his mind and beats the tar out of you right here."

"We can't do that," reminded Jeff, "we have to find a fire and return to our time ASAP."

"Can't we wait until after the burning? I'd like to say farewell and show our respects to the Maid," Ty asked.

"We still have an hour or so before sunrise," Nick added.

Nodding, all the men agreed. They made it back to the marketplace of Rouen without further incident and waited as the final preparations were completed.

The mood of the crowd was strange. Many were acting as if this was a party, others as if it were a tragedy. The brothers and the cousins got as close to the pyre as they were allowed and waited. As distraught as Nick was at the thought of watching Joan burn at the stake, he could see her brothers were even more so. Pierre appeared ready to fight, and Jean looked as if he were about to cry.

They watched as Joan was brought out and chained to the enormous stake, a rough tree trunk embedded in the ground. After she was secured to the stake, they heaped piles of wood all around her to the height of her knees.

She looked at her brothers and the cousins with recognition and determination and commanded them sternly, "Don't mourn for me. I do the will of God. Be at peace."

Immediately, Joan's sword began to vibrate in Nick's hand. He glanced down and saw a soft glow emanating from it. He looked back at the Maid and she gave him a single, small nod. He knew in his heart that her sword had given her the valor and strength she would need to endure her fate.

Nick was struck by her bravery and courage, but his inability to help her tortured him.

The fire was lit, and as the flames rose and began to engulf her, they could hear her voice crying, "Jhésus! Jhésus! Jhésus!"

Although they had been mentally preparing for this moment since they discussed the mission in the Keeping Room, Nick was overwhelmed by the horror of it. Jean and Pierre fell to their knees and began beseeching God to save her. The cousins joined them.

Nick stole a quick look at Joan as he knelt. He saw her upraised face in agony and the roaring fire glinting off the cross and chain Ty had given her. Glancing at his cousin, he hoped Ty felt some level of comfort in knowing that she thought enough of his gift to wear it during her most horrifying trial.

After Joan's screams faded away, Ty stood and said hoarsely, "We have to go."

Jeff and Nick helped the distraught brothers to their feet. "Her sacrifice and your help will not be in vain," Jeffrey consoled them. "What we accomplished tonight will result in the salvation of many people. Take heart and honor your sister's memory."

The cousins took positions in front of the still-burning pyre of Joan of Arc, raised their swords in salute to her, touched them gently together, and vanished in a flash of pure, white light.

CHAPTER SEVEN

THE SECOND RETURN

Once again, the prophet and the remaining heroes were waiting by the fire pit near the river when the three returning heroes materialized. Startled for a moment, the prophet quickly regained his composure and his eyesight and observed that all three cousins had returned safely.

The three cousins who'd been left behind rushed to those who'd returned, starting to greet them with enthusiasm. When the returning cousins didn't return their eagerness, they backed off a bit.

The prophet again sighed in relief and said a quick prayer of thanks.

"Do you have the Sword of St. Joan of Arc?" he asked the returned team.

"Yes," Nick replied. He walked to where the prophet stood, knelt, and extended the sword, handle first. "Prophet, I present to you the Sword of St. Joan of Arc, given to us with the express permission of the Maid herself, the rightful owner of the sword she received from St. Catherine."

After he said the words, he bowed his head. "It was awful; truly horrific. She was so brave and so strong. It was dreadful to see her die like that."

Then he stood and returned to the group of cousins. The prophet watched as the cousins doused the fire and began the walk back to the house. This time, there was no witty banter. No prying questions. There would be time for that later. For now, they walked in silence. Each cousin that hadn't made the trip had their arm around the shoulder of one who had.

When they arrived at the house, the prophet instructed, "Take fifteen minutes to eat, visit the bathroom, and for goodness sake, wash! You all smell awful! When you are cleaned up, meet me in the Keeping Room to debrief. Nick, bring that castle guard uniform with you. We have a collection for that sort of item. I'll put your swords away." He began gathering the swords, then paused, looking at each one of them. "As tough as this assignment was, I'm afraid they are going to get tougher." With that, he retreated to the barn with their swords and the Sword of St. Joan of Arc.

Standing in front of the glass case, the prophet studied each of the eight swords. He felt awed by their beauty and inherent power. He was proud of his sons and nephews. They had managed to succeed in both assignments. Still, worry filled his mind. He knew the next assignment would have an even greater impact on them. Moving to sit at the table, he looked at the empty circle in the middle. "I hope they're ready, Dad," he whispered.

A few minutes later, the cousins entered the Keeping Room. Quietly, they took their seats, and the hologram of their grandfather appeared in the middle of the table once again. The image looked solemn as he addressed the cousins.

"I see that you have recovered the Sword of St. Joan of Arc. Well done. I also sense that this assignment has taken a toll on the three that have returned. It is to be expected. You are going into challenging and emotionally-charged points in history. There is always a price to pay for heroism. Learn the lessons and grow into them. As you know, we monitored you while you were there. We have some questions about what we observed. Begin your tale, and we will resolve those questions as you fill us in. Now let us debrief. Jeffrey, why don't you begin?"

Jeff told of their arrival and their plans to enter Joan's cell.

Then Nick jumped in, continuing the story. "When I arrived to relieve the guards at the tower prison, I convinced them they were needed elsewhere, got the keys from them, and waited for Jeff and Ty. When they arrived, we entered the tower and found Joan of Arc there. We told her who we were and why we were there. She didn't seem overly surprised. I assume that she was used to mystical and spiritual things happening to her. She asked her voices for a sign of confirmation that we were truthful and trustworthy. We showed her our swords, and my Sword of St. Michael burst into flame."

The image interrupted. "Very interesting. We saw a couple of huge power surges related to the Sword of St. Michael and were concerned. Apparently, it has a quality we were not aware of. This may be useful in the future. Continue."

Nick resumed his report. "This, evidently, was the sign her voices had told her to expect. She agreed to give us her permission and blessing to recover her sword. She suggested that her brothers may know its whereabouts and shared how to find them.

"We were all so impressed and inspired by her that we tried to convince her to come with us. It seemed like such a crime to leave her there to suffer that horrible fate. She refused and told us that she was 'born for this'. So, we departed and met her brothers in the courtyard at the final sentencing hearing."

Ty took it from there. "They challenged our story. They were going to cut our throats, but Nick came to our rescue." He continued up to the sword's recovery and Joan's horrible demise.

All three cousins seemed exhausted as they reported on their assignment. The prophet observed their grave and drawn faces, and he felt worried. He was sure they were in no mood for too much conversation. But there were more questions to be asked.

The image spoke. "I'm pleased by your resourcefulness and your teamwork. You handled a challenging situation with great skill and sensitivity. However, I'm troubled by your attempt to save the Maid. We saw some significant quantum warning signs related to the timeline. It indicated that there was the possibility of disruption. It eventually subsided, and disaster was averted. What you attempted was impetuous and dangerous. Do you realize that if she had accepted your help to avoid the flames even for a day, it could have had disastrous effects on the timeline? We have discussed this many times. You can't change history! Let it stay as it has always been."

Nick rose in his chair and pounded his fist on the table. "What would you have done, Grandpa?" he shouted. "There is no way you would have stood there doing nothing, knowing the horror that poor girl was going to face in a few hours! I know you. You were more heroic than all of us combined. You hated bullies and injustice. You fought the Nazis, for goodness sake! You would have done more than we did. All we did was ask her to come with us. We should have grabbed her and forced her to go with us. The swords would have protected us all. Instead, we just wimped out and let that innocent young girl go to her horrible death while we all stood around watching!"

He turned and left the table. The others sat in silence. The prophet searched their faces and his heart ached at the pain he saw there.

Finally, the image spoke again. "Ty and Jeff, do you feel the same as Nicholas?"

"Yes, we do," Jeff replied.

Ty nodded, touching the empty space where his chain and cross used to hang and added, "We are ashamed of ourselves."

The prophet spoke. "Look, you were there for one specific purpose, a purpose that has global consequences. There are millions of lives hanging in the balance. We can only imagine what you must have been feeling and experiencing. The swords also had an impact on you. They increase your chivalrous natures. They inspire you to do good deeds, fill you with their virtues, and influence you strongly while you wield them. But you must use your minds.

"Separate the good from the best. Discern when the greater good is served by not doing a good deed in certain instances. Your heart may tell you that you need to do something, but your mind will tell you that it is not the right thing. You need to let the swords influence you, but you must also stay true to the mission."

At this point, Nick returned to the room. He seemed much more composed.

"Are you all right, Nick?" he asked.

"Yes, sir," Nick's voice was subdued. "I was standing just outside the door and heard everything you said, and I understand." He looked up with tears in his eyes. "I'm sorry for my outburst, Uncle Rob. I keep remembering Joan of Arc's faith and the courage she had to carry out her mission regardless of the personal cost. We must do the same. We must follow her example and walk the path we were placed upon. That includes resisting all selfish urges to change history. If I can help it, it won't happen again."

The prophet nodded and smiled fondly at his nephew.

"Well said, Nick," spoke the image. "Let's move on to the third assignment. This one will be even more impactful. It will truly and powerfully test your resolve not to change history. So, you will need to commit yourselves to it.

"Your third assignment is to recover the Sword of St. Peter the Apostle at the height of its power. It was at its most powerful when it was in the presence of Jesus Christ and was being used in his defense. The only recorded instance of those two things happening simultaneously was in the garden of Gethsemane the night before Jesus was crucified. As always, you must gain permission to return with the sword from its rightful owner or receive it directly from his hand willingly.

"As you have been told, Joseph of Arimathea gained possession of the Sword of St. Peter sometime after the crucifixion of Jesus. He took it with him to England, and it remained there under the protection of his family until it was presented to the Vatican. The Vatican allowed it to be taken to Poland to honor the birthplace of Pope John Paul. It resided in the Poznan Archdiocesan Museum in Poland. It was usually housed in the cathedral treasury, except for the few times a year when it was shown to the people.

"Five years ago, the archdiocese arranged to have the sword moved to the chapter house as a more proper place for this noble relic. During that transition, the Sword of Peter fell into the hands of the Apostles of Azazel.

"This time, it will be even harder to decide on an exact date and time for your trip into the past. We all know that Jesus was crucified in Jerusalem in the first century. Can we determine the precise day and time? Yes, we can. Our quantum computer has searched every available database and every ancient document available to the Guardians. We have analyzed and examined every possibility. Look at the monitors once again, and I will lay it all out for you so that you can make your own determination. Here is what we know.

"Seven facts point to the year, date, and time of the crucifixion of Jesus with very high probability. If we can know that with certainty, then you can make a reliable determination about the place and time of your arrival." The cousins looked at the screens while the hologram continued.

"Fact number one: The High Priesthood of Caiaphas. The gospels indicate that Jesus was crucified at the instigation of a first-century high priest named Caiaphas. We know that he served as high priest from 18 AD to 36 AD. That puts Jesus's death within that timeframe.

"Fact number two: The Governorship of Pontius Pilate. All four gospels agree that Pontius Pilate ordered the crucifixion of Jesus. We know that he served as governor of Judea from 26 AD to 36 AD. So, we can narrow down the range by several years.

"Fact number three: After the Fifteenth Year of Tiberius Caesar. The Gospel of Luke tells us that 'the word of God came to John, the son of Zechariah in the

145

wilderness'. The ministry of John the Baptist began in the fifteenth year of the reign of Tiberius Caesar. This pinpoints a specific year: 29 AD. Since all four gospels depict the ministry of Christ as beginning after John the Baptist started preaching, we can shave a few more years off our range. The death of Christ had to be within a range of seven years: between 29 AD and 36 AD.

"Fact number four: Crucified on a Friday. All four gospels agree that Jesus's crucifixion happened on a Friday before a Sabbath. That eliminates six days of the week, but there were still quite a few Fridays between 29 AD and 36 AD.

"Fact number five: A Friday at Passover. The four gospels also agree that Jesus was crucified in conjunction with the annual feast of Passover. That lets us narrow the range of possible dates to just a few. Here is a complete list of the days between 29 AD and 36 AD on whose evenings Passover began.

"Monday, April 18th, 29 AD
Friday, April 7th, 30 AD
Tuesday, March 27th, 31 AD
Monday, April 14th, 32 AD
Friday, April 3rd, 33 AD
Wednesday, March 24th, 34 AD
Tuesday, April 12th, 35 AD
Saturday, March 31st, 36 AD

"Thus, there are just two candidates left: Jesus was either crucified on April 7 of 30 AD or April 3 of 33 AD. Which was it? The traditional date is that of 33 AD. However, many people today advocate the 30 AD date. Do the gospels let us decide between the two?

"Fact number six: John's Three Passovers. The

Gospel of John records three different Passovers during the ministry of Jesus:

"Passover number one occurred near the beginning of Jesus's ministry. Passover number two occurred in the middle of Jesus's ministry. Passover number three occurred at the end of Jesus's ministry.

"That means that the ministry of Jesus had to span something over two years, but less than four. A fuller treatment would reveal that it spanned about three and a half years, but even if we assume it began immediately before Passover number one, the addition of two more Passovers shows that, at a bare minimum, it lasted more than two years.

"That means the 30 AD date is out. There is insufficient time between the fifteenth year of Tiberius Caesar, 29 AD, and the next year's Passover to accommodate a ministry of at least two years. The numbers don't add up. As a result, the traditional date of Jesus's death on Friday, April 3rd, 33 AD must be regarded as the correct one. But can we be even more precise?

"Fact number seven: The Ninth Hour. Matthew, Mark, and Luke each record that Jesus died about 'the ninth hour'. The ninth hour in today's terms is 3:00 p.m. This allows us to narrow the time of Jesus's death to a specific point in history: around 3:00 p.m. on Friday, April 3rd, 33 AD.

"Of course, there are many detailed arguments that I haven't taken space to deal with here. But this is the best that our quantum computer can determine, utilizing the highest quality historical data possible. So, to within a 99.9999996 percent certainty, this is when the crucifixion happened. Are you all still with me?" asked the image.

"Still with you, Grandpa," Robbie replied, and they

all nodded.

The image continued. "Now that we have a date for the Crucifixion, we need to determine when and where you will arrive. We know that on the evening before his death, Jesus ate dinner with his disciples. Then they gathered to pray in a place called the Garden of Gethsemane on the Mount of Olives. At some point, Jesus took three of them, Peter, James, and John, to a place separated from the rest. Here, Jesus asked the three apostles to watch with him and pray.

"We don't specifically know where this separate place was, but it wasn't too far from where the rest of the disciples remained. John 18:1 tells what happened after that. I shall read it for you.

When Jesus had spoken these words, he went out with his disciples across the Brook Kidron, where there was a garden, which he and his disciples entered.

Now Judas, who betrayed him, also knew the place, for Jesus often met there with his disciples. So, Judas, having procured a band of soldiers and some officers from the chief priests and the Pharisees, went there with lanterns and torches and weapons, surrounding Jesus and the disciples.

Then Jesus, knowing all that would happen to him, came forward and said to them, "Whom do you seek?"

They answered him, "Jesus of Nazareth."

Jesus said to them, "I am he."

Judas, who betrayed him, was standing with them. When Jesus said to them, "I am he," they drew back and fell to the ground.

So, he asked them again, "Whom do you seek?"

And they said, "Jesus of Nazareth."

Jesus answered, "I told you that I am he. So, if you seek

me, let these men go."

This was to fulfill the word that he had spoken: "Of those whom you gave me I have lost not one."

Then Simon Peter, having a sword, drew it and struck the high priest's servant and cut off his right ear. The servant's name was Malchus.

So, Jesus said to Peter, "Put your sword into its sheath, shall I not drink the cup that the Father has given me?"

"We know that there was a large group of soldiers there to arrest Jesus, so you will need to be careful. Next, we read of Jesus's arrest," the image continued.

The band of soldiers and their captain and the officers of the Jews arrested Jesus and bound him. First, they led him to Annas, for he was the father-in-law of Caiaphas, who was high priest that year. It was Caiaphas who had advised the Jews that it would be expedient that one man should die for the people.

"We see he was taken to the house of the high priest, Caiaphas. This will be your opportunity, as you will see from the following verses.

Simon Peter followed Jesus, and so did another disciple. Since that disciple was known to the high priest, he entered with Jesus into the courtyard of the high priest, but Peter stood outside at the door. So, the other disciple, who was known to the high priest, went out and spoke to the servant girl who kept watch at the door and brought Peter in.

"You must gain entrance to the courtyard of the high priest so that you can speak with Peter there. Now please confer together and decide where and when you must go," the image finished.

Joe spoke first, "It seems clear that our objective should be the garden of Gethsemane, prior to the arrest. We need to be in position before then so we can observe from a safe distance. Then we can follow the soldiers when they take Jesus. Agreed?"

Billy responded, "I agree, but what time should we arrive? I propose that we arrive just before sundown. That way we will still have some daylight to find a good place to watch for Jesus and the disciples when they arrive. We can adjust our position if need be at that point."

"What time would sundown be?" asked Robbie.

The image responded, "That would be 6 p.m., local time."

"So then, our objective is the garden of Gethsemane, on Thursday, April 2nd, 33 AD at 6:00 p.m. Agreed?" asked Jeff.

The cousins looked at each other and agreed.

"Have you reached a consensus?" asked the prophet.

Noting his cousins' nods, Jeff responded, "We have."

"Are you ready to do your duty for family and for the Guardians?" he asked them.

"Yes, we are," they replied.

"So be it," the image of their grandfather acknowledged as it faded away.

"Let us begin," said the prophet.

The cousins stood, collected their swords, and followed the prophet.

While walking to the fire pit next to the river, Jeff asked, "Uncle Rob, have you figured out who will be going on this assignment this time?"

The prophet responded, "I believe not all of you will make the trip. I can't reveal who right now, because I don't want it to impact your focus when you are performing the leaving process. My suspicions will be confirmed once the process is completed. Just focus on your objective and pray that we have chosen the right time and date."

They continued toward the river in silence. The prophet hoped they were thinking about their objective, and not being distracted by the incredible things they were about to experience, and the challenging task ahead. He knew their focus would be crucial. He also knew that the cousins, all having been brought up in the Faith, would experience intense emotions during this assignment. Based on their response to the last trip, he needed to remind them one last time to keep their desires to help in check.

When the fire was built, and the heroes were in position, he instructed them firmly, "Remember, whatever you do, whatever you feel, don't do anything to change history. We are dealing with spiritual issues as well as temporal ones this time. Are you ready?"

"We are," they responded.

"Raise your swords," he commanded.

The team complied.

"Bring them slowly together, and Godspeed," he instructed.

The cousins brought their swords together and were surrounded by the now-familiar flash of white light.

When the light faded, the prophet could clearly see that once again not all the cousins were chosen for this assignment. It confirmed his assumptions. Billy, Ty, and Robbie remained around the fire, holding the swords of Roland, Charlemagne, and William Wallace.

Only those swords that had a biblical connection were chosen this time. The sword Excalibur, which was initially the Sword of Melchizedek, the Sword of Solomon, and the Sword of St. Michael the Archangel. He must trust that the swords had made the right choice. They always had before.

CHAPTER EIGHT

THE SWORD OF PETER THE APOSTLE

———— ∾∾ ————

"Whoa!" Joe exclaimed, reflexively grabbing Nick's arm as they materialized precariously close to a sharp drop-off on the edge of an outcropping of rock. Following Jeff, they quickly scrambled to safety using the roots and trunks of the ancient olive trees to assist them. When they reached a safer place, they took stock of their situation.

"Looks like Billy, Ty, and Robbie were left behind," said Jeff.

"Either that, or they were closer to the edge of the outcropping than we were and are at the bottom of the valley," Nick replied, eyes wide.

Horrified by the thought, the cousins made their way carefully to the edge and looked over. Not seeing the broken bodies of their cousins, they looked at each other, relief in their eyes.

"Let's figure out where we are and find a place to hide," suggested Joe.

Nick frowned. "We should have asked for a virtual tour. That would have made this much easier!"

"Too late now," Joe sighed. "We need a spot where

we can get a view of Jerusalem and the Brook of Kidron. That's the route that Jesus and his disciples took on their way here."

The three cousins climbed higher and scouted out various locations on the mountain.

"What about there?" Joe asked, pointing to a thickly-wooded area nearby, just above the Brook of Kidron.

"Looks good," Jeff agreed, moving into the stand of trees and looking east. The others followed him. "It has an unobstructed view of Jerusalem, and we're about three-quarters of the way up the mountain. The odds are good that the garden that Jesus will visit is near here. This seems like the perfect location."

The sun would be setting in an hour or so, and the April air was starting to feel a bit chilly.

Joe said, "I think we have some time, so let's think this through and try to plan out the whole assignment. On the first assignment, Robbie, Billy, and I sort of winged it. I think we need to be more strategic this time. We are going to be dealing with a large group of heavily-armed soldiers and frightened disciples. So far, on each assignment, neither group interacted all that much with the people of that time. This could be different, and we need to prepare."

Nick agreed. "One of the issues is that after they get here, Jesus breaks his followers up into two groups. He and John, James, and Peter go off to a different area to pray, so we have two locations to cover. What do you think we should do?"

Jeff answered, "I think we stay with Jesus and his group. From the Biblical account we just heard, it seems that either Jesus heard the commotion and rejoined the larger group, or the others ran to where he was when the soldiers arrived to arrest him. Either way, they end up together. I think we should stick with Jesus. We know that he is the one they are looking for, and Peter will be with him. We don't want to lose sight of either of them."

Joe and Nick agreed.

"Then, after they arrest Jesus, we need to hang back and follow Peter from a safe distance. We should stay off the road. When we are sure which building they have taken Jesus to, we can try to gain entry," suggested Nick.

Joe said, "We will know what Peter looks like by his actions during the arrest. We can find him in the courtyard and speak with him there. Agreed?"

Nick and Jeff concurred, and they settled in for a few hours' wait.

While they were waiting, Joe addressed the group. "I have been thinking about a couple of things we need to get straight so that we don't mess it up. First, I have always been confused about the Bible's account of Peter's denials of Christ. Three of the gospels say that Jesus told Peter, 'before the cock crows, you will deny me three times'. However, Mark states that he said Peter would deny him three times before the rooster crows twice. So, I'm confused about how many times the rooster crowed.

"Second, what time does the rooster crow? We need to figure that out, because if the rooster crows at dawn, we need to be gone with the sword by then. Any thoughts on all of this?"

Nick responded first. "I have been confused about that, too. I just figured that maybe the three gospels that referred to only one rooster crow were talking about the final one. Or maybe Jesus knew that would be the only one Peter would actually hear."

Jeff jumped in, "I took a biblical studies class at Penn. The teacher focused on pointing out all the discrepancies in the Bible. He tried to get us to agree that those inconsistencies illustrated that the Bible wasn't a reliable source of historical information. So, I did some digging and some research of my own. I studied this incident in depth and found out a few things.

"In the first century, roosters were accustomed to crowing at least twice during the night. The first crowing usually occurred between twelve and one o'clock. Relatively few people ever heard or acknowledged this crowing. Likely, Peter never heard it.

"The second crowing likely took place around 3:00 a.m. It was this latter crowing that commonly was called 'the cockcrowing'. Why? Because roosters crowed the loudest at this time of night, and their loud cry was useful in summoning laborers to work. This crowing of the roosters served as an alarm clock to the ancient world. Mark recorded in his gospel account that Jesus spoke of this 'main' crowing when he stated, 'Watch therefore, for you don't know when the master of the house is coming, in the evening, at the crowing of the rooster, or in the morning'.

"If you lived in the first century and your boss said to be ready to labor when 'the rooster crows', you would know he meant that work begins before daybreak. If he said the job starts at the second crowing of the rooster, likewise, you would know he meant the same thing, that work begins before daylight. These are not contradictory statements, but rather two ways of saying the same thing. That is what I told the professor to refute his assertion. I'll just say that we agreed to disagree.

"I believe that there are two crowings; the first around midnight, and the second sometime around 3:00 a.m. Since sunrise will be only a couple of hours after that, we need to have the sword in our possession and be gone shortly after the second crowing. I estimate that we should not delay more than is necessary after that happens, or we could be stuck here with the sword.

"Finally, since we know Peter was in the high priest's courtyard for the two rooster crows, that means he was there for a minimum of two hours, between 1 and 3 a.m., give or take a half-hour either way. We have at least two hours to find him and convince him to give us his sword."

"Wow, Jeff, I'm impressed," said Nick. "You not only did all that research, but you remembered it. Very cool."

Jeff replied, "Remember, I'm a lawyer. I have always liked arguing and debating. But I need to tell you, I think the swords helped me a bit in bringing all of that to mind. It was a few years ago, and I'm surprised I recalled it in detail like that."

"Well, we are glad you did, Jeff," said Joe. "It is beneficial to have some reference points regarding timeframes. Now we know what we need to accomplish and when."

"Let's take turns watching the road," suggested Nick. "We don't want to miss them coming. I will take the first watch." He left Joe and Jeff alone and went to the clearing at the edge of the tree line to watch for indications of Jesus and his disciple's arrival at the Mount of Olives.

As Joe sat waiting with Jeff, he could not help but think about what was to come. He understood that Jesus already knew all that was going to transpire, and just like Joan of Arc, it was why he was born.

Yes, he was fully divine, but he was also fully human. He knew what pain was. He knew suffering. He was going to experience both to the ultimate degree, and yet he did nothing to avoid his fate. He could have easily called ten thousand angels to his side to protect him, but he didn't.

He accepted his destiny and went willingly to the cross. The only indication of his human anxiety about his forthcoming agony is the account we have of his time in the garden of Gethsemane.

Joe wondered if they would get to witness it for themselves. If they did, could they endure it? Could they observe such anguish and suffering and not want to act, knowing that Judas and the cohort were going to be there shortly to arrest this innocent man and crucify him?

He knew they would try to control themselves and remember what the prophet and their grandfather's image had told them about interfering with history, especially history that had spiritual implications, but it would be hard to do. Joe hoped that God and the swords would assist them.

After an hour had passed, Nick returned and reported, "I see movement on the road. A few dozen people with lanterns are heading this way. We need to watch them and see where they go."

The cousins all went to the clearing to watch. All Joe could see was the light of the lanterns slowly coming toward the base of the mountain. In just a few moments, the group started to ascend. As they drew closer, Joe could make out the shapes of people. The group made their way to an open spot surrounded by olive trees about halfway up the mountain and stopped. They seemed to be settling in.

"Shall we move closer?" Joe whispered.

His cousins nodded, so they quietly picked their way down the sloping terrain to a spot not far from the group, close enough so that they could hear, but far enough away not to be seen. They sat down on some rocks and listened.

The group seemed to be discussing the events of the evening, with lots of debate about Jesus's words and actions. Some seemed disturbed by them, and some were explaining the meaning to others. There didn't seem to be too much distress, but Joe felt there was an anxious edge to the conversations, a sense of something imminent.

Then Joe heard a voice speaking, and when that voice spoke, everyone in the group became silent. The voice said, "This very night you will all fall away on account of me, for it is written, 'I will strike the shepherd, and the sheep of the flock will be scattered'."

Joe was overwhelmed, realizing that he had heard the voice of Jesus Christ with his own ears. He noticed that their swords had begun to glow faintly. Not wanting to miss a word, he continued to listen carefully.

Then Jesus said to the group, "Sit here while I go over there and pray." He took three of the disciples with him and walked a few dozen yards away to a small clearing. Then he said to those with him, "My soul is overwhelmed with sorrow to the point of death. Stay here and keep watch with me."

Going a little farther, he fell with his face to the ground and prayed, "My Father, if it is possible, may this cup be taken from me. Yet not as I will, but as You will."

Joe knew that those with Jesus were supposed to be Peter, James, and John, but he couldn't identify Peter at this point. Jesus then prayed silently for a long time. He had a troubled expression on his face.

Then he rose, returned to his disciples and found them sleeping. He asked, "Couldn't you men keep watch with me for one hour? Watch and pray so that you won't fall into temptation. The spirit is willing, but the flesh is weak."

Since the scripture had indicated that Jesus said this to Peter, Joe knew one of those three disciples must be Peter. However, from their vantage point, he couldn't tell

159

who Jesus had addressed.

Jesus went away a second time and prayed again aloud, "My Father, if it is not possible for this cup to be taken away unless I drink it, may Your will be done." Then he prayed silently for a while more.

During this time, Jesus became even more distressed. He was sweating, and his body writhed. He was obviously in intense agony. During this time, Joe was severely tempted to run to him, comfort him, and just be with him. Joe looked at his brother and cousin and saw they were moved and distraught as well. Then, inexplicably, he saw them fall asleep. As he reached to wake them, his eyes closed and he, too, fell asleep.

When Joe awoke, he felt disoriented for a moment. Looking around, he saw Jeff and Nick stretching and yawning. Realizing where they were, he quickly looked towards the garden and saw Jesus standing over Peter, James, and John saying, "Are you still sleeping and resting? Look, the hour has come, and the Son of Man is delivered into the hands of sinners."

Then Jesus shouted, "Rise! Let us go! Here comes my betrayer!"

At his words, the cousins rose hurriedly, trying to shake the sleep from their bodies. So did Peter, James, and John. The three disciples followed quickly behind Jesus.

As they neared the coming group, a man approached Jesus along with a large crowd armed with swords and clubs. The man said to Jesus, "Greetings, Rabbi!" and kissed him.

Jesus replied, "Do what you came for, friend."

Then the men stepped forward and seized Jesus. One of the three men who had been with Jesus in prayer reached for his sword, drew it out, and struck the high priest's servant, cutting off his ear.

Now Joe knew for sure which one was Peter. He memorized his face and observed him carefully. As the cousins watched, Jesus rebuked Peter, reached down, picked up the ear that had been severed from the servant, and knelt next to him. Joe could not hear the words that he spoke to the man, but they saw him touch the side of his head with the hand that picked up the ear.

After a short while, Jesus steadied the man as they rose. The man's ear was healed. Jesus said to him, "Remember this, Malchus." Then he turned his attention back to Peter.

"Put your sword back in its place," Jesus said to him, "for all who draw the sword will die by the sword. Do you think I can't call on my Father, and He will at once put at my disposal more than twelve legions of angels? But how then would the scriptures be fulfilled that say it must happen in this way?"

The cousins looked at each other and their swords, which had begun to glow once again.

Then Joe heard Jesus say to the crowd, "Am I leading a rebellion that you have come out with swords and clubs to capture me? Every day, I sat in the temple courts teaching, and you didn't arrest me. But this has all taken place that the writings of the prophets might be fulfilled."

As they bound Jesus's hands and started to lead him away, the soldiers began to chase the disciples, intending to capture them also. Chaos erupted. People ran everywhere.

The cousins were drawn into the mayhem as many of the disciples ran near to their hiding place. Soldiers followed. Two female disciples of Jesus saw the cousins and ran to them, begging for their help. Three soldiers followed close behind.

The cousins raised their right arms and immediately their swords appeared in their hands. All of them glowed in the darkness. The soldiers following the women stopped dead in their tracks.

"Leave these women alone!" shouted Joe. "They are no threat to you, but we are. Take another step closer, and we will cut off more than your ears!"

The soldiers, startled by the sudden appearance of the cousins and the three glowing swords, quickly retreated without a word and began to chase the other disciples.

The two women were in tears. "They have taken our Lord," the younger one wailed, "and we don't know where they have taken him or what will become of us!"

"Help us, please!" the older woman added.

The cousins tried to comfort the women, and Nick asked, "What are your names?"

"I am Miriam, and she is Anna," replied the older woman.

Nick said, "Miriam and Anna, we will help you get safely back to Jerusalem, but we need your help, too. We are here on an important mission, and we need to get to the high priest's home. Do you know where that is?"

Miriam replied, "Are you angels of God sent to free our Lord? We see your heavenly swords, and we are frightened."

"Don't be afraid of us," said Jeff. "We are not angels. We are just men who have a job to do. Your help will be critical to our success. Will you take us to the home of the high priest, Caiaphas?"

The women agreed, and after the chaos had subsided and all the disciples had fled, the three cousins and the two women began the long trek down the mountain toward Jerusalem.

As they walked, Joe could not help thinking how, no matter how carefully the assignments were planned, things could easily change on a dime. They had to adapt quickly or fail. They had intended to follow Peter to the home of the high priest, but they had lost him in all the chaos. Now he was gone and so was Jesus. They would instead have to depend on the two distraught women leading them now.

They made their way cautiously, staying off the main path and keeping out of sight. That made the trek longer and harder. As they finally approached the walls of the city, Joe was struck by the view of this ancient place. It was aglow with torches and fires burning in various locations.

It seemed much smaller than he had imagined, but less primitive, too. Having only seen images of the ruins of first-century Jerusalem, he had believed it to be a crumbling and dying place. What he saw was different. It was fresher and newer than they thought, even though it was still ancient. It hadn't yet faced the destruction and burning that would take place at the hands of the Romans in 70 AD. It was still alive!

Miriam spoke up. "When we get inside the gate of the city, we will need to follow the road to the left. We will walk that road following near to the wall, and then we will point out to you the home of Caiaphas. We won't go with you, as we fear for our lives. If it is possible, please try to save our Lord. He has much work ahead of him, and we love him deeply."

Joe responded, "Dear sisters, we also are followers of Jesus. Even though we come from far away and have never met him, we love him also. We have been blessed to have been near to him this night, and we will do all we can to complete our mission. It is how we will honor him. Believe us when we tell you that all will be well. You will see him again soon. He will rise victorious from his trials. Billions of people will revere his name, and what he does in the next few days will change the world forever."

Anna responded, "Jesus said to us that although we believed in him because we saw and heard him, more blessed are those who have not seen him or heard him yet believe. That sounds like you three men. You are blessed. Let us go quickly to the home of Caiaphas."

They followed the road to the left staying as near as possible to the wall of the city. Soon, the women pointed to a large and elaborate home, alive with activity and surrounded by a wall of stone.

"That is the entrance to the courtyard over there," Miriam said. "Please, be careful. Don't reveal that you are followers of Jesus, or they will arrest you, also."

The cousins thanked the women, and they departed.

Jeff said, "Let's get closer and see if we can figure out how to get in."

They skirted the crowds and surveyed the area.

Nick frowned. "There doesn't seem to be a straightforward alternate way into the courtyard. Looks like we'll have to go in through the main gate with the rest of the crowd."

They joined the throng and shuffled closer step by step. There were guards at the entrance challenging people and tossing them out of line if they had no reason to be there.

As they drew closer, Joe realized they had no plan to gain entrance. "How do we get in, guys?"

"Maybe we should just try to rush past the guards when they're distracted," proposed Nick.

Joe suggested, "Or one of us could create a diversion

while the other two slip in unseen."

Jeff replied, "Those could be workable options, but I don't want us getting separated. We don't know what kind of backup these guards have, either. Let's trust the swords to give us what we need when we need it. Have faith."

As they got to the entrance, a guard challenged them. Joe answered for the group. "We are sons of Joseph of Arimathea, a member of the Sanhedrin and a respected Pharisee. We are here to bear witness for him as to the handling of the accused. Let us pass."

Upon hearing the name of such a respected elder, the guard lowered his spear and let them pass.

"That was amazing, Joe," said Nick. "How did you come up with that?"

Joe responded, "I just trusted the swords, and I guess they gave us what we needed when we needed it. Let's go find Peter."

As they wandered about searching the crowd for Peter, Joe heard a rooster crow.

"Did you hear that rooster?" he asked his brother and cousin. "Must be around 1:00 a.m."

"I heard it," Nick said with a shudder. "It was awfully shrill, kind of eerie."

Joe nodded, feeling shaken to the core. "Maybe it sounds that way because of the circumstances or the stress."

Jeff pointed to a far corner. "I feel that, too, but let's move quickly. We don't want to run out of time."

Joe looked around the crowded courtyard. It was full of all sorts of people; men in religious robes, servants stoking fires, common people, and wealthy men in fancy clothes. Everywhere he looked, he saw desperate people. Some were desperate to kill Jesus to salvage their faith.

Some were desperate to save the man who they believed was the Messiah they had all been waiting for.

Jeff remembered being back in Catholic school. During Holy Week, the nuns would take them to the church, and they would do the Stations of the Cross. He remembered the feelings of sadness and horror at seeing the suffering of Jesus, and now, here he was witnessing all of it firsthand. He had always told himself that if he were there, he would have found a way to help Jesus, but now he realized that was impossible. All he could do was find Peter and bring his sword back. That would have to suffice.

Nick sighed. "How are we ever going to find one man among all these people?"

"Remember what the scriptures said?" Jeff replied. "When Peter went into the courtyard, he sat with the guards to wait for the outcome of the trial. It also says that a young servant girl challenged him while he was warming himself by the fire. He denied that he was one of Jesus's disciples. Mark's gospel says that was when the rooster crowed the first time. So, we have missed the first denial. We need to find him right away. The second denial took place a while later. The scriptures are not specific as to who challenged Peter. Let's just find him and get this done."

The cousins increased their efforts. After a while, they found Peter near one of the fires with a group of unknown men. They approached him carefully. Joe sat down beside him, while Nick and Jeff found a seat behind him.

They sat silent for a moment, then Joe whispered, "Simon Peter, we too are followers of Jesus from far away. May we speak with you about a matter of grave importance?"

166

Peter looked at Joe with fear and desperation on his face. He was a haunted man. He rose and shouted, "I'm not with Jesus. I don't know the man!" He turned and walked quickly away.

It occurred to Joe that they had just participated in and initiated Peter's second denial. He was horrified and worried but did not have time to dwell on it now. They must convince Peter to talk to them. Joe looked at Nick and Jeff, then indicated they should follow him.

Catching up quickly, they surrounded him. He was a powerful man, and he drew himself up to his full height. "Out of my way!" he commanded.

"No," replied Joe firmly, unsheathing his sword and raising it slightly in his right hand. The others followed his lead, raising their swords, as well. All three swords appeared and began to glow dimly, hidden from the view of the crowd by their bodies.

Peter was taken aback. He said, "What is your business with me? I know nothing of this matter."

Nick responded quietly, "In the name of Melchizedek, King Solomon, and the Archangel Michael, we require the sword you carry."

A puzzled expression crossed Peter's face, and resignation came over him.

Nick continued. "Follow us to a secluded part of the courtyard, and we will explain."

Peter followed them to a spot hidden by a large olive tree.

Jeff started, "Simon Peter, we are three cousins, related by birth to Joseph of Arimathea. We come from far away and a time far in the future. We are of a family that is charged with keeping safe the ten Swords of Valor. Your sword is designated as a Sword of Valor because it was used in defense of Jesus Christ and was wielded

167

righteously for the cause of freedom."

Nick continued the tale, "In our time, evil has gained possession of your sword and three other Swords of Valor. These evil men are also in possession of the ten Swords of Terror, which are empowered by the watcher Azazel. They will use the evil swords to destroy the good ones and will thereby cause a dissipation of good to begin in the world. Evil will be recognized as good, and good will become recognized as evil, just as the scriptures predict for the end times. All the good that the Lord Jesus has begun here could be destroyed. All good people will be hunted, condemned, and destroyed."

Joe then took over for Nick. "We have been sent here on an assignment to retrieve your sword at the height of its virtuous power. That time is now. We must obtain your permission to return with the sword and receive it from your hand. You must give it up willingly. If we are successful in our mission to recover the swords we seek, we can prevent the triumph of evil. When we have completed the task, the sword will immediately return to your hand, imbued with even more virtuous power. You won't be without it for long. It will strengthen you for the trials and work you have ahead of you as leader of all Christ's followers."

Peter stared at them as they spoke. He still appeared distracted and distraught. "The Sanhedrin has taken Jesus and he is now being questioned and accused. Unless we free him, all will be lost. I need my sword to help to defend myself and free him. Do you know what they do to those they condemn as blasphemers?"

Jeff replied, "We do know all of this. We were there in the garden. We saw his agony when he was in prayer, and we watched as he was arrested and taken away. We also saw you strike the servant named Malchus and cut off his ear. We saw Christ perform a miracle and heal his wound. And finally, we heard what he said to you, Simon Peter. Do you remember? He said to you, 'Put your sword back in its place, for all who draw the sword will die by the sword. Do you think I can't call on my Father, and He will at once put at my disposal more than twelve legions of angels? But how, then, would the scriptures be fulfilled that say it must happen in this way?'

"He was telling you that this is all happening to fulfill scripture. That 'the sword' is not going to be effective in accomplishing his Father's will. Jesus is willingly submitting himself to this trial. He does not want you using worldly means to interfere with what he must accomplish. Give us your sword for now, and we will use it to continue his good work."

Peter replied, "That can't be. He would never let these men stop us. He would want us to free him, and to do that, I must be free to act on his behalf. I need this sword. If virtue empowers it as you say, then I will continue to wield it in defense of my Lord! I'm all he has right now, and I must do my part. That includes maintaining my freedom and staying armed."

Joe responded, "But at what cost, my friend? Remember Jesus's words to you last night. Think on them and reflect. Is not obedience better than sacrifice? Is not the will of God more powerful than the weapons of man? Is not the Word of God sharper than a double-edged sword? Trust in him, Simon Peter. Trust and obey."

"I can't right now," he replied.

At that point, the crowd seemed to come alive; they were bringing Jesus out of the high priest's house. Peter rose and went to gain a clear view of the high priest and Jesus. The cousins followed. They were running out of time.

The crowd hushed, and the high priest spoke. His robes were torn, and he looked angry. He stood next to Jesus, who was still bound and had his head bowed as if in prayer. "This man is accused of blasphemy! He has confirmed it with his own words! We will take him to Pilate and have him sentenced to death by crucifixion. This is what happens to all who blaspheme our God!"

At this point, a man standing next to Peter pointed to him and shouted. "Surely, this fellow also was with him, for he is a Galilean!"

Peter yelled, "Man, I don't know what you're talking about!"

At the moment he spoke, a rooster crowed. Joe realized that they had heard Peter's third denial, just as the scriptures had recorded.

Then Jesus, who was now being led away, passed Peter and the cousins. He turned and looked straight at Peter, who remembered his words at the Passover supper the night before. He had said to him, "Before a rooster crows today, you will deny me three times".

Looking horrified, Peter ran from the courtyard. Joe watched him as he exited, and then turned back to look at Jesus. He looked straight at the cousins now. His eyes were clear and steady. He looked toward heaven, closed his eyes for a moment, then looked back at them. Their swords seemed to come alive with vibrations and began to glow once again. Then the soldiers roughly pulled Jesus forward and took him away to Pilate.

Joe couldn't seem to tear his gaze away from the scene. His heart hurt, both for the torment that Jesus had already suffered, and for what was to come. He knew he would never forget the feeling of power and love emanating from Jesus's face as he looked at them. It seared his very soul, yet it also left him feeling more cherished than he'd felt in his entire life. He hadn't expected that.

"Time is running out," Jeff whispered. "Let's go."

After a short search, they found him alone next to a well not far from the high priest's house, weeping bitterly.

"Peter!" Nick shouted as the cousins approached him. He was a broken man. His worst nightmare had come to fruition.

"I told him I would never betray him! I assured him that even if all the others deserted him, I would not. He said to me that before the crowing of the rooster, I would deny him three times. He was right. I'm not worthy to be his servant. I'm a failure. What is left for me now? Did you see the disappointment in his eyes when he looked at me?" Peter sobbed.

Joe spoke up. "Peter, this is all to fulfill scripture. Jesus knew that you would use every human means possible to try to stop what must happen. He loves you and has great plans for you. This is not the end. You will see him again. You will be restored. Have faith in him. Trust in his ways. Abandon your dependence on yourself and your own strength. Trust in his word and not your sword. Give your sword into our hands so that we may use it well."

Jeff finished, "Now is the time, Peter. Release your reliance on the strength of your right arm and depend on the arm of the Lord!"

Peter pulled the sword free and thrust it at them. "Take it! Take it now! I'm not worthy to carry it further. Just go, and leave me to my misery."

Joe took Peter's sword and said, "Peter, go find and strengthen your brothers. They need you now more than ever."

Then the cousins departed to find a fire. As they left,

they looked back at Peter, who was weeping and had fallen to his knees in prayer.

They hustled back to the courtyard area, and Nick said, "We need to hurry. The sun will be rising soon, and we need to be gone by then."

They re-entered the now-deserted and unguarded courtyard, found a fire that was still burning, and stood around it. Joe took a deep breath and focused hard, eliminating the distracting thoughts about what he'd just witnessed. He thought about their objective, the fire pit by the river.

Holding the Sword of Peter the Apostle tightly in his left hand, he raised his right arm, gently bringing his sword together with those of his brother and cousin. As they were surrounded once again by the flash of light, he knew they had all been changed forever.

CHAPTER NINE

THE THIRD
RETURN

The prophet was troubled. The three heroes hadn't returned from Gethsemane yet, and enormous quantum fluctuations had disrupted the remote monitoring of them. By the computer's calculations, they should have appeared an hour ago. So, for the past hour, the prophet and the remaining cousins had gathered around the fire pit waiting.

Finally, the usual of flash light signaled their return and the prophet took a deep breath, peering into the light, hoping they were all right. At last, the three cousins materialized with their swords held high. In Joe's left hand was a short and well-worn sword. He hoped this was the right one.

"Do you have the Sword of Peter the Apostle?" he asked the returned team.

"Yes," they replied in unison.

Joe walked to where the prophet stood, knelt, and extended the sword, handle first. "Prophet, I present to you the Sword of Peter the Apostle, given to us directly from his hand."

After uttering these words, he bowed his head.

"Thank you, Uncle Rob, for enabling us to have such a powerful experience. It was incredible."

Then he stood and returned to the group of cousins. The prophet watched as they hugged one another, noting that they held on longer than usual. When their greetings were done, he instructed them in a soft voice. "I know this has been a difficult assignment. Please, douse the fire and head back to the house. Follow your usual post-return routine; wash, eat, then meet me in the Keeping Room."

Upon entering the room, the prophet placed the Sword of Peter in the glass case with the other retrieved swords. He stood staring at it for some time, wondering what his nephews were feeling. He'd sensed an undercurrent of sadness and frustration, but there was something else. They seemed strangely uplifted. He hoped they would talk about their emotions when they reported on the assignment.

When the cousins came in, they moved to the table and assumed their positions around it. As soon as they were seated, the image of their grandfather appeared in the middle of the table and began to speak.

"Welcome back, Jeff, Joe, and Nick. Congratulations on completing another successful assignment. I sense some conflicting emotions in each of you. Would you like to share what you are feeling with the rest of us before we dig into the details?"

Joe, Jeff, and Nick looked at each other.

Gently, the prophet spoke, "I know it will take time to evaluate and process all that you've witnessed. Perhaps you're not sure if you can clearly articulate what you're feeling right now, but please try. We can't help you if we don't know what's going on in your minds and hearts."

Jeff cleared his throat. "I can't speak for the others,

but what we experienced back there was life-changing for me. I have always assumed the scriptures were somewhat accurate but were not entirely perfect. What we discovered was that the scriptures are precise in every material way. I find that incredible."

Nick added, "Using the scriptures, we were able to plan out our approach accurately and were prepared for what would happen. We had to adjust due to human intervention, but overall, everything went exactly as it is described in the gospels. I was incredibly moved by the events in the garden of Gethsemane."

Joe finished, "Meeting and interacting with Peter and other disciples of Jesus, feeling their passion and zeal and love for him and each other, was incredibly inspiring. Most of all, to hear Jesus speak, to witness his suffering, to see his command of every situation, and to feel his commitment to the will of God, was life-altering. It has inspired me and has also made me feel ashamed in many ways, but I would have to say I have been uplifted more than anything else."

The prophet responded, "Thank you, all of you for sharing that. I know it was difficult. There will be more time to examine your experiences and feelings after we complete our mission. These are extremely impactful situations that challenge your assumptions and expectations of the world and history. There is no way that you could emerge unchanged. I'm sure it will take years to work through and absorb it. I will be here to help you with that. So, let's put it aside for now and begin the debriefing. Please report the details of your assignment."

Nick began, "We arrived on the Mount of Olives on the precarious edge of a rock ledge, but we were safe." He went on to describe everything they'd experienced, including the fact that they'd fallen asleep just as the apostles had.

"This must have been the point where we observed the first quantum disturbance while we were monitoring you," said the image. "We observed that your vital signs and brain wave patterns took a dive. We were quite concerned. This helps to explain that. Continue."

Jeff took over the review from Nick, summarizing the arrest of Jesus, the cutting and healing of Malchus's ear, and the trek to Caiaphas's home.

Then Joe reported. "As we approached the gate, Jeff suggested that we trust the swords to give us what we would need to gain entry to the courtyard. I told the guards we were the sons of Joseph of Arimathea and were there to observe the proceedings officially. He let us pass.

"While we were looking for Peter, we heard the first rooster crow. We knew we had missed his first denial and that we had to hurry. We eventually spotted him with a group of men by a fire and joined him there. I whispered to him that we were followers of Jesus, and we needed to speak with him about a very urgent matter. He became agitated and shouted that he 'didn't know the man', causing those around us to look our way. Peter walked quickly away to avoid scrutiny. We had been a part of his second denial."

The image interrupted, "This resulted in a slight ripple in the timeline, but according to our calculations, it has had no impact. The scriptures do not name the person or people who initiated the second denial. Please continue."

"We followed and surrounded him and drew our swords. Once again, they glowed. We told him that we were there representing Melchizedek, Solomon, and Michael the Archangel, and we needed to obtain his sword. He eventually agreed to talk. We spoke with him about our mission and why we needed his sword.

"Before we could get him to agree, the Sanhedrin brought Jesus into the courtyard to announce his crimes. They said they would take him to Pilate for sentencing. We all moved to an area nearby where we could see and hear better. After they announced the charges against Jesus, a man shouted that Peter was one of Jesus's followers. Peter was startled and proclaimed that he wasn't; his third denial.

"At this point, Jesus looked directly at Peter, and Peter was shattered. He ran out of the courtyard. Then Jesus looked straight at us before looking up to heaven, closing his eyes. He appeared to be saying a prayer. Then they took him away.

"We followed Peter and found him by a well. We tried to comfort him and to convince him to release his sword into our keeping. He eventually agreed. We returned to the courtyard, found a fire still burning, and initiated the return."

The room was silent. Not even the image of their grandfather spoke for a few seconds. The prophet was moved by the details and knew they all needed time to collect their thoughts.

Finally, the image spoke. "At the end of your assignment, the quantum diagnostics malfunctioned. We lost track of all three of you and your swords. We could not regain contact and did not reestablish diagnostics until you returned. Somehow, your proximity to Jesus and his virtue must have overloaded the quantum field. Very well done, gentlemen. Indeed, very well done. What can we all learn from this assignment that will help us on the next?"

Billy started. "It seems clear that we have been learning to trust the swords. We need to remember that they will give us what we need when we need it."

"That's right, William," responded the image. "Anyone else?"

"I have a question," said Ty. "Why did Joe, Jeff, and Nick fall asleep? What was that about?"

The image of their grandfather replied. "My assumption, based on the quantum diagnostics and what has been told, is that it was the influence of the swords. It was clear that they were on the verge of interfering with the events of the day, and they needed to be prevented from doing so. It is possible that the same thing happened to the three disciples that were with Jesus. It may have been a way for God and the swords to prevent them from interfering with or disturbing Jesus during his time of prayer. We have no way of knowing.

"But this does tell us that the swords will help you to avoid any action that would materially threaten the timeline, have adverse social or spiritual impacts on the course of history, or prevent you from accomplishing the ultimate purpose of our mission. If history does need to be changed for the ultimate benefit of mankind, we must assume the swords will allow it. But that is untested and unknown.

"Believe it or not, this is a positive development. Not only are we beginning to realize the extent of the influence of the swords, but you are all becoming more responsive and attuned to their virtues."

Finally, Robbie asked a question. "Why did Jesus look at Joe, Jeff, and Nick? And why did the swords glow during this assignment?"

The image didn't immediately respond. After a few seconds, it said, "Sorry, we were running some analysis on all of that, and it took longer than expected. What we assume about the encounter with Jesus at the end is that he somehow connected on a quantum level with your cousins. We cannot know for sure, but it is possible that he was searching their motives and evaluating their virtue.

"To your second question, Robbie, we also now understand that the swords are sensitive to spiritual emanations. The more powerful the virtue of a nearby person, the more power they are imbued with. The fact that the swords glowed and vibrated when they were in Jesus's vicinity, and even responded to his words, indicates that your cousins were near to the source of all virtue, the source of the ultimate power of the swords. They will be more powerful than ever now, and that is good. You will need all that power for the next assignment and the Final Process.

"We have learned much from these past missions, and we will need to incorporate it all into this last assignment. Are there any further questions before we delve into the information you will need?"

No one spoke up, so the image began. "Your fourth and final assignment will be the most challenging from a decision-making perspective and will test both the power of the swords and your ability to adapt to circumstances. This will be your furthest venture into the past, and the most dangerous situation thus far.

"You will be traveling back in time to the Battle of Thermopylae to recover the Sword of Leonidas I. The Spartans were fighting against the Persian army in 480 BC. I'm sure you have all studied this battle in your history classes and may have seen the movie based on the story. Forget what you think you know and listen carefully to what I tell you here.

"The quantum computer has accumulated and acquired all the facts and analyzed them in detail. It has separated fact from fiction. What I present to you today

179

is reliable, and you can make quality decisions as to place and time based on it. Let's start with some information and history of the sword itself.

"The Sword of Leonidas was supposedly taken from his body by Xerxes upon the culmination of the Battle of Thermopylae. He was so enraged by the difficulty of defeating the Spartans, and so in awe of their bravery and fighting skills that he demanded that they find the Sword of Leonidas and that no one touch it but him. He believed that for Leonidas to have accomplished what he did, he must have possessed some form of magic. He thought that the power must reside in the sword.

"When the corpse of Leonidas was identified, Xerxes retrieved it from his broken body. The sword he believed to belong to Leonidas remained in Xerxes's possession and was passed down through the ages.

"However, the sword that Xerxes recovered wasn't Leonidas's sword; it was the sword of one of the Spartans' brave generals, Alpheus of Sparta. Alpheus, when he saw his king fall, took Leonidas's sword from him and replaced it with his own, so that it would not fall into the hands of the Persians. The Spartans later verified that this was the real Sword of Leonidas, identified by the engravings on the bronze blade. These engravings of leopards attacking were symbolic of Leonidas' courage and strength.

"The sword was kept in Sparta for many years, then was stolen by Phillip of Macedonia, the father of Alexander the Great. When Phillip died, it became the possession of Alexander himself and was always kept by his side.

"Alexander traveled with this sword until his death. One of his generals, named Ptolemy, stole Alexander's corpse when it was sent to Macedon for burial. He spirited the body and the sword away to Egypt. He hoped he could secure the prophecy that the land where his body was laid to rest would be prosperous and unconquerable. This general would found the Ptolemaic Dynasty in Egypt. That dynasty lasted until 30 BC, ending with the death of Ptolemy's descendant Cleopatra VII. The sword remained in the vast Library of Alexandria.

"Even after the fall of Carthage following the Punic Wars, when Rome became supreme and Alexandria fell under her sway, the city remained prosperous and continued to attract visitors from all over the world. The increasing tensions in Rome between Nero and Pompey first impacted Alexandria negatively in 48 BC. In the civil war, the famous Library of Alexandria where the Sword of Leonidas was kept was burned. The sword was assumed lost.

"However, some amazing artifacts survived. Among these were the source charts later used by Christopher Columbus to draw his maps of the new world, and the Sword of Leonidas. These artifacts changed hands many times, but eventually, King Ferdinand and Queen Isabella of Spain gained possession of them. The maps and the Sword of Leonidas were given to Christopher Columbus as gifts when he made his voyages to America.

"They remained in his possession until the wreck of the Santa Maria off the coast of Haiti on December 25th, 1492. They saved the maps, but it was then that the sword was lost. It remained in the wreck of the Santa Maria for centuries.

"Then, in May 2012, an underwater archaeological explorer belonging to one of the families of the Apostles of Azazel claimed that his team had found the wreck of the Santa Maria. In the following October, an international team of experts published their final report, concluding that the wreck could not be Columbus's vessel. They stated that the fastenings used in the hull and possible copper sheathing dated it to the 17th or 18th century. This was a falsehood perpetrated by the Apostles of Azazel. They had actually found the Sword of Leonidas and have had it since that time."

"Any questions?" the image asked the team.

"No question," said Ty, "just an observation. I'm astounded by the number of historical figures involved in the histories of the swords. Learning all of this is amazing. It opens up our eyes to the fact that there is much more going on out there in the world than we realize."

"That it does, Ty," said the image. "That is true for much else besides the swords. Our political and sociological history is much different than you have been led to believe. There will come a time when we can review all of that with you, but that time is not now. Let's continue and focus on this assignment. I will now tell you about the Battle of Thermopylae.

"Under Xerxes I, the Persian army moved south through Greece on the eastern coast, accompanied by the Persian navy sailing parallel to the shore. To reach Attica, the region controlled by the city-state of Athens, the Persians needed to travel through the coastal pass of Thermopylae. In the late summer of 480 BC, Leonidas led an army of six to seven thousand Greeks from many city-states, including three hundred Spartans, in an attempt to prevent the Persians from passing through Thermopylae.

"Leonidas established his army at Thermopylae, expecting that the narrow pass would funnel the Persian troops toward his own force. For two days, the Greeks withstood the determined attacks of their far more numerous enemy. Leonidas's plan worked well at first, but he'd counted on a local Phokian contingent to defend another route through the mountains to the west of Thermopylae that would have allowed the enemy to bypass his fortified position along the coast.

"A local Greek told Xerxes about this other route. Xerxes decided to send his 'Immortals', his chosen *baivarabam*, or army of ten thousand, through this pass. They defeated the Phokians, enabling them to surround the Greeks.

"An army of Spartans, Thespians, and Thebans remained to fight the Persians, but now Leonidas had to split his attention. That proved to be their undoing. Leonidas and the three hundred Spartans with him were all killed, along with most of their remaining allies. The Persians found and beheaded Leonidas's corpse, an act considered to be a grave insult. To add insult to injury, Xerxes did it with the sword they thought was Leonidas's own.

"After the battle, Leonidas's sacrifice, along with that of his Spartan soldiers, didn't prevent the Persians from moving down the Greek coast. Nonetheless, Leonidas's action demonstrated Sparta's willingness to sacrifice itself for the protection of the Greek region.

"For his personal sacrifice, Leonidas achieved lasting fame. Hero-cults were an established custom in ancient Greece from the eighth century BC onward. Dead heroes were worshipped, usually near their burial site, as intermediaries to the gods. After the battle, Sparta retrieved Leonidas's remains, and built a shrine in his honor. The Greek poet Simonides's epitaph on the Kolonos hillock, the site believed to be the location of the last stand reads:

GO TELL THE SPARTANS PASSERBY,
THAT HERE OBEDIENT TO THEIR LAWS WE LIE

Of those who died at Thermopylae renowned is the fortune, noble the fate: Their grave's an altar, their memorial our mourning, their fate our praise. Such a shroud neither decay nor all-conquering destroy.

This sepulcher of brave men has taken the high renown of Hellas for its fellow occupant, as witness Leonidas, Sparta's king, who left behind a great memorial of valor, everlasting renown.

"Another author wrote about the battle:

The most valiant are sometimes the most unfortunate. Thus, there are triumphant defeats that rival victories. Nor did those four sister victories, the fairest that the sun ever set eyes on, Salamis, Plataea, Mycale, and Sicily, ever dare match all their combined glory against the glory of the annihilation of King Leonidas and his men at the pass of Thermopylae.

At the memorial site of the battle, below the statue of King Leonidas, is a marble frieze, depicting the defenders of Thermopylae who died during the campaign. The heroes that distinguished themselves and who were recorded by Herodotus have been immortalized by name and the respective city-state that each warrior represented.

> *Alpheus, Sparta*
> *Demophilus, the Thespian*
> *Dienekes, Sparta*
> *Dithyrambus, the Thespian*
> *Eurytus and Maron, Sparta*
> *Megistias, the Arcanian*

"This memorial is situated atop the hillock where it is believed that the Spartans and Thespians made their last stand. The Greek archaeologist, Spyridon Marinatos, found a large concentration of arrowheads in 1939, confirming the location. So, we know the site of the battle with reasonable certainty.

"Now we need to determine the date. But before we get to the dates in question, let me tell you a bit more about Leonidas himself. You will need to know all you can about him, since there are no pictures or paintings that have survived, and the sculptures of him are unreliable.

"Almost everything known about Leonidas comes from the work of the Greek historian, Herodotus. Leonidas was the son of Anaxandrides, the Spartan king. When his older half-brother, Cleomenes I, died, he became king. King Leonidas was probably born in about 540 BC. This would mean that King Leonidas would have been in his fifties, or perhaps as old as sixty, when he died at Thermopylae in 480 BC.

"Although Leonidas lost the battle, his death at Thermopylae was considered a heroic sacrifice, because when he realized that the Persians had outmaneuvered him, he sent most of his army away. Three hundred of his fellow Spartans stayed with him to fight and die.

"King Leonidas was not just a political leader. He was a military leader, as well. Like all male Spartan citizens, Leonidas had been trained and prepared mentally and physically since childhood to become a warrior. In battle, the Spartans used a formation called a phalanx. Rows of warriors stand directly next to each other so that their shields overlapped with one another. During a frontal attack, this wall of shields provided significant protection to the warriors behind it. However, if the phalanx broke or if the enemy attacked from the side or the rear, the formation became vulnerable. It was this fatal weakness to the otherwise formidable phalanx formation that proved to be Leonidas's undoing.

"Now, on to the dates. There is some debate about the date of the Battle of Thermopylae, with two dates under contention. The dates in question are either August 8th through the 10th, or September 8th through the 10th of the year 480 BC. Our studies and the analysis of the quantum computer have settled on the September dates with high certainty. The time of day is also in question. We know that the height of the battle took place for three days. You know you will only have until the sunrise after the day you arrive to accomplish the assignment. We need to be precise, so choose carefully and be committed to it. Consider the facts and reveal to me your decision."

The cousins began to discuss their options at the table. The prophet listened as they reviewed all the known facts about the battle, Leonidas, and the sword. He wasn't surprised that this took more time than the other assignments. There were many more variables, including the fact that they were being sent into a war zone so far back in time. They would be in an extremely unfamiliar setting, to say the least.

Finally, Billy announced, "We have come to a decision. We have chosen to return to September 10th, 480 BC. We also choose to arrive at sunrise once again, to maximize our time there and give us room for error. The place of our choosing is the Kolonos hillock where the memorial is today."

The image asked the group, "Is everyone in agreement?"

"Yes," they responded in unison.

"So be it, but remember, the Battle of Thermopylae

has been called the 'battle that changed the world'. Make it so once again today," instructed the image as it faded from view.

The prophet stood and watched as the heroes collected their swords from the glass case. The prophet smiled as he watched the cousins chatting on the way to the fire pit by the river. It seemed they were all energized by the inspiring story they had just heard and the incredible courage of King Leonidas and his three hundred.

"I'm having mixed feelings about this," Billy told Ty. "I'm eager to get on with the assignment, but I'm also wary of what we'll encounter."

Ty nodded. "We'll be going into the teeth of a crucial battle in history."

"You have to admit, we've had some good success on our past assignments, though," Robbie said.

"I won't argue with that," Jeff said. "I, for one am even more confident in the power and influence of the swords. Still, I'd be lying if I didn't tell you I'm a little afraid, too."

"This won't be easy," Joe added. "I wonder which of us will go this time."

Nick's response was somber, "And which of us will return."

CHAPTER TEN

THE SWORD OF LEONIDAS

———— ✦ ————

For the fourth time, the fire was lit in the pit by the river. Once again, the prophet and the heroes gathered themselves around it. This time, the prophet felt he needed to say something to all six heroes before they attempted the departure.

"Gentlemen," he started, "as we have discussed, this will be the most challenging and dangerous assignment you have undertaken yet. The twin aspects of distance in time, and that you are traveling into the height of one of the most vicious conflicts in history make it so. As you know, I have been analyzing the choices that the swords have made regarding who has been sent on the previous assignments.

"Utilizing the power of the quantum computer, I believe that all of you will be selected this time. I see no other way. The power necessary to travel so far back in time, and the vast number of variables involved with such a dangerous assignment, will require not only the combined power of all the swords but all the virtues associated with them. So, it will be necessary for you all to work with and trust each other and the swords completely. Do you understand?"

"We do," the heroes replied.

"Good," stated the prophet. "Let us begin!"

The heroes raised their right arms slowly. They gently brought their Swords of Valor together. When the last sword touched the others, there was a huge flash of pure, white light. When the prophet could see clearly once again, he saw that all the heroes had indeed departed. This time, the flash of light was so powerful that the fire they had been standing around was extinguished.

"Godspeed, my heroes," was all he could say. He returned alone to the Keeping Room to monitor their progress and prepare for the Final Process.

The heroes arrived as planned on what Joe assumed was the Kolonos hillock. But something felt different this time. He felt a sense of exhaustion. Looking at the others, he saw they all looked tired.

Robbie spoke first. "Wow, that was different. I feel drained."

Billy nodded. "Yeah, kinda weak."

The others said they all felt the same exhaustion.

"What do you think that's all about?" asked Ty.

Jeff responded. "I guess that the power required to get us here was so great that it drained us a bit along with the swords, but I can't be sure. I assume the swords will recharge themselves while we're here, but we can't worry about it now. Let's just take a moment to gather our strength and figure out where we are. Then, when we feel a bit better, we can get moving."

Joe looked around and noted they stood on top of a

hill beside two large boulders. The knoll was thick with trees along the lower parts, with fewer trees at the top. From where they stood, he had an unobstructed view of the surrounding area and could see a body of water in the distance to the north. Looking toward the west and below them, he observed a massive cloud of dust and heard a battle raging. That, he realized, was where they needed to be.

Billy addressed the team. "Look, we need to get down there as quickly as possible, but we also need to be careful. We should stay together and keep quiet. Remember, the whole point of this assignment, the only point of this assignment, is to recover the Sword of Leonidas. We are not to be combatants. We are not to put our lives in danger. This is the last day of the battle, and the fighting will be the fiercest. We need to identify Leonidas and ask him for his sword."

Joe asked, "Billy, you think he is just going to give us his sword because we ask him? I can't imagine that a warrior like Leonidas would give up his sword without a fight. In fact, we might have to fight the general that took it from his dead body."

Billy shook his head. "That won't work. The rightful owner must give it to us willingly. Leonidas can't give it to us willingly if he's dead. We must get it before he's killed."

"Joe is right about one thing, though," said Nick. "Let's get down there and get some perspective. We can discuss this when we get a better view of the battle."

Jeff added, "As we head down there, try to spot the camp of the Spartans. Not all the soldiers may be involved in the battle at this point. I'm sure there are wounded that need attention and storage for supplies and such. I suggest that we head to the camp first and try to blend in.

Maybe we can question some of the men there to get more intelligence before we make our next move."

The other cousins recognized the wisdom in this suggestion and agreed. Their first objective would be the Spartan camp.

Cautiously, they began their descent, staying well hidden in the trees. The lower they descended, the louder the sounds of battle became. Joe was nervous, but a surge of adrenaline filled him and the exhaustion dissipated. All his senses were engaged and on high alert.

As the cousins reached the base of the hillock, Joe saw that they were in a narrow pass. He looked left and right and saw that the dust of the battle was heaviest to their left, to the west. Looking right, he could make out more dust rising, and in the distance, wounded men being helped. He assumed this was the camp of the Spartans.

"Let's join that group of wounded soldiers and help them back to camp. With the cloaking powers of the swords, we should fit right in," said Nick.

"Except for the fact that we're not wounded," observed Ty.

"Or wearing armor" added Joe.

The cousins moved swiftly along the road and stayed in the tree line. When they were close enough, they joined the slow-moving group of injured soldiers helping each other back to camp. They each went to the neediest of the wounded and relieved the ones that were carrying them.

Joe realized that all these men needed significant medical attention. There were puncture wounds from spears, deep gashes from sword strikes, and some even had arrows still protruding from their bodies.

Nick asked the soldier he was helping, "How goes the battle, my friend? Are we holding strong?"

"We are holding, but the Persian numbers are

starting to overwhelm our phalanx. We need reinforcements, but none are coming. The Persians seemed to be backing off a bit when I was wounded, and General Alpheus fears they are regrouping for a final attack later in the day. I think they might split their forces and attack from different directions," the soldier replied.

As they rounded a bend in the road, the Spartan camp lay before them. Joe saw hundreds of tents, dozens of campfires, and not more than thirty men. Most of these men were wounded, and some were already dead. A few were attending to those whose injuries were most severe. He observed one of these men cauterizing an open wound with the broken blade of a sword that he'd heated in a nearby fire. The wounded soldier didn't make a sound, even as the hot iron sealed the gash in his leg. These Spartans are certainly tough, Joe thought.

The cousins discharged the wounded men to various tents and then gathered together to talk.

Jeff said, "I will find whoever is in charge and gather more information. You guys attend to the wounded and see what they can tell about Leonidas's whereabouts. But don't leave the camp, and try to stay in sight of each other at all times."

Before they took off, Ty spoke up. "Look, I know you guys joke about me being a neurologist and all, but seriously, I have dissected a lot of bodies and have a good understanding of anatomy. I'm the only one with anything close to medical training. If you have a question about how to help a wounded soldier, come and ask me.

"The most important thing is simple cleanliness. Keep the wounds clean. The second most important thing is to stop the bleeding. Do those two things, and that is all we can do. Start by finding pots to boil water. Then find some reasonably clean cloth and use that for tourniquets and bandages. Finally, the method that we observed on the way into camp where the man used the heated sword blade to cauterize the wound is a valid one. Not the cleanest, but certainly effective. Do that if the wound is severe, and you can't stop the bleeding."

The cousins indicated their understanding and moved to help the wounded. Jeff left to find the person in charge.

Joe looked around to determine where he should start. The camp had a deserted feel to it and an aura of defeat, like a body during the last moments of life. It was still there and serving a purpose, but it was dying for sure.

He entered the tent where he had laid the wounded soldier he was helping along the road to camp. He had gathered a pot on his way there, filled it with water, and set it to boil on the fire just outside the tent. He searched for clean cloth as Ty had instructed, but found none. So, he took off his T-shirt and ripped it into strips. He examined a soldier writhing on the floor and saw two wounds. One was a huge gash, clearly visible, probably fatal, in his side just below the last rib. The second was a puncture wound from a spear in his right thigh.

After assessing his wounds, Joe retrieved the boiling water from the fire. While there, he found a couple of pieces of pig iron lying near a fire. They looked like they'd be perfect for cauterize the gash in the soldier's leg. He placed the rods in the fire to heat up as he had seen the attendant do upon arrival in the camp. When he returned, he used one of the strips from his T-shirt for a tourniquet for the puncture wound, and then used the water and some cloth to clean both wounds.

"I'm going to stop the bleeding from your side," he told the soldier. "It will hurt, but it will work. Be strong."

The soldier replied. "Do what you must. I'm a

Spartan and fear nothing but dishonor. All I ask is that you do it quickly, so that I may return to my position." Joe left the tent to retrieve the pig iron rods. They were hot, but not red-hot. Perfect... I hope, he thought.

Joe returned to kneel next to the soldier and without a word, he gently pressed the hot metal onto the wound. The soldier's body tensed, his jaw clenched, and his eyes closed. Joe held the rod in place for just a couple of seconds, then pulled it away to see if the wound had been sealed. The bleeding had slowed, but not stopped, so he repeated the process. Again, checking the wound, he started to repeat the process, then had the feeling he should use Excalibur.

Drawing the sword, he placed it on the wound, just as he had the pig iron rods. After a couple of seconds, he pulled it away, and sure enough, the bleeding had stopped. He sat for a few minutes, in awe of the power of these swords. He hadn't even known they had the power to heal!

He quickly wrapped the wound with the strips of his shirt. When he finished, he asked the soldier if he was well enough to answer some questions. The soldier nodded his assent.

"Tell me how the battle goes. Will we hold the position until nightfall?" Joe asked.

The soldier replied. "Alpheus said that we could hold the position for a while longer, but that we must drop back closer to the camp. Because it's near the narrowing of the pass near Kolonos hillock, we will have a further strategic advantage. He was about to give the order to do so when I was wounded. I believe they must be withdrawing to that spot at this point. Help me rise so I can go to them and rejoin the battle!"

Joe responded, "You are in no shape to do that yet.

Rest a while longer, and I will return to check your wounds. Then we will see if you can return." Before he left, he asked the soldier's name.

"I'm Eurytus, friend."

Just then, Jeff stuck his head into the tent.

Joe looked up and motioned him over, "You'll never guess…"

Jeff interrupted him, "Later, Joe. Right now, I need you to come out here, I have found the man in charge, and we need to talk with him."

"But…" Joe started.

"Come on!" Jeff insisted.

Joe looked at Eurytus apologetically. "I'm sorry. I'm needed elsewhere."

The Spartan shook his head. "Don't worry about me. You have done all you can do. Go. Do your duty."

Joe stood and sheathed Excalibur, then left to meet the others in the middle of the camp.

Jeff was standing with a short, stocky man in full armor. He introduced the man as the commander, then addressed the cousins.

"I have told the commander that we have been sent to determine the status of the battle and that we must speak with Leonidas himself, as we have an important message for him."

Then he turned to the commander and asked, "Does the king have any plans to return to camp this evening?"

The camp commander just stared at him like he had two heads. "Not unless he is brought here upon his shield. The king won't leave his men. You should know that if you are truly from Sparta. If you want to speak with him, you will have to go to where he is." Then he turned away from them to return to his duties.

Before he had gone far, a soldier came running up

to the group of cousins and grabbed Joe.

"Sir, I return to battle, thank you for your help and healing!"

Joe recognized the man he had just helped. "Eurytus, you are not yet healed. Go back to the tent."

Eurytus then reached down and uncovered the wound in his side. To the cousins' amazement, it was fully healed! He showed them the puncture wound, and it also was completely mended. Joe and the other cousins were in shock.

"What's this?" the camp commander turned and asked. "What's this about healing? Let me see."

As he examined Eurytus, the heroes huddled together for a moment.

"What? How?" sputtered Billy.

"It must have been Excalibur," Joe whispered. "I touched the wound with it."

"I did the same with the soldier I treated," Ty added.

Robbie nodded, looking stunned. "So did I, and I didn't know why. It just felt right."

Joe agreed. "Same here. I'd tried to cauterize the wound, but then I felt like I should lay Excalibur on it. I thought it just sealed it like cauterizing it. I didn't expect it to heal it… to heal all of his wounds!"

"The swords have healing powers?" Nick shook his head. "That's useful!"

The commander confirmed the soldier's fitness to return to battle. He shot the cousins a look of amazement and newfound respect, then turned to Eurytus. "Take these men with you; they need to speak with Leonidas himself."

Following behind Eurytus, the group of six cousins began the walk to rejoin the campaign, joined quickly by the other healed Spartans. As they neared the Kolonos hillock, Joe could see the larger group of Spartans falling back to that position, just as Eurytus had said they might. They picked up their pace and arrived just as the first wave of retreating combatants reached the camp.

Eurytus ran ahead toward one of the men. "Maron!" he shouted as he embraced him. "You are well! When I was wounded, I thought you were next! Thank the gods you are safe!"

Maron replied, "It is you who we should be thanking the gods for. We believed you mortally wounded and lost to us forever. How is it that you are here… and healed?"

"I have been healed by the power of these…" Eurytus's voice hitched as he turned to the heroes. "I know not what to call you. Healers? Gods?"

Uncomfortable with the inference, Joe raised a hand to stop him. "We are not gods, my friend." He thought for a moment. "Perhaps 'messengers' is the best way to describe us."

"But I don't understand," Eurytus shook his head. "How is it…"

Again, Joe stopped him. "It's a long story, and we have an important message for Leonidas. Please, will you take us to him?"

"Of course! Immediately!" Eurytus replied, then turned to Maron. "Where is the king?"

Maron replied, "The king is protecting the rear. He should be here soon."

Eurytus nodded. "Good, I will take them to him, then I will return to you, my brother, so that we can fight our last battle together."

They embraced again, then Eurytus turned to the cousins and said, "Follow me."

As they started to leave, Maron touched Joe's arm. "Thank you, my friends, for returning my brother to us.

Now we can die with honor together instead of separately."

Touched by Maron's gratitude and unable to speak, Joe swallowed hard, put his hand on Maron's for a moment and simply nodded before turning to join the others. The men made their way through the retreating troops looking for signs of the king.

Eventually, Eurytus spotted General Alpheus. He called out, "General, where is the king?"

Alpheus responded, "He comes quickly, what is your business?"

Eurytus replied, "I have six reinforcements with a message from Sparta. They must speak with the king at once!"

Alpheus approached the group and looked them over. "Where is your armor?" he asked them.

The cousins looked at each other in surprise.

Billy spoke up, "Our message is of such great importance that we left in a hurry… and did not take time to put it on."

Alpheus looked at them with disgust and ordered Eurytus, "Get them properly dressed. I won't have them appearing in front of the king so ill-prepared."

Eurytus said to the cousins, "Let's get you equipped for battle. We will gather what you need from the dead."

"Why doesn't he see us in armor?" Nick whispered to Jeff as they followed Eurytus.

"Remember the experience with the uniform boots when we rescued Joan of Arc?" Jeff responded. "I believe the cloaking ability of the swords allows him to see us in common Spartan apparel, but apparently we need to obtain physical armor as well."

Nick nodded. "Illusionary armor probably wouldn't protect us from real swords, would it?"

Jeff raised an eyebrow and grimaced. "I don't know, but it's not going to hurt to wear the real thing if we have to fight."

They spent some time wandering about choosing and reverently removing what they needed from the dead soldiers who had been carried back to the position by the retreating troops. When they finished donning the appropriate armor, they followed Eurytus back to the general.

Alpheus looked them over, approved, and then ordered, "Follow me."

Eurytus turned to the cousins. "May the gods be with you. If you require nothing more from me, I'll return to my brother."

Joe held out his hand and clasped Eurytus's. "I hope to see you again, my friend."

Eurytus grinned. "Perhaps on the battlefield?" He squeezed Joe's hand, then took off at a run.

The cousins followed Alpheus a short way to a large, makeshift tent. He entered first, telling the cousins to wait outside. After a moment, he appeared back at the entrance and commanded sharply, "Enter."

The heroes slowly filed in. As Joe's eyes adjusted to the gloom of the tent, he saw King Leonidas seated before them, dressed in full battle gear, looking worn but powerful. He appeared to be in his fifties but very fit, with a commanding presence. He finished drinking from a metal cup, then looked at the cousins, appraising them.

"What is your business with me?" he asked them directly.

Billy spoke for the group. "Great king, we are here on a mission of paramount importance. May we speak with you privately?"

The king responded, "Whatever you have to say to

me can be said in the presence of Alpheus." Then he dismissed the others in the tent and ordered Billy to speak.

Billy began. "Great king, what we have to tell you is strange. We are travelers from a faraway land and a time far in the future. We have come here today to complete our mission of gathering the Swords of Valor from throughout history. It is imperative that we complete this mission before sunrise tomorrow, or all will be lost. The sword you carry is the only remaining sword we need to complete our assignment. If we are to achieve success and defeat evil, you must release it into our hands of your own accord. Will you agree?"

Leonidas's eyes grew wide, his nostrils flared, and he fixed the cousins with a steely glare. "Do you waste my time with such tales of nonsense?" he shouted. "Am I to believe that you are gods sent here from Olympus to strip me of my sword so that I may go into battle defenseless? Alpheus! How dare you bring these men to me with such a request?"

Alpheus responded, "My King, they were brought to me by Eurytus, who as you know, was mortally wounded earlier in the day. He is now fully healed and has returned to the fight. He has said that these men are responsible for his healing and the healing of four other warriors. Eurytus is trustworthy. I suggest we question them further about this healing."

Joe took advantage of this opening and suggested, "Great king, may we show you the Swords of Valor we carry? These swords are responsible for the healing of Eurytus and four other men who have now returned to battle. These swords also have great power and might."

Leonidas replied, "I don't see any swords. Where are they?"

The cousins drew their swords and raised their right arms. The Swords of Valor appeared.

Alpheus reached for his sword immediately upon seeing them.

Nick announced, "These are the Swords of Valor. They have been used throughout history in defense of freedom and righteousness. They have won many battles and changed the course of history. Men and women of valor and virtue have wielded them. We wish to add your sword to their number this day. Please, consider our request." Then the cousins lowered their arms, but the swords remained visible.

The king and his general were awestruck for a moment. Then Leonidas gestured for Alpheus to come near. They whispered together, then Leonidas looked at the cousins and said, "I will consider your request, but I have one condition. You have stated that the swords you carry are swords of valor and virtue. That may be so, but that does not mean that you, yourselves, possess valor or virtue. If I am to agree to your request, you must prove to me that you possess both qualities. You will join us in the battle soon to resume. If, at the end of the day, you have proven your bravery and valor, I will release my sword into your hands."

Surprised, Joe looked at his cousins. They weren't prepared for this request. The swords hadn't previously led them into actual combat. But this was different, and there didn't seem to be any other option.

With a raised eyebrow, Robbie nodded at each of them. Joe returned his nod, as did the other cousins. Robbie then looked at the king. "We agree. We will, this day, add our Swords of Valor to your cause and will stand with you in battle. Whatever the outcome, this day will be remembered as one that changed history forever, I assure you. May we fight with virtue and valor."

He raised the Sword of William Wallace. His cousins raised theirs also, and the swords glowed gently in the gloom of the tent. Then they bowed to the king and followed Alpheus outside.

"I want you men at the front of the battle," Alpheus told them. "I don't know what experience you have, but you possess swords like none I have ever seen. You will stand in the row behind the phalanx and kill anyone who breaks through or climbs over. I will be there with you. Today may be our last day. Only the gods know what our fate will be. Just know this; if you run or if you prove yourselves cowards, I will kill you myself." He turned and left the cousins there alone.

Joe looked at the others with raised eyebrows. "Sounds like he meant it."

Billy nodded. "Time to stand up and be counted."

The others nodded, then went to find Eurytus and Maron.

They found them sitting by a campfire just finishing their meal. Eurytus looked up and asked, "How went your visit with the king? Is all well?"

Ty responded, "We had hoped for better, but all will be well. We have been assigned to fight behind the phalanx and use our swords in the cause today. Will you take us there?"

"I will," said Eurytus. "That is where Maron and I have been positioned. We will fight together side by side with you until the end. With the eight of us standing shoulder to shoulder, we will repel the Persians! Long live Leonidas! We have been told to assemble at the mouth of the pass where it narrows just under the Kolonos hillock. I will come and get you when the time comes." He took his last bite, then stood. "Right now, Maron and I must go and help the others move boulders across the road to block the path of the Persians. We intend to narrow the pass even more. Be ready when I come for you."

Joe watched them depart, then moved to sit beside the fire. He realized that this was their first opportunity to speak privately since they had first entered the camp. There were some weighty matters to discuss. He didn't know where to start, though, so remained silent for a few moments.

Finally, Jeff spoke up. "Look, I need to say something to you guys before we go into battle. To be honest, I have thought that this may very well be the last time we are all together. Who knows what's going to happen out there? We are going to be in the thick of the fighting, and it will be fierce. The Persians are coming in for the kill. They intend to end this today with the complete annihilation of the remaining Spartans, and now that includes us. We know from history what happens today.

"Our only hope is to survive long enough to get Leonidas to give us his sword before he dies. That means we need to keep him in sight at all times. I will do my best to protect each of you and myself, but I fear that it may end up being every man for himself. Remember, I love you all. If I fall in battle, please, tell Carolyn that I loved her with all my heart and make sure my children know that, too."

Billy put his arm around his younger brother and said, "Love you too, Jeff, but nothing will happen to us. You can tell Carolyn and the kids that you love them yourself. The swords will protect us, and I will have your back. Solomon and Roland, an unbeatable team!"

Joe found his voice and spoke next, "Billy, we appreciate your confidence, but Jeff is right. The Spartans are the best of the best, and the Persians crushed them today. Realistically, we have a very slim chance of survival. You heard what Leonidas said. He will be watching us for any sign of weakness or fear. He and Alpheus will be expecting us to engage the enemy aggressively. We can't win his respect by just defending each other. That is part of it, but we will have to kill people or at least stop them from killing Spartans.

"I agree with Jeff. We need to say our goodbyes now. I love you all and could not imagine a better way to die if it comes to that. Side by side with my brother and my cousins to the end. Let's do this!"

Nick spoke next, "Joe and I will fight together. That is how we need to deal with this, in three teams of two. Eurytus and Maron are brothers, and they will fight side by side also. What better way to die than at the side of your blood brothers? We need to be prepared to die in this effort. Anyone who is not ready for that better not go. Also, let's make sure to keep track of everyone's swords so that if they fall, we can collect them. That way, the survivors can return home. I love you guys, and I will see you all for the return trip."

Robbie nodded. "Brother by brother. I like that, Nick. Billy, you said that the swords would protect us, but I don't think we can assume that we have complete protection from the swords. The swords will influence us, and we need to trust that influence, but we must do the work. We must fight.

"Also, Leonidas was right when he said that just because the swords are imbued with valor, that does not mean we are. Remember what my dad said during our indoctrination. He told us the swords can magnify or enhance the qualities we already possess. He didn't say the swords would give us their qualities. I am grateful that

Leonidas said that to us and challenged us in that way, so we would realize it before the battle and not go in assuming complete protection from harm.

"God made the Hebrews fight for their victories, even though he assured them that they would be victorious. Some of the Hebrews lost their lives in those battles. We need to be prepared to do the same. Trust the swords, trust each other, fight hard, and remember the mission. That is what I will do. Ty, what about you?"

"I'm with you, bro," said Ty. "Side by side till the end. I love all you guys and will do whatever I can to help us all make it through this. Whatever happens here today, we will know that we gave it our best and did it together. What more could anyone ask? We will also be a part of history!" He hesitated, then grinned.

"Personally, I am hoping we live long enough for me to get back in time for finals. I look forward to reading about ourselves in the history books. Let's make sure that we make Grandpa proud."

The cousins chuckled at Ty's attempt to lighten the mood, then huddled together, knelt, said a few prayers, and stood to see Eurytus heading their way. "It is time! The Persians approach! Come this way!"

They checked their armor and hustled after Eurytus.

Joe's heart was beating wildly, and the blood pounded in his ears. Excalibur felt alive in his hands, and that gave him hope. They had all been in various championship games before. They had all known the heat and excitement of competition when everything was on the line, but never to this degree. This was new and different. Joe knew they would be tested in ways that they had never imagined, all the time knowing from history that everyone on their "team" would die today. It all felt so surreal!

They ran together with Eurytus to take their positions. General Alpheus awaited them. He noted they were standing in pairs and nodded his approval, then instructed them quietly, "Don't move forward. Stay back from the phalanx. Let the men up there do their work with their shields and spears. They need room to flex backward at times, and if you get too close, you will get in their way. We are the second line of defense. Only engage the enemy who breaks through.

"If that happens, the phalanx will close the gap quickly to trap them on our side of the line. Attack the man in a team of two. Dispatch him quickly and move the body away from the line so that the men in the phalanx won't trip over it. Remember, teams of two at all times. If we become overwhelmed, only then should you fight alone and fight for your lives. If you can help a fellow Spartan, then do so, otherwise, protect yourself and keep on killing, understood?"

The cousins nodded their understanding.

He then positioned the teams of brothers behind the phalanx with Maron and Eurytus. He admonished all of them. "You have been given your instructions. I will be watching, and so will the king. Prove yourselves this day!"

Looking up, he pointed his sword over their heads. The men all looked where he was pointing as he shouted, "The enemy arrives. Engage!"

The phalanx of two hundred men snapped into formation creating a two-shield-high wall that bristled with spears. They were about ten feet behind the wall of boulders that they had hastily rolled across the pass. This would allow them to skewer with their long spears any Persian that made it over the boulders.

There was a massive, sheer wall of rock to the left flank and a less imposing one to the right. If the Persians wanted to get past them, a lot of them were going to die. But there were thousands of them. The odds and history were in the enemy's favor.

The first wave of Persians reached the boulders and quickly climbed over. It slowed them down long enough for the Spartans to dispatch them with ease with their long spears. They could not attain enough speed to break through the phalanx. It had held.

The next wave had even more men. They easily surmounted the boulders positioned across the pass. Half of them started to push at the boulders to move them aside while the other half fought to protect their fellow soldiers from the Spartan spears. In short order, they dispatched all of the second wave, but the Persians had succeeded in moving some of the boulders from the middle of the pass.

Alpheus shouted orders for the phalanx to move rearward five paces. As they moved, they realized the Persian bodies would create an additional obstacle for the next wave and would give them more room to use their spears.

The third wave approached. This time, they poured through the opening in the boulders much faster. The wave of Persians hit the middle of the phalanx hard, and it buckled backward.

The Persians spread out left and right, attacking along the full length of the phalanx. This was more than a mere wave; it was a tidal wave of Persians. From this point on, it would be a constant battle.

The cousins were positioned behind the middle section of the phalanx. It was all Joe could do to resist rushing up to the line to help them repel the attack. But he remembered Eurytus's instructions and hung back.

Soon, the first Persian broke through by climbing

over the back of one of his comrades impaled on a Spartan spear. He leaped over the top of the line in front of Joe. The Persian was dead before his feet hit the ground. Joe had thrust Excalibur right through his heart as he descended from his leap.

Nick looked at Joe for just a second with an expression of amazement and then proceeded to help him move the body to the rear.

The middle of the phalanx was holding, but the number of Persians was increasing. A dozen Persians had breached the phalanx at various points along the line, but the Spartans were making quick work of them. As Joe and Nick returned, they passed Robbie and Ty, who had just eliminated one and were dragging him away. Billy and Jeff were currently engaged with one of their own. Joe witnessed Billy slicing off a Persian's sword arm with a mighty blow from Durandal, then Jeff finished the job. They, too, began to drag the body to the rear.

Nick said to Joe, "Looks like each team has their first kill. Only nine thousand more to go."

They resumed their positions, and the Persians continued advancing. They breached the right flank and streamed in from that side. The fearless Spartans killed them in high numbers, but Joe knew that before long, their sheer numbers would be a problem.

Robbie and Ty moved to aid Eurytus and Maron who were fighting with three Persians. By the time they arrived, Maron had been killed. Robbie stepped over Maron's dead body, drew back the Sword of William Wallace, and beheaded the man fighting with Eurytus.

He turned to Eurytus and said, "Let's make them pay!" Then he, Ty, and Eurytus dispatched the other two Persians.

Joe and Nick now engaged two Persians of their

own. As they were fighting, Nick tripped over a dead body and fell on his back. As he fell, the Persian tried to leap on top of him.

Nick planted the hilt of his sword on the ground next to him, the point jutting upward. The Persian skewered himself on the blade. Nick then rose, freed his sword from the dead Persian, and joined Joe. He struck the Persian fighting Joe with a slicing blow to his right side. Simultaneously, Joe hit the man with a slicing blow to his left side. They ended up cutting the Persian into three pieces.

But Joe had been wounded in the fight; his left arm was covered in blood. Nick checked it. The artery hadn't been cut, but the muscle was damaged.

"Joe," he said, "you need to get out of here and get that worked on."

Joe replied, "I'm not going anywhere until this is finished."

Billy and Jeff were struggling with two Persians and were having trouble. Jeff appeared to have a leg injury, but it wasn't slowing him down. He rained blow after blow with the Sword of Solomon upon the Persian. Finally, he prevailed and ended it with a thrust to the heart.

He then turned to help Billy, whose head and face were now covered in blood and sweat. Billy appeared to be fighting blindly because of the blood flowing from his head into his eyes. Jeff rushed to his side, and together they finished off the Persian.

The fighting continued for over an hour. There were hundreds of Persian bodies covering the ground, along with dozens of Spartans. The phalanx was a mess. They had tried to retreat and regroup, but there were not enough of them left to fill the gap between the rock walls.

All they could do was slow the Persians down long enough to give the Spartans behind them enough time to kill the ones that broke through.

Joe was tired but not exhausted. He and the others continued defending each other and their Spartan brothers, fighting valiantly. Joe kept a watch on Leonidas as much as he could. The king was in the thick of it, a killing machine.

As Joe and Nick finished pulling their latest kill out of the way, Joe looked up to see three Persians suddenly attack the king simultaneously. Without thought or discussion, the brothers rushed to aid the king. They dispatched one of the Persians as soon as they got to him and watched as Leonidas skewered the one he was fighting. As he tried to pull his sword from the body of the Persian he had just killed, the remaining one raised his sword to strike at the king's head.

At the same time, Joe and Nick leaped into action. Joe grabbed Leonidas around the waist and tackled him, while Nick blocked the descending sword of the Persian with the Sword of Michael the Archangel. Immediately upon contact with the Persian's sword, it burst into flame.

Joe rolled off Leonidas and thrust Excalibur through the heart of the stunned Persian, causing a gaping, fatal wound.

The battle paused as all the combatants turned to stare at the sight of Nick's flaming sword in the quickly descending darkness. The Persians began fearfully yelling for retreat and ran as one through the gap in the boulder wall back to their camp. The battle was over, at least for today.

Joe helped Leonidas to his feet with his undamaged right arm. The king looked at Joe and then Nick, who was holding high the still-flaming Sword of St. Michael.

He said to them, "Well done, men. Help me find Alpheus, and we will meet in my tent. We have much to discuss." Joe and Nick walked with him to find Alpheus.

As they walked, Joe saw Robbie and Ty raise their swords and shout a victory cry. Almost simultaneously, Jeff and Billy did the same and ran to where they were standing. They hugged each other and took a knee, breathing hard.

Joe knew the adrenaline was still coursing through their veins, as it was his. It would soon start to subside, allowing exhaustion to set in. He was sure his cousins wouldn't be talking about what had just happened. Like him, they wouldn't want to relive the horrors they had just experienced and witnessed. There would be no rehashing of "great plays" or "game-saving heroics". This hadn't been a football game; it had been war, and it had been brutal.

Once they had the king settled in his tent, Joe sat on a nearby rock. Almost as if by magic, a soldier appeared by his side and began bandaging his wound. He looked over at Nick, who was sitting on another rock, looking at his sword. Its blade had just returned to normal.

Joe started to say something to him when the other cousins arrived at the tent led by Eurytus. They greeted each other with great hugs and powerful pats on the back. All except for Joe, who was still being bandaged. He offered a fist-bump and broad grin to each of them.

"Glad to see all of you made it out alive," he said.

Before anyone could answer him, Alpheus exited the tent and announced, "The king will see you now." He held the tent flap open for them as they entered, then joined them inside.

The king addressed the cousins. "Today, I have witnessed heroic displays of valor and bravery. We have turned back the Persian army once again for the third day in a row while being outmanned thirty to one.

"You six men and your swords made the difference. I witnessed your bravery and skill. I witnessed your fidelity to your brethren, and two of you saved my life. I am forever grateful and in your debt. You have met the requirement for the release of my sword into your hands, but I cannot honor it."

Joe was devastated. Jeff spoke up. "Great King Leonidas. In our time you are revered. There are monuments to you and your men upon the hillock where the battle just took place. You are the standard for military leadership, and your battle strategy is taught in the most prestigious military academies in the world. Most of all, they revere you as a pillar of virtue, valor, and honor. How is it that today you choose to dishonor yourself by refusing to follow through on your agreement with us?"

Leonidas responded, "I don't have to explain my actions to anyone, but because of your efforts here today, I will do so now. It is plain to me that I need my sword for further battles. Having turned the Persians back this day gives me hope that we can win tomorrow and the day after.

"We will request reinforcements from Sparta. They will call upon the rest of the city-states to join the cause, and if we can hold out for a few more days, we will have all the men we need to win this war. Victory is within our grasp. I won't give up my sword while victory is still possible, you may have it when I'm dead."

Joe responded. "King Leonidas, please listen. What happened today, this victory wasn't supposed to happen this way. History records that you and all your valiant men died here in this narrow pass today. The only reason that didn't happen is that we intervened with the Swords of

Valor. If you had given us the sword when we first approached you, history would have run its course, and you and all your men would be dead heroes, forever enshrined in the memory of men. But that has now changed. What has not changed is that you will fall. You will be defeated. We wish that were not so, but it is the truth, it is history."

Robbie then followed Joe, "In fact, history states that the Persians have obtained information from a sheepherder they captured about the alternate way through the mountains. They have split their forces and intend to come up behind you with one army, while the other will attack from the front. They will trap you between them, and none of you will escape. This is history. This will happen."

"It will do them no good," Leonidas dismissed Robbie's argument with a wave of his hand. "The local Phokian contingent will repel them. Our flank is safe."

"I'm afraid you're wrong," Robbie insisted. "Xerxes will send his Immortal,s and they will defeat the Phokians. Time is running out, and you need to give us your sword quickly or history in our time may come to an end. Xerxes will have the final, irrevocable victory. Don't let your victory today turn into ultimate defeat for all mankind."

The king said nothing. He just stared at his sword, looking thoughtful.

After a few moments, Ty spoke, "King Leonidas, if I may, please allow me to recite from the inscription on the monument that will be built on this spot to honor you and your men. It will illustrate for you how all men will remember your defeat, and the impact it will have on humanity for thousands of years to come."

Leonidas said, "Proceed."

Ty started. "These are the words written by the

Greek poet Simonides on the Kolonos hillock memorial dedicated to you and your men. 'Go tell the Spartans, passerby, that here, obedient to their laws we lie. Of those who died at Thermopylae renowned is the fortune, noble the fate: Their grave's an altar, their memorial our mourning, their fate our praise. Such a shroud neither decay nor all-conquering destroy. This sepulcher of brave men has taken the high renown of Hellas for its fellow occupant, as witness Leonidas, Sparta's king, who left behind a great memorial of valor, everlasting renown.'

"This, oh great king, is your legacy! It is a legacy of honor and valor. One of glorious defeat that outshines the greatest victories in history. Let this future stand. Let your men live out their glorious fate. Don't succumb to vanity and delusions of grandeur. Release your sword into our hands so we may prove the truth of all we have told you, so your glorious memory will be preserved along with a bright future for all mankind. Xerxes will be defeated forever."

Leonidas looked thoughtful. Finally, he said to the cousins, "Yes. You may take my sword to prove to me what you say is true. If you can do as you say, you may keep it. If you can't, you will return my sword to me and join us tomorrow at dawn to share the fate you have declared for us all. Either way, you will either have been proven to be men of truth and will have what you seek, or liars that will be remembered as heroes. What say you?"

Jeff answered for the cousins. "We accept your conditions, King Leonidas. Meet us at the large fire at the center of the camp. Bring your sword with you, and we will prove our claims beyond any doubt. You and all your men may watch."

"Agreed," King Leonidas replied.

Then he turned to Alpheus. "Assemble the men

around the fire. We have seen that these are men of valor. We will now see if they are also men of virtue."

Alpheus left to assemble the troops, and the cousins bowed to King Leonidas and followed him.

When the cousins and the troops were assembled around the now-roaring blaze, the king appeared. He walked slowly from his tent to the fire, handed his sword to Jeff, and took his place next to Alpheus. The king addressed the assembled group of men.

"Today, we have been victorious. Tonight, we may witness the confirmation of our future fate. We will always fight to the end with valor and virtue. May our swords sing on the morrow."

He turned to Jeff and ordered, "Begin."

Joe knew what Jeff had planned. They would perform the return process, and if they were successful, they would depart in a flash of very impressive, pure, white light that would give Leonidas all the validation he sought. They would also have the sword. Joe hoped it would all go well one last time.

Jeff took the sword from Leonidas in his left hand, then spoke to the assembled group. "We will now prove that we have spoken the truth with virtue! We will demonstrate that all we have told the king will come to pass. When you witness the flames consume us, you will see us no more. But remember that on this day, you have all secured your place in history as men of valor."

He then spoke to his cousins. "Gentlemen, raise your Swords of Valor."

The cousins complied.

"Now bring them slowly together."

They once again complied.

When the swords touched, nothing happened. They stood still as statues holding their position. Joe knew that if the process failed this time, they would be branded as liars and would join the doomed forces of Leonidas in their fate at sunrise. Joe wondered what Jeff would do. He remembered the lesson about trusting the swords, but the swords seemed to be betraying that trust now.

Then, slowly, the Sword of Leonidas rose! Joe couldn't be sure, but it looked as if it was rising of its own accord. Jeff's expression seemed to reflect the shock that Joe was feeling. When it met the other six Swords of Valor, a huge flash of light enveloped the cousins, and they disappeared.

Leonidas, Alpheus, Eurytus, and the other men covered their eyes to protect them from the blinding light. When they could see clearly once again, they saw that the cousins were gone.

Leonidas turned to Eurytus and said, "Bring me the sword of your brother, Maron. I wish to use the sword of a hero of Sparta when I face death tomorrow." Then he slowly retreated to his tent to contemplate all that had transpired.

CHAPTER ELEVEN

THE FOURTH RETURN

The prophet sat near the fire by the river, waiting once again for the return of his charges. He had been working feverishly in the Keeping Room monitoring the cousins, as well as making calculations and preparations for the Final Process. He had almost all that was needed to assure successful completion of the mission.

He had used the quantum computer to analyze and confirm all the virtues of the Swords of Valor and had compared them with the corresponding evils of the Swords of Terror. He believed that with the acquisition of the Sword of Leonidas, they would succeed in forever extinguishing the threat that the Swords of Terror posed to humanity.

The prophet had done everything he could think of to validate his understanding, but as always, when dealing with things of a spiritual nature, nothing was guaranteed. The disturbing feedback from the quantum diagnostics during this last mission indicated much death and a troubling impact on the timeline.

Suddenly, a brilliant flash of white light blinded him. The fire was extinguished, and standing around the fire pit in the moonlight were his two sons and his four nephews. He was overjoyed! They had returned; all of them! He rushed to them, and they rushed to him.

Before he could ask, Jeff knelt before his uncle and said, "Prophet, I deliver unto you the Sword of Leonidas, given to us by his own hand."

He extended the sword, handle first, to the prophet. The prophet accepted it. Jeff then stood and returned to the others.

The prophet examined the sword. It was worn and battle-scarred. There were still traces of blood around the hilt. The blade was made of bronze and had intricate engravings on both sides, depicting two leopards attacking. This confirmed that it, undoubtedly, was the Sword of Leonidas.

The prophet looked up and saw that the cousins wore full Spartan battle armor. It was also apparent that Joe had been seriously injured. His left arm hung limply at his side and was covered in blood. Billy also had significant wounds to his head. Jeff had a gash on his right thigh.

Nick, Ty, and Robbie were mostly uninjured but had many scratches and bruises. Blood, hopefully not their own, stained their clothes. They were all drenched in sweat and dirt. He was concerned and puzzled. Why such extensive wounds? Why were they wearing the armor? Had they had to compete for the sword, or had they been forced to enter the battle?

He spoke to the heroes, his tone one of worry. "Is everyone all right? Does anyone need medical attention?"

Joe answered for them. "We are all right. We may be bloodied, but we are not beaten!"

The prophet looked doubtful but nodded. "If you're sure you're all right, I have many questions, and we need to debrief immediately and prepare for the Final Process. Bring the armor with you."

The heroes helped each other back to the Keeping Room.

"I'm exhausted," Nick sighed as they walked, "but I'm glad we've completed all four assignments successfully!"

Joe nodded. "I didn't dream it was possible."

"I'm just grateful we all survived," Ty said.

"And that we're together again back on Grandpa's land," Nick added.

"I've never been so grateful to see this old barn!" Robbie said. He touched the barn door almost reverently as he and Ty entered.

Ty looked thoughtful. "It's strange. Coming home feels more magnificent than the battle victory, doesn't it?"

The others murmured their agreement as they entered the Keeping Room, laid the armor beside the glass case, and returned the swords to their respective resting spots within it. The case now contained all ten Swords of Valor. Each of them felt a sense of pride in their accomplishments.

Continuing to the round table, they took their seats alongside the prophet. Immediately, the image of their grandfather appeared and spoke.

"Welcome home, my heroes! I see you have recovered the Sword of Leonidas, and that we are now in possession of all ten Swords of Valor. Well done. I also observe that some of you have received significant wounds. All of you show some evidence of a struggle. Haven't the swords demonstrated to you their healing powers yet?"

Billy answered, "Yes, Grandfather, they did. But a lot happened after the battle. We didn't even think to heal each other."

"Understood," the image replied. "Use them to heal each other. But you must use a sword other than the one carried by the wounded person. You can only be healed by the sword of another. That is one of the basics of virtue. We use our own strength to heal the wounds of others. When you are healed, we will continue with the debriefing."

When the heroes rose, the prophet stood, too. Although their wounds didn't seem to be fatal, he was worried about them.

"Are you coming, too, Uncle Rob?" Joe asked. "I think we've got this."

"Yeah," Nick grinned. "We've done this before."

Smiling fondly at the young men, the prophet shook his head. "Mind if I watch? I've never seen a sword heal a wound before."

"That is pretty ironic, isn't it?" Joe laughed.

They entered the room where the swords were kept and gathered them from the glass case once more.

"Okay, let's start with Joe; he's wounded the worst," said Nick, holding the Sword of Michael the Archangel in his hand. "Do you guys remember how this worked?"

"I don't know," said Billy. "I just had the idea to hold the sword against the wound, and it healed it."

Jeff replied, "Same here. Let's just do what we did before and see what happens."

They all agreed that that was a wise choice. Joe sat down, and Nick held Joe's arm away from his body. He placed the blade of his sword flat against the laceration on Joe's bicep. Immediately upon touching the wound, the sword began to glow. Joe winced slightly and closed his eyes. After a couple of seconds, Nick removed the sword. As the cousins watched, the gash shrank and closed, and

SEASON OF THE SWORDS

after a few seconds, it had healed completely.

"Amazing!" the prophet marveled.

Joe flexed his arm and announced, "Good as new! Thanks, Nick."

Nick replied, "No worries, bro, anytime."

They proceeded to treat the rest of the wounds they'd obtained in the battle, each one using their sword to heal their own brother. They thought that was most appropriate, given that they had fought and been wounded fighting side-by-side with their brothers.

When all were healed, they returned the swords to the case and reassembled around the table.

The image immediately addressed them. "The prophet and I observed a few disturbing and significant quantum fluctuations during our tracking of this assignment. Please enlighten us as to what transpired so we may understand and input the information for analysis."

Billy reported first, sharing the details of their arrival, spotting the camp and deciding to help the wounded to gain access to the camp. Then he added, "Joe worked on a man named Eurytus who had sustained a potentially mortal wound to his side. He used his sword to cauterize the wound, then cleaned him up. Later, while we were speaking with the commander, Eurytus walked up and announced he was returning to battle. He was fully healed from his wounds. As you guessed, Grandfather, Excalibur had healed him."

The image interjected, "That was the first major quantum fluctuation we observed. Except for Jeff's sword, all the swords' quantum activities spiked rapidly then fell just as quickly. Please continue."

Robbie jumped in. "We asked to be taken to King Leonidas. Eurytus took us to General Alpheus. He

221

demanded that we dress appropriately to speak with the king, so we collected armor from the dead. It seems Leonidas did not meet with anyone on the battlefield unless they evidenced their willingness to fight by wearing armor.

"Then we were presented to the king. We told him that we were there on a special assignment of utmost importance and needed his permission to take his sword back with us. He demanded proof, so we raised our swords. They appeared at once and softly glowed. We explained about the swords, but he challenged us.

"He stated that although the swords might be imbued with valor and virtue, that didn't mean that we were virtuous men, nor that we possessed valor. He agreed to give us his sword on the condition that we stand with him in battle against the Persians that very day and prove ourselves worthy. He said that he and Alpheus would be watching us closely, and if we didn't display courage and valor, Alpheus would kill us himself. They assigned us to fight behind the phalanx."

Joe spoke next. "We were given our instructions by Eurytus and broke up into teams of two. Brother stood with brother. They positioned us behind the middle of the phalanx. When the Persians attacked, the line held firm for the first two waves. After that, the Persians began breaking through the phalanx. We did what we had to do to survive and to prove ourselves to Leonidas and Alpheus. We killed many Persians with our swords. We protected each other. We avenged the death of Maron and saved the life of Leonidas." Joe stopped, unable to go on.

The prophet gave him a moment, then spoke. "While I was observing the mission, there were indications of widespread death and suffering. I hoped it was just because of your proximity to the battle, and that your swords were picking up the quantum emanations. We never thought you would have to participate in the battle. From what I have heard so far, it sounds like you had no other choice. Please, continue."

Nick resumed the description. "Joe and I saw that three Persians were attacking Leonidas. He was holding his own, but he was in trouble. We ran to his aid. As we got there, Leonidas killed one of the Persians with a thrust of his sword. I killed the first one I came to. Leonidas's sword was stuck in the Persian he had just killed, and he struggled to remove it. The remaining Persian was raising his sword to deliver a death blow to the king when Joe leaped forward and tackled Leonidas to the ground.

"As the blade of the Persian was descending on them, I blocked the blow with my sword, which then burst into flame. As the Persian stood there in shock, Joe jumped up and finished him off. The sight of the flaming sword lighting up the darkness caused panic among the Persians, and they retreated. The battle was over, and the Spartans had won."

"So, you saved Leonidas's life? He did not die that day in battle?" asked the prophet. "This seems to be the cause of the significant timeline disturbance I observed. We will need to analyze this quickly. Computer, begin the analysis utilizing the information we just received!" he commanded.

Jeff continued the story. "We then gathered at the tent of Leonidas, expecting that he would now give us his sword, and we could be on our way. But based on the victory we had won earlier, he was now filled with the hope that they could ultimately prevail and win total victory over the Persians, driving them from the land. He told us that he would not honor his agreement and that he needed his sword to fight again.

"We revealed as much as we could remember about how the day should have gone according to our history. We told him that he wasn't supposed to have won the battle and that the Persians were already on their way to flank them and surround them. They would die tomorrow. He still didn't comply."

Ty added his perspective. "At this point, I remembered the verses from the inscription on the memorial at Kolonos. The sword brought it clearly to my mind, and I recited it word for word, hoping to give some perspective to Leonidas about his ultimate place in history if he followed through with his fate and released his sword to us.

"I don't know if it was that or the point that Jeff had made about letting Xerxes have the last final victory if we failed, but he compromised with us. He said if we could prove that all we said was true, we could have the sword. If we failed to convince him, we would have to join them in the morning to fight against the Persians once again.

"We figured the best way to convince him was to perform the return process successfully. So, we, Leonidas, Alpheus, and all the men gathered around the fire in the middle of the camp, and Leonidas gave Jeff his sword before we started the return process. However, the process didn't work."

Billy now finished the tale. "We were standing around the fire, as still as possible, holding our swords together waiting for the process to start. It didn't. Then I saw Jeff raise his left arm, holding the Sword of Leonidas. He slowly touched the sword to the others, and we were enveloped in the bright flash of light and returned."

The prophet nodded, looking thoughtful. "That is one amazing tale. You certainly exhibited personal and collective bravery and valor, but do you realize that you have significantly changed history?"

"We do," Joe replied as the others nodded.

"But what else were we supposed to do?" asked Robbie. "You heard what Leonidas said. We had to agree with him. We had no other choice. To recover the sword, we had to fight alongside them. We had to prove ourselves. We did that and ended up with the sword. It was the only way!"

Joe added, "We couldn't steal it from him as that would have violated the rules and resulted in us bringing back a worthless sword. If we had let him die, we could have risked losing it, or we could have died before we could return. We took the flaming of Nick's sword as confirmation that we had done the right thing for the right reasons, and all would turn out well. If we are wrong, please enlighten us as to why that is so, and what we might have done differently."

The image of their grandfather replied. "We are not saying that you made the wrong decision. Regardless of the appropriateness of your choice, the fact remains that history has been changed. The quantum computer's analysis of history as it now stands shows that the Battle of Thermopylae lasted for four days, not three. The Spartans were, as you revealed to Leonidas, outflanked and surrounded on the fourth day, and every Spartan lost their life that day except your friend Eurytus.

"When he realized all was lost, he returned to Sparta on Alpheus's orders. Eurytus related a tale to the elders of the bravery of the Spartans in their defeat and of the intervention of the gods. He told them that the gods sent Achilles, Ajax, and the other heroes of the Trojan War to fight side by side with them in defeating the Persians on the third day of battle. He told them that the gods gave the heroes healing powers and flaming swords and that one of them had healed him. When the battle was won, the heroes departed for Olympus with Leonidas's sword as their reward.

"That is just one example of how you have changed history. The story of the Battle of Thermopylae has now changed forever, and you have changed history by one day. You added an additional day to the lives of the Spartans you helped to save, and to the life of Leonidas. We don't know what the impact of this will be on the timeline, or on the calculations for the Final Process. Anything can happen in a day. Anything!"

"I will need to spend some time working with the quantum computer to assess the impact," announced the prophet. "You guys head back to the house and regroup. When I have completed my work, I will come for you, and we will reconvene by the river. Before you leave, put the Spartan armor in the storage room and take your swords with you into the house."

Humbled and a little worried, the cousins did as they'd been instructed. The storage room contained many other historical items that had been collected over the centuries by the Guardians. There was a collection of Roman armor, a Civil War uniform, an ax that appeared to be Viking-related, and a possible crusader or Templar flag stained with blood, along with many other strange and interesting items.

"Wow," said Ty, "I sure could have used this stuff for show-and-tell when I was growing up! We'll have to spend more time here... some other day." They laughed and returned to the house.

They cleaned up and ate, then settled around the fire in the family room. Now healed and reasonably rested, they had time to compare notes about their experience. Robbie turned to Jeff. "How did you know that we needed to add Leonidas's sword to ours to initiate the return process? I would have never thought of that."

Jeff replied, "I was as puzzled as you guys standing there. I wracked my brain to think of what could have happened. While I was thinking of it, my left arm started to rise of its own accord. I didn't interfere with what was happening and let it continue. I assume it was the influence of the swords. They knew that either we needed more power, or that whatever virtue was inherent in Leonidas's sword was necessary to complete the process. Just another lesson, I suppose. We must always trust the swords."

"I think we also learned something else on this assignment," Joe added. "Not only do we need to trust the swords, but we need to act. We need to obey the leading of the swords. Trust, obey, and take action."

During their conversation together, they talked about the various aspects of the assignments they had been on, each telling a different fact or observation. What they didn't talk about was the killing. That was something they would individually need to process for a very long time.

CHAPTER TWELVE

THE FINAL PROCESS

———— ✺ ————

The prophet entered the family room carrying the four Swords of Valor they had brought from the past. He said, "It is time, gentlemen. Collect your swords, and let's head down to the fire pit. The Final Process of the destruction of the Swords of Terror will begin shortly."

The cousins ran to the Keeping room and hastily retrieved their swords, then followed the prophet to the river. When they reached the fire pit, the prophet looked at each of them. His expression was somber.

"As you know, I've spent some time working with the quantum computer assessing our assumptions and calculations. Your actions at Thermopylae have resulted in some timeline changes that have pushed our schedule a bit. So far, we have seen some significant ripples in the fabric of time and the quantum foam. We can't yet predict the eventual total impact. We are fortunate that the day you changed was so far back in history, because it will take a few hours before it has an impact here. If you had changed something significant on your first assignment in 1940, the ripples would have already been felt. Still, we need to hurry. We must complete the Final Process before those ripples reach our time. Let's get this done as quickly as possible."

The heroes put down the swords, lit the fire once again, and waited for it to start burning fiercely. The prophet felt anxious and a little excited as he contemplated the coming process. Soon, this would all be a memory and the world would be safe.

When the fire was ready, the prophet addressed the team of heroes. "What we will be trying to accomplish is the destruction of the Swords of Terror. We now have all ten of the Swords of Valor, and the four of them you recovered are at the absolute height of their power. We also have more virtuous energy than ever before, and we have all the swords together in one place. Today is the day of victory.

"Tonight, we will attempt to completely obliterate the source of much of the evil in the world; the division, the hatred, the fear, and the envy. We will effectively disarm the Apostles of Azazel and thwart their plans to subjugate the world. Of course, we can't change their hardened hearts. That is above our pay grade, but we can take away their power. We can cripple their ability to implement their plans. Let's get to it."

The prophet instructed the heroes to lay the swords around the fire with their blades in the flames. They followed his instructions, and the swords were finally appropriately arranged and positioned precisely.

When the prophet was content with the arrangement of the swords, he called the heroes to him. "I have researched all the information available to the Guardians regarding the virtues inherent in each of our swords and all the evils imparted to the Swords of Terror. I have been as precise as possible and believe that each of the Swords of Valor corresponds well to a specific counterpart sword.

"I will call the name of the first Sword of Valor after reciting the Initiation Protocol. It should arise of its own accord and float freely over the fire. It will summon or 'sing' to its counterpart Sword of Terror, and if all goes well, that sword should appear.

"The Sword of Valor will oppose the Sword of Terror, and if victorious, the result will be the dissipation and destruction of the evil sword. The Sword of Valor will then return to its proper time and its rightful owner for its use at the time of their greatest victory. The process should then proceed of its own accord without our intervention. One by one, each Sword of Valor will rise and call to its evil counterpart and then destroy it.

"When the process is complete, we should be standing here by ourselves, and out of a job. As a reminder, I have here a list of the swords that will be involved in the Final Process. As you are observing, try to identify each one so we can keep track. We will want to compare notes with the quantum computer afterward to make sure that we have accounted for all of them."

The prophet hesitated, then continued, "Now, mind you, I have never seen this process work. It has been planned for centuries by the Guardians and thoroughly modeled by the quantum computer. I'm confident it will succeed, but nothing is guaranteed. After I call for the first sword to rise, we will retreat a safe distance away to observe. I don't know what kind of fallout there may be. Do you all completely understand?"

The heroes nodded.

"Excellent, let's get this done," directed the prophet. "We only have a few hours before the ripples in the time stream start to impact us. I will now begin the Final Process by reciting the Initiation Protocol."

"Hear me, oh Swords of Valor!
Rise, for the day is at hand.
Ancient evil has once again wakened,
And terror now threatens the land.

Rise and display all your virtues.
Your power now use to defend.
The world now has need of your service.
The rise of this terror must end

Rise and show forth your glory!
Rise and have victory today!
Fulfill your valorous purpose,
So that virtue will triumph this day."

As the prophet finished reading the Initiation Protocol, the fire rose higher. He then called out the name of the first Sword of Valor.

"The Sword of St. Peter, rise!"

At the prophet's command, the Sword of St. Peter the Apostle rose from its place near the fire, hovering about ten feet above the flames. It began to spin, slowly at first, then with increasing speed. Another sword appeared opposite it above the fire, spinning at the same velocity. Immediately, both swords stopped spinning.

The prophet whispered, "I recognize that sword. It is the Sword of Cain, the first sword ever created."

The Sword of St. Peter struck the Sword of Cain with a resounding clang. The Sword of Cain quivered for a moment, vibrating to the blow. It began to turn black from the tip to the handle. Finally, it turned into dust and crumbled, the remains falling into the fire, where they were consumed.

The virtues of reverence and brotherly love had defeated the evils of envy and murder. The Sword of Peter then faded from view and returned to its proper place in time and to its rightful owner.

The next sword rose of its own accord. This was the Sword of Roland, Durandal. Slowly, it rose ten feet above the fire. It began to revolve in the same manner as the Sword of St. Peter. Soon, its opposing Sword of Terror appeared spinning opposite it. The swords stopped turning and faced off.

The prophet again whispered. "That is the Sword of Herod the Great."

The Sword of Roland approached the Sword of Herod, which retreated as if afraid. Durandal approached and struck it multiple times with mighty blows. In only a few moments, the Sword of Herod turned black and crumbled into dust, falling into the fire, where it was consumed.

Temperance and diligence had defeated the evils of bloodlust and sloth. The Sword of Roland then faded from view and returned to its proper place in time and to its rightful owner.

Next followed the rise of the Sword of Tristan, Curtana. The sword assumed its position above the fire and began to spin. Its opposite Sword of Terror appeared spinning across from it. The swords both stopped their rotation and faced off.

This time, the Sword of Attila the Hun attacked the Sword of Tristan, sensing an advantage. The Sword of Tristan absorbed the blow from the Sword of Attila and responded with a mighty strike of its own. The Sword of Attila fell backward. It slowly became black as night and quickly crumbled into tiny particles floating down into the fire, where they were consumed.

The virtues of mercy and meekness had defeated the evils of cruelty and anger. The Sword of Tristan then faded from view and returned to its proper place in time and to its rightful owner.

The prophet observed every detail intently. Three of the Swords of Terror had been accounted for and had been destroyed.

The next sword to rise was the Sword of Joan of Arc. It, too, took its place above the fire and began to call to its opposite Sword of Terror. The sword responded to the call, and both swords stopped spinning and faced off.

The prophet murmured again, "That is the Sword of Ivan the Terrible."

The Sword of Joan of Arc waited for the Sword of Ivan the Terrible to approach. As it was drawing back to strike, the Sword of Joan of Arc struck a tremendous, slashing blow, shattering the Sword of Terror into fragments. It turned black and floated into the fire and was consumed.

The virtues of self-control and chastity had defeated the evils of depravity and lust. The Sword of Joan of Arc then faded from view and returned to its proper place in time and to its rightful owner.

Joyeuse, the Sword of Charlemagne, rose, took its place above the fire and called to its opposite Sword of Terror. It appeared, spinning in tune to the song of Joyeuse.

When the swords stopped spinning, Robbie whispered, "That's the golden Sword of Midas, isn't it?"

The prophet nodded as he watched Joyeuse swiftly approach the Sword of Midas and gently touch it with its tip. The Sword of Midas immediately turned into lead. Then it became a black shadow of itself, and the whole shadow drifted into the fire and was consumed.

The virtues of generosity and ethics had defeated the evils of ambition and greed with the slightest touch. The Sword of Charlemagne then faded from view and returned to its proper place in time and to its rightful owner.

The Sword of William Wallace rose and took its position. The great two-handed sword spun wildly, calling out to its opponent to appear. It didn't come right away. When it did, it immediately stopped spinning and attacked.

The prophet couldn't be sure which of the Swords of Terror had appeared. It should be the Sword of Nero, but it was hard to tell, because the swords were madly exchanging blow after blow. After a few minutes, the battle slowed, and the prophet could see it was indeed the Sword of Nero, and it was weakening.

Finally, the Sword of William Wallace struck a final mighty blow, and the Sword of Nero hung still and unmoving in the air. It gradually crumbled into hundreds of small black pieces, floated slowly into the fire, and was consumed.

The virtues of persistence and fortitude had overcome the evils of fear and corruption. The Sword of William Wallace disappeared and returned to its rightful owner and proper place in time.

Next, the Sword of Solomon rose majestically into the air. It hung for a moment in the proper position, then began to rotate slowly and cautiously, gaining speed until it was a blur. It continued until its opposing sword appeared, then it slowed its rotation and stood still and straight. The two swords stood unmoving for a few moments then began to circle each other.

The sword facing off with the Sword of Solomon was the Sword of Nebuchadnezzar, the swords of the two greatest kings of all history. They assessed each other and then attacked simultaneously. They rained blow after blow, neither showing signs of stopping.

Then, without warning, Solomon's sword sliced through the Sword of Nebuchadnezzar, cutting it in two. The handle crumbled first, as it was made of a mixture of iron and clay. Next was the base of the sword, made of iron. The lower half of the blade was next, as it was made of silver, and finally the top and tip of the sword crafted of gold. When all of it had turned black, it floated into the fire to be consumed.

The virtues of wisdom and faith had defeated the evils of idolatry and gluttony. The Sword of Solomon then faded from view and returned to its proper place in time and to its rightful owner.

The next sword to rise was the mighty Sword of Leonidas. It moved to its position swiftly and began spinning violently and feverishly. It called for a long time to its foe, the Sword of Genghis Khan.

Finally, with a rush of wind, the Sword of Terror appeared and was spinning as feverishly as the Sword of Leonidas. The prophet only saw it for a second before it attacked. The two swords began slashing and thrusting at one another. The Sword of Genghis Khan appeared to be driving the Sword of Leonidas backward farther and farther, almost beyond the flames of the fire. The Sword of Leonidas advanced and kept pounding the Sword of Terror.

With a final heroic effort, the Sword of Leonidas battered the Sword of Genghis Khan with multiple strikes. It shattered into fragments that first turned red, then faded to black, and then fell quickly into the fire and were consumed.

The virtues of bravery and prudence had defeated

the evils of wrath and licentiousness. The Sword of Leonidas departed to return to its rightful owner and its proper place in time.

The prophet observed that only two swords remained. He was glad to know that this would be over soon.

The sword Excalibur rose next. It rose and hovered, taking its place above the fire. The beautiful, legendary Sword of both Arthur and Melchizedek, benevolent and exemplary kings, began its calling spin. It was answered with a whirlwind, threatening to extinguish the fire. Dust and leaves and embers of the fire rose to join the spinning sword Excalibur.

Then, suddenly, in a burst of red flame, the opposite Sword of Terror appeared. The prophet had feared this moment. He recognized the Sword of the Prince of Persia, a demonic spirit alive with red flames that represented the territorial spirit of ancient Persia and other nations. It was a violent and powerful entity, inspiring many evil deeds throughout the centuries. It immediately attacked Excalibur with vicious aggression. Excalibur bravely fought back and held its own. The battle went on for more than ten minutes.

The prophet was worried for the first time. He could not tell if Excalibur would prevail.

The fire below the battle was dying, and the demon sword was burning brighter. At this moment, the Sword of Michael the Archangel burst into flame. It flew quickly to join the battle. The space above the fire was filled with flashing flames of red and purest white. The sounds were deafening as the demon sword fought against the sword of the archangel and the sword Excalibur.

Finally, the flames of the demon sword began to die out. Excalibur and the archangel's sword stepped up their efforts, and then, with a mighty blow from the Sword of Michael, the Sword of the Prince of Persia was demolished.

It lay in pieces floating in the air above the now brightly-burning blaze. Hanging there, it tried to put itself back together as the two Swords of Valor waited and watched. Slowly, the pieces of the sword floated down into the fire, which erupted in bright red flames that turned quickly to bluish-white. At last, the sword was consumed.

The virtues of benevolence and love combined with the virtues of justice and courage were enough to defeat the deadly evils of perdition and confusion.

The prophet watched as Excalibur and the Sword of Michael the Archangel faded out of view, returning to their rightful owners and proper places in time.

There were no more Swords of Valor left around the fire. They had all been used to defeat nine of the Swords of Terror. That was a problem.

"What happens now?" Joe asked. "There's still one Sword of Terror left, right?"

The prophet had accounted for all the Swords of Valor, but only nine of the Swords of Terror. The Final Process hadn't worked. The remaining Sword of Terror was the one he feared the most. The Sword of Goliath of Gath, the giant descended from the Nephilim from the dawn of history.

"Yes," the prophet replied. "Come. We must consult the computer."

They ran to the Keeping Room, quickly taking their seats at the table. The image of their grandfather appeared and spoke, "I see we have a problem. A giant problem."

CHAPTER THIRTEEN

THE FIRST VIRTUE:
FINDING A SOLUTION

Agreeing with the computer's assessment, the prophet replied, "Yes, we do have a giant problem. Two of the Swords of Valor were required to defeat the Sword of the Prince of Persia. We hadn't accounted for that in our calculations, research, or quantum modeling. We must now figure out how to deal with the remaining sword. We have no Sword of Valor to counteract its influence on the world. Without that, its influence will infect mankind freely. We must find a solution and initiate the Final Process once again."

"That is so," said the image, "but to do so will require another Sword of Valor. We are not in possession of another one, and we have never been made aware of another's existence. This will take time and possibly require another assignment for the team. Prepare them for that, and I will search the data we have collected over the centuries for a clue.

"This will require significant creativity and intuition. We don't have much time. The ripples in the time stream are accelerating. I estimate it will be upon us in a matter of hours. We can't know the impact that will have on us, so we must finish the job before the impact reaches our time. After that, it will be locked in and unchangeable. Let's get to work."

"Where should we start?" asked Robbie. "Shouldn't we try to determine what virtues the sword we seek should possess to be able to counteract and vanquish the Sword of Goliath? Isn't that how the other swords were victorious over their opposite Swords of Terror?"

"Yes," replied the prophet. "That is the appropriate starting point. Computer, please tell us all the information available about Goliath and his sword. Let's examine that first so that we will understand the threat that it poses."

The image complied. "All of what we know of Goliath comes from the Jewish scriptures. We are told that he was a man who was exceptionally tall for his culture, to the point of being seen as a giant to those around him and to his enemies. Along with his height, we are told that he was also very powerful. Powerful enough to carry weapons of a size that would have been difficult for ordinary men to wield or even defend against.

"We also need to look at Goliath with spiritual eyes. He symbolizes the worldly, depraved, rebellious part of mankind that worships the power of the material world. He embodies the ongoing struggle between the forces of light and the forces of darkness. Goliath exemplifies the forces of evil throughout history who stand in full defiance and mockery of people of virtue. These are true representatives of the kingdom of evil and the spirit of darkness.

"Goliath clearly stands for those who are full of pride, self-power, and self-glory. Think of the cult of celebrity today. Have pride, egotism, and self-glory ever been on greater display than now? The spirit of Goliath is rampant. Goliath, in all his arrogance, gave Israel the

DOMENIC MELILLO

following challenge. That same challenge is valid for us today:

'If he be able to fight with me, and to kill me, then will we be your servants: but if I prevail against him, and kill him, then shall ye be our servants, and serve us.'
1 Samuel 17:9.

"This is the goal, this is the danger, and this is the intent of the Apostles of Azazel; to enslave mankind. It was true in Goliath's time and is true today."

"We've all heard the story, Grandpa," Ty said. "But I don't remember why Goliath was calling for a challenger? What was the point?"

"This was the way many wars were settled in ancient days. Instead of entire armies going to battle, they would choose a man from each side, who would then fight to the death. The victor was celebrated as if he had conquered the entire army. If we can identify a sword to stand against and defeat the Sword of Goliath, we will effectively defeat all the Apostles of Azazel.

"Your grandfather wrote something in his diary a few months before he died. He input it into the quantum computer before his passing. I will now read what he wrote.

We are coming very rapidly to the time when there will be another clash between the forces of darkness and the forces of virtue. We know God is raising up another David, and a small flock of 'sheep', soldiers for the Guardians of the Swords of Valor, who will engage in this battle. This clash will be greater than anything we have ever witnessed. In his letter to Timothy, St. Paul foretells what we must become to be part of this end-time army:

240

Thou therefore endure hardness, as a good soldier of Jesus Christ. No man that warreth entangleth himself with the affairs of this life; that he may please Him who hath chosen him to be a soldier. And if a man also strive for masteries, yet is he not crowned, except he strive lawfully. II Timothy 2:3-5.

To be victorious in this battle, preparations must be made. To become a good soldier, we must endure hardness, or suffer afflictions. We must not allow the affairs of this life to entangle us. We must strive for masteries, and we must strive lawfully. This means we must seek virtue in everything we do. We must be a part of this end-time army to defeat the giants of the spirit of darkness.

"That is where the diary entry ended," the image said. "It is obvious that your grandfather foresaw the possibility of your dilemma, as well as the struggle you now find yourselves in.

"We know that David defeated Goliath with a stone from his sling and then finished the job by cutting off Goliath's head with Goliath's own sword. That won't work for us. We are in a different battle. We are dealing with Goliath's sword, not flesh and blood. We are fighting against an inanimate object that influences men. We need to fight it with a similar object with the opposite and stronger influence.

"Unfortunately, we know relatively little about the Sword of Goliath. We can surmise that since he was a very large man, he carried a very large sword. But it couldn't have been ridiculously large. Remember, being made of the most commonly used metal at the time, bronze, it still had to be usable in battle. We can assume that it was large and heavy but not so large that David could not use it. As we know, David used it to cut off the giant's head,

"We are also told in scripture that David eventually obtained it for himself. While he was fleeing from Saul, he went to the priests at Nob to get some food. After he ate, he requested a sword. Ahimelech, the high priest, gave him the only one he had, the one used by Goliath. The scriptures tell the story.

David asked Ahimelech, 'Don't you have a spear or a sword here? I haven't brought my sword or any other weapon, because the king's mission was urgent.'

The priest replied, 'The Sword of Goliath the Philistine, whom you killed in the Valley of Elah, is here; it is wrapped in a cloth behind the ephod. If you want it, take it; there is no sword here but that one.'

David said, 'There is none like it; give it to me.' I Samuel 21:8-9

"Ahimelech retrieved it, wrapped in cloth, from behind the ephod. It had become a sacred national possession for Israel. David apparently felt comfortable using and carrying the sword, so we must assume it was of a size that he could utilize properly, although with effort. It must have also been used as a deterrent, due to its reputation and size. I think it is safe to assume that it was about the same size as the Sword of William Wallace, although heavier and possibly broader.

"David kept this sword the rest of his life. It became his sword. That is one of the reasons it has never become one of the Swords of Valor. It was tainted. It was evil. A Talmud scholar has stated that Goliath's sword, which later became the Sword of David, had marvelous powers.

"So, when exactly did the sword of Goliath become a Sword of Terror?" asked Billy. "It seems odd to me that when Great-Grandpa picked up the sword of Herod back in 1940, it vanished as soon as his hand touched it. He said that Swords of Terror cannot abide the hand of virtue. So how could David have wielded the sword and how could he have carried it his whole life?"

The image of his grandfather smiled. "Yes, very good question! And the answer is shrouded in mystery. All of the Swords of Terror are assumed to have been given to their bearers by Azazel himself and therefore were Swords of Terror from the beginning of their existence. However, the Sword of Goliath seems to have become a Sword of Terror many years after the death of David. There is more to the history of this sword, so please hold any further questions until I complete the story.

"What became of it after David died? We are familiar with the fact that many of the Israelite Tribe of Dan migrated through Europe after captivity. We have in our archives an ancient document stating that a people called the Tuatha de Danan, also known as the Tribe of Dan, had migrated into Ireland.

"The document also mentions warriors migrating to Ireland. In this ancient document, we find these Tuatha de Danan people had genealogical records dating back to the time of Noah.

"Finally, it states clearly that these people brought with them the sacred sword and spear. We now have confirmed that these objects were the sword and spear of Goliath, the giant. Sometime after the sword was brought to Ireland, it became an important ritualistic item for the Druids. It was said to have been utilized as the main implement of human sacrifice. It is very possible that it was at this time that it became one of the Swords of Terror.

"This is the last indication we have of the

whereabouts of the Sword of Goliath, although we know it eventually fell into the hands of the Apostles of Azazel.

"Does that answer your question Billy?" asked the image.

"I believe it does" Billy replied. "Thank you."

"I have given you a lot of background information," continued the image. I'm hoping it will stimulate some ideas about how we can defeat the Sword of Goliath and what we can use to do it."

Joe spoke first, "When the image read to us from Grandpa's diary, I wondered if we are the sheep that are being raised up and that you, the prophet, are the David in the entry. Could that be a clue? When I think about sheep, the first thing I think of is that they follow, they don't lead. They are completely dependent on the shepherd. They are meek and mild animals."

Nick interrupted, "Um, bro, we are anything but meek and mild!"

Ty chuckled.

"I don't mean it literally, Nick." Joe snapped. "I'm just trying to make a point here."

"Sorry," Nick looked chagrined. "Please, go on."

Joe continued, "Uncle Rob, if you are the David part of his entry, we know that David ultimately defeated Goliath. So, he is telling us that you must lead us in the defeat of Goliath's sword."

"That's logical," the prophet nodded.

Jeff added, "That leads me to some questions. What virtues are sheep symbolic of? What were the virtues of David? Those could be the virtues we need to seek to be successful."

The prophet replied, "Those are important questions, Jeff. We must determine the qualities needed to defeat the Sword of Goliath, and your questions point us in the right direction. Let's look at what evils the Sword of Goliath is imbued with and what it represents.

"First of all, it represents rebellion and blasphemy. It is the embodiment of faithlessness and pride. So, which virtues are the opposite of these evils?"

Jeff spoke up, "The opposite of rebellion would be obedience or submission. The opposite of blasphemy would be holiness or faith."

"I don't think that's exactly right," Robbie disagreed. "I think the opposite of blasphemy is bearing testimony of God."

"But testimonies stem from having faith and faith leads to holiness," Jeff argued. "When one has faith and holiness, they bear testimony."

Robbie looked thoughtful. "I see where you're going with this. Can I take it a step further? If someone is holy, they are humble and submit to God. The opposite of pride is humility."

"So, what I'm hearing," Billy chimed in, "is that we need to look for a sword that has the virtues of faith and humility, right?"

Ty frowned. "Didn't the Sword of Solomon embody faith? Why would there be two swords that represent faith?"

"What's more fundamental in the fight against evil?" Joe asked. "Without faith, the rest of it falls pretty flat, I think. So, perhaps a double dose of faith is needed."

But, don't we also need to determine if we have chosen properly? Let's confirm that David and the sheep represent those qualities, too. Grandpa, can we get that information?"

"Certainly," replied the image, "Let's just review the virtues of sheep and of David. Sheep are obedient and trusting animals. You could call them the humblest of the animal kingdom, thus the virtue of humility fits.

"What about the virtues of David? We know that he was the youngest of eight brothers and was always the reject. He was obedient to his father and to God. That shows humility. We know he accepted and owned his mistakes; he repented and asked for forgiveness. That also proves his humility. David also had great trust, or in other words, faith. To go out and fight a giant with only a sling and stones shows great faith and trust. So, he definitely had faith and humility. I believe we have confirmed that we are seeking a sword that represents those virtues. Well done!"

"Where can we find such a sword?" asked Ty. "And can we find it in time?"

"We must," the image of their grandfather responded. "There can be no doubt. We must, and will, uncover the solution to our problem. I will conduct a search to determine which sword has represented these virtues throughout history. The quantum computer has never failed to find a solution. I'm confident it will find one now. I will commence the search."

While they were waiting for the image to gather the information, Nick asked a question. "I'm wondering something. If Grandpa knew what was coming, and he suspected that we might have to deal with the Sword of Goliath, why didn't he just tell us what sword to use or to look for? That would have made all of this so much easier."

The prophet responded, "As always, this process requires you to learn. It is important that you struggle as you go through the steps necessary to find your own solutions, as you have for every assignment so far. You must own the choices you make and live with the outcomes. This is the ultimate lesson, whether you are fighting against the Apostles of Azazel, or just facing a tough challenge in life. Doing the hard work, understanding all the facts and options, and coming to your own solution is the only way you can live with the consequences, be they good or bad. Your grandfather knew that and lived by it. It was one of his greatest legacies."

The image reappeared and spoke. "The quantum computer has failed. It has not returned a reasonable solution for us to act upon."

Jeff frowned, then asked, "Can you tell us what the computer found? Let us decide the validity of the information. It could be that the logic of the computer needs some human evaluation and wisdom. Let us decide for ourselves!"

"As you wish," replied the image of their grandfather. "The quantum computer searched and only found one match, but it is not valid. The only sword that matches the criteria we selected was the fictional Sword of Don Quixote."

Jeff threw up his hands. "In what world does that make sense? I confess it's been a long time since I read the book, but as I recall, Don Quixote was about as prideful as they come, and was wildly disobedient and rebellious. Beyond that, his only real faith was in his own delusions. That his sword would represent faith and humility is absurd."

"Besides that," Billy added, "that sword's not even real, just a figment of a writer's imagination. That certainly creates a challenge. I can see why the quantum computer determined it wasn't a viable option."

Ty said, "But, Billy, we don't have any other choices. It's that or nothing. We can't get the other swords back and use them individually or together. We are defenseless.

If not the Sword of Don Quixote, then what?"

"Your grandfather would not have left us defenseless," the prophet interjected. "He obviously knew that we would have to battle the Sword of Goliath. Let's dig deeper into this. Tell us about Don Quixote," he said to the image.

"Where shall I start?"

"Please start with the story itself. Tell us about the book," suggested the prophet.

"So be it," responded the hologram. "Part I of the book was published in 1605 and was written by Miguel de Cervantes Saavedra. *Don Quixote* is often touted as the first modern novel, and many would argue that it is the greatest novel ever written. But compared with other masterpieces, *Don Quixote* is remarkably uninspiring. It is in its lowly simplicity, and the humility of the storyline, that its greatness lies."

Jeff snorted. "There's another stretch."

"Sh!" Joe hissed. "I want to hear this."

The computer continued, "It tells the story of a nobleman with chivalrous ideas far beyond his limits, infected with a madness that focused him on the bygone era of knight-errantry. Don Quixote leaves home to enact a new golden age of chivalry. He says to his loyal squire:

"Friend Sancho, I would have you know that I was born, by the will of heaven, in this iron age of ours, to revive in it an age of gold, or golden age as it is often called. I'm the man for whom dangers, great exploits, valiant deeds are reserved."

"Oh yeah, there's a bastion of humility," Jeff muttered.

The prophet glared at him, and Jeff held up his hands in surrender as the image resumed the story. "He and Sancho take to the road to right all wrongs and to do great acts of selfless service. Don Quixote sees things as they should be, not as they are. In doing so, he helps to lift people out of their 'realistic' views of themselves and eventually, they impute to themselves the same worth that Don Quixote believes they have.

"An example of this is his adoration of his Dulcinea. To herself and everyone else, she was nothing more than a lowly, common servant. To Don Quixote, she was royalty, his 'Lady'. Eventually, she grew into his view of herself. She began to see herself through his eyes and was better for it.

"He is seen as mad by the people who are committed to the reality around them and the status quo. This quote from the novel tells it all:

When life itself seems lunatic, who knows where madness lies? Perhaps to be too practical is madness. To surrender dreams, this may be madness. Too much sanity may be madness and maddest of all, to see life as it is, and not as it should be!

"His very first encounter is against windmills, which he sees as giants. Here is a quote related to this adventure:

"Destiny guides our fortunes more favorably than we could have expected. Look there, Sancho Panza, my friend, and see those thirty or so wild giants, with whom I intend to do battle and kill each and all of them, so with their stolen booty we can begin to enrich ourselves. This is noble, righteous warfare, for it is wonderfully useful to God to have such an evil race wiped from the face of the earth."

"What giants?" asked Sancho Panza.

"The ones you can see over there," answered his master, "with the huge arms, some of which are very nearly two leagues

long."

"Now look, your grace," said Sancho, "what you see over there aren't giants, but windmills, and what seems to be arms are just their sails, that go around in the wind and turn the millstone.'

"Obviously," replied Don Quixote, "you don't know much about adventures."

"Don Quixote could not be persuaded. He believed he was battling giants and that he would succeed. Regardless of the cost to himself, he would fight against greater foes in the cause of virtue and valor. Another quote is:

The wounds received in battle bestow honor, they don't take it away.

"He risked bodily harm, shame, and humiliation to do what he believed needed to be done. In the end, although most of his efforts were in vain, he succeeded in changing the lives of those around him for the better. He did accomplish his dream, even if it was for only a few people."

The image paused and added, "And that, my heroes, is the core of the tale. Take from it what you will."

"Let me see if I can summarize this for us," said Joe. "We have possibly the greatest book of all time, but also the humblest storyline. It is about a nobleman who is also humble and is committed to bringing back a golden age."

Jeff interrupted again. "Now, wait. That's highly debatable. Many have seen this book as a grand satire against the cultural climate of Cervantes's age. Nothing very humble about a satirical poke at the social status quo."

Joe nodded. "Maybe Cervantes was poking fun at the social status quo. But the beauty of true art is that each of us brings our own perspective to the interpretation. Where you see a satirical joke, I see an entirely different perspective of the story and the main character. I have been fascinated by Don Quixote for years.

"Yes, on the surface he could be seen as prideful. He is considered mad. He fights giants. But, what was it you said, Jeff? 'His only real faith was in his own delusions.' Quixote's delusions could be seen as a manifestation of his desire to create a better world; his faith that the world could become a better place if we acted like it already was.

"He esteemed valor, virtue, and honor above all else. He was ready to experience pain and suffering for his righteous cause. He was willing to be thought of as a fool, a madman, in order to live out his dream of making this world better by making the people around him see themselves as he saw them, as more than they thought they were.

"I believe that his chivalry, service to others, and his ability to see the best of and in others could only be driven by true faith and humility. Remember what Grandpa always said, 'Humility is not thinking less of yourself. It is thinking of yourself less'."

"I'm still not convinced," Jeff argued. "Humility is defined as a modest or low view of one's own importance. By its very meaning, humility is about thinking less of oneself."

"Ah, there's the difference," Joe replied. "By your own definition, humility is a low view of one's own 'importance'. That's not the same as thinking of yourself as inferior, or less than everyone else. It's realizing that your importance isn't any greater than anyone else's. A humble person can have a healthy self-esteem and a strong will to fight for what he believes in. A person with faith believes in a better future and will be willing to fight for it. Can you see the connection?

"Don Quixote envisioned a better future. Maybe they were delusions. Maybe not. But nobody could argue that he had faith in them and was willing to fight for that future. I believe he was also humble because he wasn't fighting for his own grand reward. He didn't think he was more important than anyone else. He just knew he had to act to bring the future he envisioned into existence for those around him, so they could see it, too."

Jeff still looked skeptical. "But..."

Joe shook his head, interrupting him. "We could debate this for a very long time, Jeff. But that's time we just don't have."

He turned to the others, "I don't know about you guys, but I see a pattern and a message here. I think we are on the right track. There is no way this can all be coincidental. This is where Grandpa was leading us. I feel it. It is like when I get a great lead on a story, I just know it. We have to follow this lead."

"But, Joe, this is just a story, a fictional character. It's not real," argued Robbie.

Joe looked thoughtful for a moment, then asked him, "What was one of the stories that Grandma always read to us when we were kids? Her favorite story to read to us, do you remember? She read it almost every time we were together at her house. It was *The Velveteen Rabbit*."

"Yeah," said Billy, "so what? What does that have to do with Don Quixote?"

"I get it!" cried Robbie. "It's about how a toy rabbit became a real rabbit because of the years of love and belief by the child. It wasn't real, but it became real."

"Right," agreed Joe. "What was another story that

she always read to us?"

Jeff replied, "*Pinocchio*. She loved reading *Pinocchio*."

"And?" asked Joe. "See any connection?"

"Yes," Jeff responded. "Once again, a toy, an inanimate puppet, becomes a real boy. But seriously, what are you implying here? We can't fight Goliath with rabbits and puppets. Are you suggesting that if we believe hard enough, we can make the Sword of Don Quixote become real? Come on, Joe! We are in fantasyland here! We need real answers and a real sword to get this done."

"Oh, ye of little faith," replied Joe. "I believe in Grandpa. I believe that he would not have left us unarmed. I believe that he must have known that we could figure this out."

"Joe could be onto something," added Nick. "This whole thing starts and ends with Grandpa. His fingerprints are all over it. Perhaps it's not important that we believe that Don Quixote had faith in something real, or even that he was humble. Perhaps it's only relevant that Grandpa did, and that we believe in Grandpa."

"Exactly!" Joe exclaimed. "I believe that he believed in us. I, for one, am going to ramp up my own faith in us. I intend to make his dream of putting an end to the threat of the Swords of Terror a reality."

"I wonder, do we know everything there is to know about him?" Robbie mused. "There must be some clue, something he left behind. There must be something we have overlooked. What could it be, and where would it be?"

The prophet thought for a moment, then remembered what his father had said on his deathbed about "hope in his office". That wasn't the first time he'd referenced that. Rob recalled his father had used that phrase the night he was first indoctrinated into the

Guardians, as well.

Speaking softly, the prophet said, "Throughout all the years that we have been coming to this house, the one place none of us has ever been in is Grandpa's office. You guys know that every time we came here with you as kids, you were never allowed to go to the third floor. That was where Grandpa's office was, and he wasn't supposed to be disturbed when he was up there. I think we need to look in that office and see if we can find further clues. There may be something that validates our focus and maybe points us to the next step. We are running out of time here, gentlemen, so let's do this quickly. It may just be our one last hope."

The prophet and the cousins moved quickly to the house, ascended the stairway to the third floor, and approached the thick, oak door.

Ty whispered to Robbie, "It's kind of exciting to be able to enter Grandpa's exclusive domain."

"I know," Robbie whispered back. "I never questioned the restriction. I just assumed that there were business papers and records that Grandpa didn't want disturbed. Anyway, everything else we need is on the first two floors."

Opening the door, the prophet turned on the lights and saw that the room took up the entire third-floor space. Stepping into the modestly-appointed office, he observed a row of three wide windows behind a simple wooden desk. Ancient oriental carpets like the ones in the Keeping Room covered the floor.

He also noticed that the walls were covered with framed quotes and signed pictures of famous people like Frank Sinatra and Marilyn Monroe, along with a huge picture of his parents dancing together at some huge social event. They were both laughing and looking at each other as if there was no one else in the room, although it was obvious that the floor was overcrowded.

Upon seeing the picture, the prophet remarked, "They certainly loved dancing together. They were so in love. Take note, men. This is what true love looks like."

There were file cabinets lined up along the wall on the right-hand side, and bookshelves filled to overflowing with books of all sizes and ages on the left-hand side. The other half of the office was furnished with a sofa and chairs for relaxing and reading. There wasn't any technology to speak of except a phone sitting on the left-hand corner of the desk.

"Where to begin?" Jeff queried.

"Let's split up the task," the prophet suggested. "Jeff, you and Billy look in the files, Ty and Robbie can look through the books, Nick and Joe can review all the pictures and stuff on the walls. I'll go through the desk. That way we can identify any possible leads quickly. Let's get to it."

They began their tasks, carefully and meticulously examining the contents of the office, setting aside anything that might have the slightest relevance to the Sword of Goliath, the Sword of Don Quixote, or the Final Process.

During the search, Joe called out to the team, "Hey, listen up. Most of the quotes on the walls are from *Don Quixote* or are Bible verses. Not much else. Some stuff from Cicero, some from C.S. Lewis, but the majority are from *Don Quixote* and the Bible. Listen to these. They're from *Don Quixote*."

For neither good nor evil can last forever; and so it follows that as evil has lasted a long time, good must now be close at hand.

Virtue is persecuted by the wicked more than it is loved by the good.

It's up to brave hearts, sir, to be patient when things are going badly, as well as being happy when they're going well.

Truth, whose mother is history, who is the rival of time, depository of deeds, witness of the past, example a lesson to the present, and warning to the future.

"These seem to be related to what we are dealing with now. There is another from that book that seems related to the cycles of history idea that the image of Grandpa told us about during the indoctrination. Listen.

To think that the affairs of this life always remain in the same state is a vain presumption; indeed they all seem to be perpetually changing and moving in a circular course. Spring is followed by summer, summer by autumn, and autumn by winter, which is again followed by spring, and so time continues its everlasting round. But the life of man is ever racing to its end, swifter than time itself, without hope of renewal, unless in the next that is limitless and infinite.

"And here are the Bible verses that seem related to our situation," Nick said.

God resisteth the proud, but giveth grace unto the humble. James 4:6

But let it be the hidden man of the heart, in that which is not corruptible, even the ornament of a meek and quiet spirit, which is in the sight of God of great price. Let him eschew evil,

and do good. Let him seek peace, and ensue it.
    I Peter 3:4

Blessed are the poor in spirit.
Matthew 5:3

"This one's great!" Joe exclaimed. "It's called The Knight's Code." He took it off the wall and showed it to them, then read it aloud as the others read over his shoulder.

THE KNIGHT'S CODE

Our quest is the preservation and restoration of the family... for without those families there is only a nation in chaos, and we will have more of the evil we face now. Keep your word and be true to your principles. Protect innocence and punish the wicked. Stand your ground.

TRUTH
The foundation of virtue, one who seeks out the truth *within him or herself* will surely discover *other knightly virtues, such as justice, courage, strength, and humility. Without truth, there is no light, only self-deception, self-delusion, and the spiritual darkness that must surely lead to other vices.*

HONOR
The standard against which we measure ourselves and are measured by others. It is a treasure that if kept grows in value and grandeur, but once squandered can rarely be regained, and even then only at great cost in time and effort. The knight's word must be more certain and sure than any written contract. Let every knight and dame consider carefully before making an oath,

and never do so lightly or without due reflection. But rather let every knight strive to fulfil every oath undertaken or stand bereft of honor.

JUSTICE

Since time immemorial, the knight's duty has been to protect the innocent from harm and to punish the guilty, as symbolized by the sword. In past times, fulfilment of this duty often required physical combat, today the battles are fought differently but are no less important. The knight must strive in all areas of life, insofar as possible, to fight injustice and help the right to prevail.

CHARITY

The knight will strive to aid those in need, be it in the form of largesse or simply giving succor and assistance to such as may need it, giving as his or her means permit and without ostentation or display. True charity encompasses more than the material. A word of encouragement be more valuable than jewels. The spirit of charity may cause the knight to forgive a wrong done to himself if the act is truly repented. Charity will help the knight to avoid the errors of gluttony and avarice.

LOYALTY

The brother and sister of honor, once dubbed a knight, has made a commitment, let him or her not waiver or withdraw, but realize that a knight does not compromise his or her loyalty. Let no such commitment be lightly made.

COURAGE

The knight is charged with fighting for the good and right, and thus is destined to face many opponents. The battles may be of the body, and the knight may face physical dangers;

but courage is as greatly in demand with the more subtle opponent of the mind or spirit. Whichever circumstances the knight enters, he or she must always face the enemy with valor.

HUMILITY
The knight who looks upon his or her life without evasion or self-deception, and exercises the virtue of truth, will surely be humbled by the great gulf that lies between the chivalrous ideal and the reality of what is. Thus chastened, the knight will surely be against the errors of pride.

EXCELLENCE
The knight and dame strive always to do and be their best, no matter what the area of endeavor. They do so not for pride's sake, but to infuse even the most mundane task with nobility and thus uplift themselves.

NOBILITY
A man may be ennobled by a prince; but a soul is elevated only by living according to standards higher *than those of the* common man. To achieve the chivalrous ideal is *not* possible; *but the very striving uplifts the spirit and purifies the soul; and marks the true knight.*

FAITH
The knight or dame must be true to that which he or she believes in above all else, for with faith comes strength *against every adversity.* Faith is the lifeblood *of courage and nobility, without it, life has no meaning.* With faith, no force, not even death, can defeat the knight.

As Joe read, the prophet realized the relevance to their problem. "I believe we are on to something here," he said. "This seems to confirm that we're on the right track. Taken in context with all the other quotes on the wall, I'm sure we need to find a sword that represented humility to fight against the Sword of Goliath, since it symbolizes pride."

"Okay, so we seem to be looking for the right sword, but where should we start? Where can we find it?" asked Ty.

Robbie, who had been peering at the Knight's Code closely, spoke up. "Hey, did any of you notice the highlighted words in the Knight's Code? They seem pretty random and don't seem to be normal words that someone would highlight. Take a look."

He showed the team what he was looking at. They scanned the document together and suddenly the prophet jumped up, grabbed a pen and paper, then returned to the group.

"What's up, Dad?" Robbie asked.

"I think there's a message here," the prophet answered as he copied down the highlighted words. When they were all copied, he arranged them into sentences, then read it aloud.

One who seeks out the truth will surely discover the sword required to aid those in need. Fighting for valor, humility against the errors of pride is elevated higher. To achieve the chivalrous ideal is possible. With faith comes strength. Faith is the lifeblood. With faith, no force, not even death can defeat the knight.

"Yahoo!" Billy cheered. "That message is certainly encouraging!"

Joe looked at the message again. "Yes! He mentions a sword, humility and fighting against pride."

"Don't forget the part about faith," Ty pointed out.

"What does he mean 'elevated higher'?" Nick asked. "And what does that have to do with the sword we need?"

The prophet observed, "If Grandpa took the time to do all of this highlighting to send us a message, then he must have known what sword was needed and where it was. Does anyone have an idea about what could be meant by 'elevated higher'?"

"Could it mean that it is venerated?" Billy offered, "or worshiped in some way?"

"I don't think so," said the prophet, "that would not fit with the concept of a humble sword."

Nick pulled out a dictionary from the bookshelf. He turned to the definition of the word "elevated" and read the first entry.

Elevated: situated or placed higher than the surrounding area.

"To me," he mused, "it seems that we should be looking for something situated or placed up high, maybe here, or in the Keeping Room."

"Excellent," said the prophet. "Let's start here. Quickly, scan the room above eye level and see what you find."

The cousins spread out and began the search.

After a moment, Robbie shouted from the sitting area, "Quick, come in here. I may have found it!"

The others hustled in to where he was. There, on the wall behind the stairwell where they had ascended, hung a sword that could not be seen when entering the office. The prophet hurriedly walked up to the sword hanging there and removed it from its wooden display.

As he removed the sword from its scarred, black leather scabbard and examined it, he had a strange feeling

261

that he'd seen this sword before. He shook off the feeling and continued his examination. It was well worn, nicks and rust infected its blade. It was a rapier-type sword about forty inches long with an ornate, clam-shaped guard for protecting the hand during combat.

On the black and gold hand-guard were engravings depicting two scenes. The main face had a scene of Sancho Panza and Don Quixote heading out on their adventures, and the opposite side had an engraving of Don Quixote engaged in battle with his imaginary giant foe, also known as the windmill.

"Well, gentlemen, it appears we have a candidate for the Sword of Don Quixote. This does not appear to be a sword intended for use in actual combat. My guess is that it is just a replica of the type of sword that was used at the time *Don Quixote* was written. It is a sword typical of Spanish descent, a cut-and-thrust sword as efficient at cutting and slashing as it is at thrusting and piercing. Shall we consider it or move on to look for another?"

Joe spoke up. "If we take all the information the quantum computer and Grandpa's clues have given us, I think it is obvious that this is the sword that Grandpa believed we needed. It may not be a 'real' sword, or have been used by an actual historical figure, but it is a humble sword. It will undoubtedly require a lot of faith for us to put the fate of the world in its fragile and rusty blade. It will be going up against the huge and incredibly powerful Sword of Goliath, but hey, didn't David face the same problem? He had faith, he trusted, he believed. So should we."

"I don't know," said Jeff. "This sword is not like the others we used. We could feel the power in those swords. They had influence. They looked powerful and intimidating. This one couldn't scare a squirrel. Grandpa probably had it here for inspiration along with all those other quotes. This seems awfully foolish."

"I'm not so sure about that," replied the prophet. "Grandpa never did anything without a purpose."

"Besides, Jeff, what about the fact that everything points to this being the sword?" said Robbie. "Really, it all makes sense to me. Remember what Joe said about *The Velveteen Rabbit* and *Pinocchio*? Everything Grandma and Grandpa taught us all our lives has been about faith. It's about believing in things we cannot see but know to be true. Now is the time to put that into action. I, for one, am going to believe that this sword is the sword we need. No doubt."

The prophet said, "We are running out of time, gentlemen, the ripples in the time stream should hit us soon. We need to come to a decision. You must all be committed to it and believe in it, or we will fail. Decide now."

The heroes looked at each other, then at Jeff.

The prophet almost held his breath as he watched Jeff's expression carefully. He hoped and prayed that his nephew would join them in this. If he didn't, well…

Jeff looked at each person around the table. He sighed. "What I believe is that we don't have time to find another sword. This one fits the bill. Even though it looks puny, fragile and rusty and, on the surface, appears to be inadequate for the task, I'm going to commit to this sword. I choose to see things as they should be, not as they are. All in favor of using this sword to conduct the Final Process against the Sword of Goliath, say 'aye'."

All the cousins said, "Aye," and raised their hands.

"Good!" said the prophet. "Let's hurry to the fire pit and commence the second Final Process. Believe like you have never believed before!"

CHAPTER FOURTEEN

THE SECOND
FINAL PROCESS

~~~

The prophet and the heroes ran down to the spot by the river carrying the Sword of Don Quixote. Together, they quickly built a fire in the fire pit and waited while it caught and began to burn furiously.

While they were waiting, the prophet spoke to them all. "As before, we don't know what to expect. The first Final Process was unprecedented, and no one has ever contemplated a second one. We will have to play this one by ear. In the past, you have all stood around this fire and kept your objectives clearly in mind to accomplish the leaving process.

"Since we only have one sword this time, I suggest that you all stand before the fire while touching the sword and clearly, with all your strength, and utilizing all the virtue that has been imparted to you by the Swords of Valor, visualize the power of this sword. Will into it all the virtues of the other Swords of Valor. Believe that this sword, this humble and unassuming sword, will accomplish the task set before it this night.

"See it as a beacon of hope against despair. See it as a symbol of faith against blasphemy. Know that humility can overcome pride. Then trust in it. Know that it will be victorious and that it will finally, and for all time, defeat and eradicate the threat of the Apostles of Azazel.

"Remember that your grandfather had faith in you. He had faith in this sword. Know that whatever the outcome, I'm proud of you all."

The fire roared, and the embers rose into a night sky that was bright and clear, filled with stars and a beautiful full moon. The heroes assembled around the fire. They each put their hands on the sword as they held it high. The prophet spoke an improvised version of the Initiation Protocol.

"Hear me, oh sword of humility!
Rise, for the day is at hand.
The pride of Goliath has wakened.
His evil now threatens the land.

Rise and display all your virtue,
Your power now use to defend.
The world has need of your service.
Upon you alone we depend.

Rise and show forth your glory!
Be strong, don't fear or retreat.
Be assured of our faith in your triumph
And that pride will now face its defeat."

As the prophet finished reciting the Initiation Protocol, the Sword of Don Quixote began to vibrate. It started to change. The rust disappeared from its blade, and it seemed to swell and then return to its original size. It took on a golden glow, but it was hard to tell if that was from the reflection of the fire or if it emanated from the sword itself. Then the sword was abruptly pulled from the cousins' hands. It hovered, taking a position about ten feet above the fire, and began to spin very slowly, then picked up speed as it spun. It called to the Sword of Goliath using its humility as bait for the prideful giant's sword.

The Sword of Goliath appeared in a howling rush of wind and debris. It spun like the most powerful windmill imaginable. The spinning sword was massive. The wind from it pushed the Sword of Don Quixote out away from over the fire, and it fell to the ground, having lost its spinning motion.

The prophet ran to it, picked it up off the ground, and with a mighty effort hurled it at the wildly spinning Sword of Goliath.

The Sword of Don Quixote smashed into the Sword of Goliath with incredible speed, driving it out from over the fire. It stopped spinning as it clattered to the ground.

The Sword of Don Quixote swiftly approached the Sword of Goliath as it lay in the dirt.

Goliath's sword started to rise, but the tip was missing. The blow from the prophet had broken it off.

Now the Sword of Don Quixote went in for the kill. It dove onto the Sword of Goliath as it was rising and struck a devastating and resounding blow. The Sword of Goliath was broken in two. It shuddered for a moment, then lay still. The process of disintegration and decay began, finally turning the prideful sword completely black. The remaining particles were carried away on the wind into the night sky.

As the prophet looked skyward, he saw the Sword of Don Quixote disappear.

"Thank you," he whispered. "I hope you find your rightful owner and proper place in time, the time of your owner's most significant victory."

When both swords had disappeared, there was a moment of silence filled with awe.

Finally, the prophet spoke. "It seems that the Sword of Don Quixote had become real enough to have a rightful owner, and it apparently is now a Sword of Valor. Well done, gentlemen, well done."

He looked at his watch and continued, "Now, there is no time to bask in our glory. We need to get to the Keeping Room. The ripples in the time stream are due to arrive any moment. Let's get in front of the quantum computer so that we can monitor the impact. Hurry."

The heroes and the prophet hustled to the Keeping Room and assembled at the round table.

The image of their grandfather appeared. "First," it said, "congratulations on a complete success. You have accomplished a legendary feat this day, one many centuries in the making. If I were human, I would tell you that I'm proud of every one of you. As it is, I must turn your attention to the monitors around the room. From here, we can watch for changes that take place in the world when the time ripple hits.

"We will be insulated from those changes here in the Keeping Room. It has been designed to protect us, as it has thus far protected us from physical, mental, and spiritual attacks while we have been within its walls. The quantum computer has an insulating quantum vibrational pattern that blocks all negative energies at the subatomic level. In here, the changes will have no impact on us, and we will remember history as it has been, but out there in the world… well, we will see."

The monitors lit up with pictures from around the globe; New York, Paris, London, Rome, Tokyo, Jerusalem, Sidney, and others. The quantum computer counted down, "Five, four, three, two, one…"

Then the vibrations of the time ripple hit. The Keeping Room felt like it was riding a tidal wave; just one wave, and then it stopped. The monitors blinked for a moment, then reset. At first, the prophet didn't detect any changes on the screens.

The image spoke, "We are assessing the impact of the ripple. It may take weeks to assess it all, but I can tell you that some things are definitely different. I will show you some of the most obvious changes."

He showed them New York on one of the monitors. The screen showed the skyline of New York City, and there were the Twin Towers of the World Trade Center standing tall and proud.

The cousins cheered! That was a huge positive! The prophet wondered what that implied, but he knew one thing right away, that all the loss of life on 9/11 never happened. The pain and agony felt by the almost three thousand people who died in that horror, as well as the grief and despair felt by their families, never happened. It was gone.

"Yes!" Billy crowed. When the others looked at him, he explained. "I was in New York City on that terrible day. I'd been working only a short distance from the Twin Towers. A few of my friends died in that tragedy, and now, our actions of the past few days had helped erase that horrible day. I can't tell you how much joy and hope this gives me!"

"Is this representative of the impact in other places?" Joe asked. "This is such a wonderful change that I'm hopeful the other changes will be just as positive."

The image responded, "It is not completely representative."

Then a picture of New Orleans appeared on a

monitor. It showed complete devastation, a ghost town. "In this new timeline, Katrina still devastated New Orleans, but it was never rebuilt. It was abandoned, and the people were relocated. There is talk of bulldozing it completely and rebuilding it into the model city of the future, complete with a staging spaceport for the colonization of Mars.

"From what we can cobble together with current history books and a quick scan of news reports for the last thirty years, the wars in Iraq and Afghanistan never occurred. The money spent on those wars has instead been funneled into the effort to colonize Mars and rebuild the crumbling infrastructure of the U.S. The economy had a small recession in 2007 and 2008, but it recovered fast, due to the infrastructure spending.

"Terrorism is a minor issue. Without the wars in Iraq and Afghanistan, and with the destruction of the Swords of Terror, there is no ISIS. Al-Qaida remains a problem only in Afghanistan. Saudi Arabia has begun to donate billions of dollars to the Palestinians to help with building their economy and infrastructure. The Middle East still does not have peace, but there is a positive movement toward eradicating the root causes; poverty and some small groups of religious fanatics.

"Here is another fascinating change. It appears that the Native American nations, after initial wars with the government, agreed to a treaty that didn't result in them being restricted to reservations. That treaty gave them the right to form states. They were incorporated fully into the nation, given full rights and participation in government.

"The Native American states were instrumental in helping the U.S. to avoid the Civil War. It seems that the Apostles of Azazel drove much of the division and hatred that fueled both the Indian Wars and the Civil War. With that influence eradicated, the Civil War never happened, and the U.S. is much stronger because of it.

"Additionally, the Native American states in the west and southwest opened their doors to all slaves. They welcomed them as free men and incorporated them into their economies and culture. Those states are now among the most prosperous and stable in the nation.

"Worldwide, the impact of pollution on ecosystems and the health of people is minimal. We see no significant rise in cancer rates, autism rates, ADHD, autoimmune diseases, or any other adverse impacts on human health from environmental factors. These remain at or below historical norms.

"Again, this seems to be related to the obliteration of the Swords of Terror. The greed, pride, and selfishness that have been driving factors in the destruction and poisoning of the environment have been controlled. Concern for the well-being of others over profit has been allowed to flourish."

The prophet was thrilled by the news of the decline in autism rates. The epidemic rise in autism was the reason that he and Billy had started his company, to address all the pain and struggle that the families impacted by this disorder endured and to give them hope. He felt as if all his own struggles of the past hours had been rewarded. He asked the image, "Is there more to reveal? I am feeling encouraged by all I am hearing."

"We could go on, but my initial analysis shows that changing history by one day, combined with the destruction of the Swords of Terror, has had a powerful and overall positive impact on the course of history. Clearly, if you hadn't completed the Final Process in time, the results could have been very different.

"Once again," continued the image of their

grandfather, "you have all performed admirably and accomplished the task set before you with valor, virtue, and bravery. More impressive than anything else, you did it in unity. Your family, the Guardians, and the world owe you a great debt of gratitude."

The prophet looked at each of the cousins and added, "The timeline changes you are responsible for have so far had a positive impact. The world is a better place because of your heroism and hard work, but it can't end there. The world is still in need of heroes, because evil will always exist.

"The forces who created the Apostles of Azazel, and who gave the Swords of Terror their evil influence, won't stop trying. Their efforts will take a different form. The tools they use may change. But the core of their assaults will always focus on destroying the building block of civilization; the family.

"Azazel knows that to destroy the fabric of society, he must attack the family structure. In order to enslave people, he must deaden their souls to love. That love is first learned and taught within families. Goodness and virtue are first taught and nurtured in the family setting.

"Without that ever-present structure, the seeds of discord, evil, and vice will be sown freely in society. Chaos will eventually ensue, so be on guard. Protect the unity of this family. It starts with us and flows out from there. Can I get a commitment from each of you?"

Billy spoke first. "I agree with you, Uncle Rob. I know I can be distant and a little self-absorbed at times, trying to get my career and life in order. I commit to taking more time to focus on this family. I will make the effort."

His uncle replied, "You were the first grandchild, Billy, and all these guys look up to you. Time to step up.

Regain your place. We can all be self-absorbed at times, just take steps to make this family a priority and to heal old wounds."

Jeff was next. "I love this family too, Uncle Rob, and I commit to using wisdom in bringing up my children in a way that will always point them to virtue and unity."

"Well said," the prophet replied.

Robbie then added, "The diversity we have in this family, our experiences and talents, make us unique and special. We need to use the talents, perspectives, and experiences of all of us together to strengthen our bonds. I commit to that."

"Thank you, Robbie," said his father.

"And," Ty commented, "we must make sure none of us falls behind. We need to pick each other up when we are at our lowest point. We have to be passionately concerned for the welfare and success of each other. I commit to that."

"Beautiful," said his father. "Very true, Ty."

Nick added his thoughts. "I have always been too independent. I keep all my struggles and challenges to myself. We shouldn't put up false fronts, but instead, show our humanity to each other. I commit to sharing my fears and worries with the family and not be so distant. I will make sure that everyone knows that I have an ear for listening to their struggles, too."

"Great!" said the prophet. "Nick, you are a strong young man, but you don't have to be strong alone. There is more strength in a cord of multiple strands than there can ever be in a single strand. Thank you for your commitment."

Finally, Joe added his promise. "Uncle Rob, I have observed that forgiveness is the greatest power we have to create unity in this family. I have experienced

272

forgiveness, and I have given forgiveness, but neither is easy. It takes commitment and effort. As a family, we must be committed to forgiveness. It will be the greatest gift we can give to ourselves and other family members. Additionally, we should give each other the grace to make mistakes. None of us are perfect, and we need to remember that. Forgiveness and grace will help us overcome and avoid the bitterness that poisons families. I commit to those things."

"Amazing, Joe," said the prophet. "Those are the building blocks of unity. Without them, no family or nation can survive. Thank you for reminding us of that."

The image of their grandfather then declared, "Well, if we are finished here, then I will depart. You all need your rest. As you head out from here and into the new world you have helped to create, remember all that you have learned.

"Apply the perspective and knowledge you have gained from your assignments and your interactions with each other to help keep this family strong, growing, and safe. Never forget who you are and where you came from, but most importantly, stay humble. Humility will be your shield. It will be your greatest quality."

Then it added, "Before you leave, I want to show you the images that I recorded during the two final processes. I think you will find them most enlightening!"

Then the monitors changed from the images around the world to a computer-generated view of the fire pit area by the river. It showed images of the prophet and the heroes preparing the fire and laying the Swords of Valor around it. The prophet saw himself recite the Initiation Protocol and call for the first sword to rise. What he saw next startled him.

A ghostly image of Peter the Apostle appeared,

picked up his sword, and then rose ten feet above the fire. As he stood there, he released the sword, and it began to spin.

When the Sword of Cain appeared, the image of a man accompanied it. The prophet assumed this must be the image of Cain. A black representation of a snake marked his face. Cain grabbed his sword, and it stopped spinning.

The prophet watched the images of the men doing battle with the swords. He saw Peter defeat Cain and destroy his sword just as he had observed while standing by the fire pit. Then he saw the dissolution of both the Sword of Cain and Cain himself. The particles of both fell into the fire and were consumed by the flames. He stared in disbelief. Then he looked around the table and noticed looks of shock and amazement on the faces of the heroes, as well.

He watched as all the other battles of the first Final Process took place. He saw all the heroes of the Swords of Valor appear to do battle with the owners of the Swords of Terror.

When the first Final Process battles were complete, the prophet asked the image of his father, "Is this an accurate representation? How were you able to record the images of Peter, Cain, and all the others? We had no idea that the spirits of the owners of the swords themselves would show up to fight the battles. Was this known to the Guardians?"

The image replied. "This was not known to the Guardians, but I can infer that your father may have known. From his diary entries and his preparations before his death, that is a possibility. I was able to record this because the quantum emanations from the swords are so sensitive and so connected to the essence of the owners that when they appeared, the images were detectable by the quantum computer. They, in effect, became visible on a subatomic level.

"I converted those emanations into visually accurate representations of the people who appeared. It is their virtuous essences that did battle against the evil essences of the other swords. I will now show you the last battle."

The screens now showed the cousins and the prophet once again by the fire pit. The Initiation Protocol adapted for the Sword of Don Quixote was spoken, and when it was complete, an image appeared. It walked to the fire and took the Sword of Don Quixote from the hands of the cousins who were holding it. As it rose with the sword to take its place above the fire, the prophet recognized the hero.

It was his father! His father was the one who stood against Goliath! The sword spun in front of him, and it called to the Sword of Goliath. Immediately, the giant appeared, along with his colossal spinning sword.

He watched the essence of his father and the Sword of Don Quixote get blown from above the fire by the powerful gust created by Goliath's spinning sword. He saw both fall to the ground and the sword drop from his father's hand. He watched himself run to the sword, pick it up, and hurl it at the Sword of Goliath.

He observed the essence of his father watch, rise, and follow the sword. He grabbed it after it struck the Sword of Goliath and before it fell to the ground. He descended with it to the fallen giant and his sword. He delivered the final blow just as the giant had picked up his sword to attack.

Then he saw the final destruction of both Goliath and his sword. The essence of his father looked at the cousins and the prophet, smiled, then he and the sword disappeared from the screens.

The quantum computer-generated image of their grandfather spoke. "That, gentlemen, is the end of our journey, the final chapter. What happens from here on is up to you. Go live your lives with virtue and valor, and honor your grandfather's sacrifice." Then the image faded from view.

The Keeping Room was silent. The prophet tried to process what he had just witnessed. Finally, one word stood out in his mind. Softly, he repeated what the computer image had just said, "Sacrifice."

Then he addressed the heroes. "My father obviously knew that he was the one that would have to face Goliath, which explains why he would not let me try to heal him. He must have known that the only way for him to have his ultimate victory was to die, and then have his essence return to fight Goliath. What incredible courage! What amazing faith! He truly was a giant of a man."

"Agreed!" Joe exclaimed. "It's going to take many years to process all of it, but I'm certain of one thing; we have been blessed to be the grandchildren of such a courageous and heroic man."

"No joke," Nick added. "I, for one, will forever remember all that he taught us. I'm going to strive always to make him proud."

Ty spoke softly, almost reverently, "We must honor his memory with our lives."

"I'm going to miss him," Robbie murmured. "I've grown almost as fond of the holographic image as I was of Grandpa. It interacted with us just like he would have. It gave me comfort to hear his voice and have him there to direct, inform, and challenge us."

Jeff nodded, "Of course, it wasn't really him, just an image conjured up by the quantum computer. Still, I'm sad to see it go, too."

"Will we ever be able to interact with the quantum computer-generated image of Grandpa again? Just for fun, I mean," asked Ty.

His father replied, "Of course, anytime."

"I can't wait to bring Alexandra and Olivia here to speak to him," said Joe. "They will get such a kick out of it."

"I think we should all gather here at Thanksgiving and have dinner around this table, that way the image of Grandpa can join us," said Ty.

The prophet smiled. "As nice as that sounds, I think, for now, we should still keep all this stuff between us, including the secrets of the Keeping Room. The family needs to decide when to bring your sisters into it. Remember, they are of the Hero generation, too!"

"Speaking of sisters, shouldn't we check on the family to determine what impact the timeline changes have had on them?" asked Jeff. "Since the changes have been so positive, I think we can assume that all is well, but still, I want to make sure they are okay."

The prophet replied, "I agree, Jeff, but I want to give it at least twenty-four hours. We have never experienced a timeline change like this before, and I believe we need to let it settle in and stabilize. I will have the quantum computer alert us if there is anything we need to know about the status of our loved ones. Now, let's see what this brave, new world has to offer."

"I hope it offers some of Grandpa's meatballs," Billy groaned, holding his stomach. "I'm starving!"

When they entered the area with the glass sword case, Nick stopped and did a double-take. "Hey, our swords are back!" he exclaimed.

Joe, who was walking behind him, nearly ran into

him. "What?" he asked, peering over his brother's shoulder. Sure enough, the swords were safely in their cases.

"What gives, Uncle Rob?" Nick asked as he stepped aside to let the others pass. "Are those the Swords of Valor? Why are they here?"

The prophet smiled. "These are the replicas of your swords. Remember, you always had the real swords but were told they were replicas. Well, these are the replicas. I placed them here before the first Final Process to fool the Apostles of Azazel if things did not go well, in case they found a way to infiltrate this place."

Then he opened the glass case and handed them each their sword. "Take these with you to remember this day and to remind yourselves of all you learned. You no longer need the influence of the real swords. Their virtue and valor are inside of you now."

"Awesome!" Robbie exclaimed.

"Yeah," Jeff nodded. "It's strange, but holding this makes me feel whole again, even though I know it's just a replica."

Joe hefted the replica of Excalibur, "Replica or not, I'm not letting this baby out of my sight!"

Laughing, the heroes and their Prophet climbed out of the Keeping Room, ready to tackle the world... and some meatballs!

CHAPTER FIFTEEN

END OF A
SEASON

Nick watched as Uncle Rob turned off the lights, shut the massive trap door, and waited for confirmation that it was locked in place. He helped slide some old wood over the top of the door to hide it from view and then followed the others out of the old barn.

As they made their way to the house, he felt fatigue setting in fast. His feet felt like they were made of lead. He couldn't remember ever feeling this tired, even after a week-long hunting trip. Traipsing all over a mountain in search of deer was nothing compared to what they'd just gone through!

Once they arrived, Uncle Rob volunteered to fix them some pasta and meatballs. Nobody argued, so they settled in the family room around the fire to decompress.

"What a crazy few days we have had," Nick remarked. "It feels like we have been going nonstop for a week! I could sleep for two days."

"I know," agreed Ty. "The last time I felt this tired was last year during finals. I'm beat."

"I have to figure out what day it is, so I can determine what meetings I have missed and which clients

I have lost because of my absence," added Billy.

Robbie shouted, "Hey, Dad, what day is it, anyway?"

His father stuck his head out of the kitchen. "It's Saturday, just coming up on midnight, believe it or not. All of this has taken just a little over thirty-six hours from the time we started on Friday morning. That is the result of the time dilatation I said you'd experience during your time travel assignments. You still have all day Sunday to rest and relax. None of you have missed any time at work or school. Cool, huh?"

"Definitely cool," agreed Ty. Then he turned to his cousins. "So, what should we do with our day off?"

Jeff suggested a few rounds of golf.

Then it started. First with Joe, then Robbie, then Nick, and soon all the cousins were chanting, "Sunnyhill, Sunnyhill, Sunnyhill…"

Sunnyhill Resort had a terrific golf course. It was only about five minutes away, and they loved playing there. That was where they'd learned to golf, thanks to their grandfather. He'd taken each of them there for their first attempts at the sport. Then he'd continued to teach them everything he knew.

Nick loved those times, because he got to spend time alone with his grandfather, and it was always about more than just golf. It was about togetherness, new experiences, and family.

"It's decided, then," declared Joe. "Golf tomorrow at Sunnyhill, but not too early. I'm too exhausted to even think of an early morning tee time!"

"Agreed," said Robbie. "Let's plan on a noon tee time. We should still be able to get in twenty-seven holes if we hustle and nothing slows us down."

Nick frowned. "But we will only have six people, and at noon, the starter will want us to have two full foursomes."

"Robbie, ask your dad if he wants to play, too. Then maybe he will let us slide with one foursome and a threesome," Jeff suggested.

Robbie shouted into the kitchen again, "Hey, Dad! Do you want to join us for golf tomorrow around noon?"

His dad replied, "Sure, you guys need massive supervision on the golf course. Every time I play there, they bust my chops about the Golf Cart Incident of 1995."

"But we didn't do it!" objected Nick.

Ty shook his head. "Wasn't us!"

Robbie threw up his hands. "Not our fault!"

"Who said we did it?" Billy asked, looking around suspiciously.

"Definitely not us," Jeff declared emphatically.

"Yeah, it was that other family!" Joe grinned.

"Sure it was," grinned Uncle Rob. "Keep sticking to that story, and maybe someday it will be true. Come on, let's eat."

They sat around the dining room table once again. Holding hands, they listened as Uncle Rob prayed.

"Father, we thank you for this food. We thank you for your protection. We thank you for being here together, and we thank you for our family. May we always be together."

The cousins responded "Amen," then everyone ate until they could eat no more.

Joe slept like a dead man that night. Not even the bright sun shining through the windows of the bedrooms bothered him. About 11:00 a.m., Uncle Rob knocked on his door, rousing him.

"Joe?" he called. "You'd better hurry or you'll miss our tee time."

Joe threw on some clothes. He started to leave the bedroom but glanced back to see the replica of Excalibur lying on the dresser where he'd left it the night before. On a whim, he stepped back into the room and grabbed it, then ran down the stairs to join the others for a quick breakfast.

"What's with the sword?" Nick asked, shifting a little in his chair.

"Yeah, what's with the sword?" the others chimed in, almost in unison.

"I don't know," Joe replied honestly. "I just felt the urge to bring it along. It's just that I feel so comfortable with it. Even though it's not 'real', I'm comforted by having it close."

Laughing, his brother and cousins pointed to their own swords hanging in their sheaths from the back of their chairs.

Joe shook his head, grinning. "What's with the swords, guys?" he mimicked, as he sat and loaded his plate with toast, eggs, and bacon.

After they ate, they went to the storage room to gather the golf clubs their grandfather always kept there for guests to use. Before they climbed into their grandfather's SUV, Joe suggested that they put their swords in their golf bags. Everyone agreed, so they loaded up their grandfather's SUV and headed to Sunnyhill.

They arrived just in time for their tee time. When Uncle Rob asked the starter if they could play with a threesome, he said that it was just too crowded today. He put a single with the group that had the threesome.

Part of the threesome, Ty complained a little. "Great. I hope he doesn't put us with someone who will slow us down too much. I really want to get twenty-seven holes in before I head back to school."

"Me too," said Jeff, "I haven't played in months, so let's just make the best of it." They put on their golf shoes, got their carts, and headed out to the first tee.

As they were warming up and stretching, the starter pointed into the distance and said, "Good, here comes your fourth, just in time. The first group can start."

Looking where the starter pointed, Joe saw an old guy pulling his cart behind him, slowly walking toward the tee box.

"Looks like a long day." Joe sighed. "This guy is really going to slow us down." He didn't mean to, but he had said it loud enough for their fourth to hear.

As the old guy drew closer, he responded to the affront. "Sounds like someone needs to teach you youngsters some humility!"

Joe stared in disbelief, squinting to try and make out the face. The voice sounded so familiar! When he finally saw the man's features clearly, his jaw dropped. He looked at the others to see if they were seeing the same thing. Everyone looked just as shocked as Joe felt.

The old man smiled and said, "What are you guys staring at? You would think that you have never seen your own grandpa before."

Then he reached into his golf bag and drew out the Sword of Don Quixote. "Anyone for a little adventure?"

Simultaneously, they dropped their clubs and ran to him.

"Grandpa!" cried Joe. "Is it really you? Is this real, or are you a hologram?"

Grandpa responded, "It's me, buddy, and as always,

I'm better than good!"

The cousins tried to hug him all at once, nearly crushing him in the process.

"Easy there, fellows," Grandpa laughed. "There's plenty of me to go around, but not all at once!"

Backing off a bit, the cousins let Uncle Rob greet his father. Their hug was long and heartfelt.

"I missed you, Dad," Rob said with tears in his eyes.

His father just smiled and patted his back.

When they stepped apart, Nick stepped up. "I don't want to interrupt, but I don't understand. How is this possible? I know we changed a day in history when we saved King Leonidas from being killed at the battle of Thermopylae, but how did that result in Grandpa's return?" Nick asked his uncle, bewildered.

"That is something we will need to ask the quantum computer," replied the prophet. "There are too many variables for me to even begin to guess, but as you can see, changing history by even one day can have far-reaching consequences. Let's get everyone together and head back to the house to sort this all out."

He then went to his father and stood before him. For the first time in his life, he was unsure of what to do or what to say to him. His father, the returned Meglio Di Buono of the Cincinnatus Family of the Swords of Valor, smiled.

"It seems that all is well, Rob. I assume the mission was a success?" his father asked.

"Yes, I mean, obviously. I mean, don't you know that? After all, you are here with us now after having…"

His voice trailed off. He was unwilling to say the words.

His father finished the sentence for him. "After having died?"

"Well, yes, after having died," repeated the prophet. "The last time I saw you was in the hospital just before it happened. Do you remember that? Do you remember anything we talked about? The plan? The Apostles of Azazel? The Swords of Terror? Your office?"

"I remember everything up until that point," replied his father. "What I do not know is the result of your actions since then. I must assume that if you have taken our heroes out for a day of golfing, that all must have gone well, or you would still be in the Keeping Room, working feverishly to save the world from destruction. Am I correct?"

"Yes, Dad, you are correct. But there is more to the story than that. There are a lot of things that happened because of our victory. We need to bring you up to speed. All did not go as you had planned." He sighed. "It appears that you withheld some vital information, which I, for one, did not appreciate."

His father smiled. "But you succeeded regardless! And I'm sure you learned some very interesting lessons because of it. Believe me when I tell you that it was all part of the plan. Let's dispense with golfing today and head back to the house, okay?"

Then he turned to his grandsons and said, "I am very proud of all of you. I knew the hero in each of you would rise to the challenge. You can catch me up on all of your adventures."

As they walked back to the parking lot, Robbie spoke. "Guess what, Grandpa? I got us into Windsor Castle!" Billy and Joe just rolled their eyes.

Billy said, "Okay, Fabio, I guess the rewriting of

285

history has already begun! Grandpa, don't listen to his version. We will have the quantum computer tell you the real story."

"Don't worry, Billy," replied the Meglio. "I know all of you well enough to know when I am being played. Remember, it was me who chose you, and that took a lifetime of very careful observation. I know you better than you know yourselves. I hope you realize that I may have been dead, but I was not born yesterday. Well, not technically anyway. By the way, I'm hungry. Is there any food left in the house, or did you barbarians eat it all?"

"We put a pretty good dent in it, Grandpa," replied Jeff. "But there is still plenty of chicken cutlet parmigiana left. Uncle Rob wouldn't let us eat that. He was keeping it for himself."

"Well," said the Meglio, "it looks like your uncle will have one more thing to deal with because of my return." They all looked at Uncle Rob, who had a big smile on his face, and laughed. They got into the vehicle and headed back to the house to debrief their grandfather.

When they arrived at the family compound, the cousins unloaded all the golf bags, removed their replica swords, and headed into the kitchen to prepare lunch. While the cousins headed to the house, the prophet and his father had a chance to speak alone on the front porch.

"It really is good to see you, Dad," said the prophet. "You can't imagine how hard it was to watch you die like that, knowing that I hadn't done everything I could to heal you."

"I know, Rob," his father said. "I am sorry for that, but it had to happen that way. There was so much at stake. Believe me, if I could have done it any other way, I would have never put you all through that. I hope that at least the holographic image I left for you helped to ease the pain."

"Yes, it did. That was a stroke of genius, Dad," replied the prophet. "It felt like we had you there right by our side, guiding and directing us. It was very comforting, but not as comforting as actually having you back with us. Of course, there is no worldwide catastrophe to deal with now, so we can just focus on relaxing and getting on with our lives."

"Are you sure of that?" asked his father.

"Well, yeah," said the prophet. "I mean, we destroyed the Swords of Terror, so what could cause trouble now?"

The Meglio stopped. He looked his son in the eye and replied, "Have you destroyed Azazel?"

Rob was surprised. "No, but we have taken away his most powerful weapons, the Swords of Terror. All the Swords of Valor have been returned to their rightful owners and proper place in time, and the timeline changes appear to have had an overall positive effect."

"Changes to the timeline you say? Tell me about that," queried the Meglio. "I realize that something significant has been altered, since I am here with you. That was not part of my plan. But as you know, changes in the timeline are deceiving. They are never what they appear to be. I have taught you that, so I don't understand your cavalier attitude."

The prophet put his arm around his father's shoulder. "We can talk more about this later. Why don't we get something to eat first, and then we will lay it all out for you? You will see that I am right, and that your plan worked to perfection despite, or maybe even because of, the timeline change."

"We shall see," said the Meglio. "Just remember, evil never changes its nature, just its form. As long as Azazel exists, we must be ever vigilant. Never doubt that Azazel and his minions are already planning their next move. We don't know how long we have to prepare, as they might strike any day."

"Surely, they won't strike this soon," the prophet argued. His father's warning look was stern.

"Anything can happen in a day. Anything!"

COMING SOON

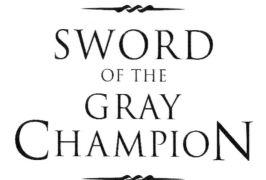

SWORD
OF THE
GRAY
CHAMPIoN

BOOK TWO
THE SWORDS OF VALOR

DOMENIC MELILLO

ACKNOWLEDGEMENTS
AND
AUTHOR'S NOTE

———⁓———

Thank you, dear reader, for taking this journey with me. The genesis of this story lies in actual family history. Well, some of it at least.

It has always been a tradition of mine to present swords to the young people in my extended family. When they reached their sixteenth birthday, I would carefully choose a replica of a historical sword, basing the choice on the characteristics I observed in them while they were growing up. I always felt that receiving such a significant symbol of character, virtue, and valor would crystalize those attributes inside of them and serve as a reminder of their better natures as they grew up. So, this book has a solid basis in fact and family history.

All the main characters in the story are reasonably accurate representations of my family members, and their interaction and interplay are very true-to-life. They are all great young men, and I am proud to be their uncle and father, respectively. Uncle Rob is a fictionalized version of my own brother and accurately portrays some of his greatest attributes; his love of family, his loyalty, his love of mentoring, and his inspirational leadership skills. I could truly see him taking on the responsibility given to him in the story and completely succeeding.

Also true-to-life is the representation of Joseph, the

Meglio Di Buono. My own father was known as Mr. Better-than-Good. It was a phrase he would always use, and over the years it became his identity. He had a lifelong love of literature. He really did read to us all the poetry mentioned in this story and made sure we remembered and understood it. He knew that there was great wisdom in literature, and it certainly had a major impact on my life. He also had a great affinity for the story of Don Quixote. He had a bronze sheet metal statue of him in his office for many years. He prized humility above all other virtues.

My mother Catherine, Grandma in the story, really did read the stories of *The Velveteen Rabbit* and *Pinocchio* to us as kids and to the grandchildren. I am glad I was able to work that into the story.

My grandfather, Robert Ogilvie Petrie, was an immigrant from Edinburgh, Scotland. He did fight in WWI and was with the Black Watch, the Royal Highland Regiment. He, however, was not with General Allenby at Jerusalem as the story mentions. Although for many years he was a hard-working coal miner and later a security guard at a bank in Brooklyn, he was always a hero to me.

Tall, soft-spoken, and slightly intimidating, he reminded everyone of Gary Cooper. He was also a fine welterweight boxer, and even into his seventies, he could hit you with three hard slaps to the head before you knew what hit you. Yes, I would say he was a real stud and could have easily handled Simeon as he did in the story.

As you can see, this is really a very family-based book with a solid basis in reality.

All the historical references to people and times are also as accurate as possible, and I encourage you to explore all the events in the story if your interest has been piqued.

Princess Elizabeth really did address the children of

her nation from Windsor Castle on the date mentioned, and the Sword of Tristan really was there at that time.

Everything that happened to Joan of Arc is also accurate, as is the tale of how she obtained her sword.

The story of Jesus in the Garden of Gethsemane and the denials of Peter are also accurate representations of what is told to us in the New Testament gospels. It is true that it is not clearly stated who initiated Peter's second denial, so why couldn't it have been the cousins?

The Battle of Thermopylae is also as accurate as I can make it. The story of this battle is better known today as the "Story of the 300" and was made into a film a few years back. I rendered the tactics and weaponry as accurately as possible, and the descriptions of the battle site are also based on hard facts and evidence.

The description of Leonidas's sword and all the other swords described in the story comes from the historical record.

The story is set in a time that I have described as a "Crisis" period in history. This and all the references to saeculum, generational archetypes, and the cyclical nature of history taking on the form of seasons described as Highs, Awakenings, Unravelings, and Crises, all come from the book, *The Fourth Turning*, by William Strauss and Neil Howe.

I first read it in 1997 when it was initially published. It made a huge impact on me when I realized how accurate the descriptions of the times and archetypes were. It told me that I was a member of the Prophet generation and that my children were all part of the Hero generation. That always stuck with me. As the years went by and all the cultural and social changes that they described began to happen, I started to prepare for the Crisis season that was to come beginning around 2005-2007. When the financial crisis hit around that time, I wished I had taken the advice in the book much more seriously. I encourage you to read it for yourself. You will rarely read a more impactful book.

"The Knight's Code" was taken from a website that I found many years ago which I cannot properly attribute today, but to the best of my recollection was the site of the Sovereign Military Order of the Knights of the Temple of Jerusalem. I always found it inspirational and profound. I am hopeful that the sentiment inherent in the code will become prevalent in our society once again.

Also, the seven clues that identify the actual date and time of Christ's crucifixion were taken from an article in the National Catholic Register. It is from an article entitled "7 Clues Tell Us *Precisely* When Jesus Died (The Year, Month, Day, And Hour Revealed)" by a man named Jimmy Akin. I found these proofs to be compelling, and they fit with the storyline. Again, I believe they are reasonable representations of accurate facts.

Finally, all the poetry in the story is of my own creation, unless otherwise stated. As I mentioned earlier, my love of poetry and my affinity for the truth it can so gracefully and gently impart was given to me by my father. He passed away in 2013. I wish he was here with us today, because I know he would have loved this tale of family honor, virtue, valor, and humility. He truly was a giant among men.

I have given you a sense of what is real and factual in the story. The time travel, quantum computers, and quantum emanations are not reality… yet, but they are just on the horizon.

I hope this story has inspired you to love your family, live with virtue and valor, and to believe that with love, honor, humility, and courage, we can make this world all that God intended for it to be. It might be as simple as making a difference in one person's life by improving their circumstance for one hour or for one day. After all, anything can happen in a day. Anything!

ABOUT THE AUTHOR

Domenic Melillo is a husband, father, son, and brother living in Wake Forest, North Carolina. He graduated from Villanova University, where he received his Bachelor of Science in Accounting. He also received his MBA in Banking and Finance from Hofstra University. He has worked in the mortgage industry for thirty-six years.

His passion for writing and poetry was inspired by his father, Joseph Melillo, who read to his children many of his favorite poems from the all-time greats. All of Domenic's writings take inspiration from real life events.

Through his writing, he strives to highlight and contrast the light and dark sides of life, or as he calls it, "the duality of our existence". He is drawn to the themes of family, faith, heritage, loss, and redemption. He is an avid student of history and in many ways strives to embody many of the characteristics of one of his heroes, Don Quixote, in that he longs to see things as they should be, not as they are.

Domenic has been described as a soul living out of his time, and yearns for the days of chivalry, virtue, valor, and honor, writing in the hope of inspiring families and society to return to these foundational qualities.

CPSIA information can be obtained
at www.ICGtesting.com
Printed in the USA
FSHW02n1704111018
52851FS